Also by K. Aten:

THE ARROW OF ARTEMIS SERIES
The Fletcher
The Archer
The Sagittarius

THE BLOOD RESONANCE SERIES
Running From Forever

THE MYSTERY OF THE MAKERS SERIES
The Sovereign of Psiere

OTHER TITLES
Rules of the Road
Waking the Dreamer

Burn It Down

K. Aten

Yellow Rose Books
by Regal Crest

ISBN 978-1-61929-418-9

First Edition 2019

9 8 7 6 5 4 3 2 1

Cover design by AcornGraphics

Published by:

Regal Crest Enterprises

Find us on the World Wide Web at
http://www.regalcrest.biz

Published in the United States of America

Acknowledgments

I have no idea where this novel came from but I know it wouldn't exist in its current form without the emotional guidance of my beta reader, Ted. I'd also like to thank Micheala and Mary for being the amazing editors they are. And lastly, thanks to Regal Crest for their continued faith in my novels.

Dedication

This one is for all the people who have been broken and put back together again. Never give up.

"It doesn't take weakness to accept help from the people who care about you. On the contrary, it takes incredible strength to know when you are not quite strong enough."

Part One: Flame

Chapter One

"TELL ME IN your own words why you're here today."

I looked at Dr. Sarah Caplin, aka 'just call me Sarah,' and played the bored and uncooperative firefighter that she was expecting. "You already know why I'm here." My hands were clenched into fists in my lap, the cast on my left wrist heavy and foreign. I didn't want to come across as belligerent so I relaxed my fingers and moved my hands to my sides. The stereotypical leather couch had warmed almost immediately with my body heat after I sat down. I was physically comfortable and I had to act like it.

She smiled at me. There was a slight gap between her teeth and she looked maybe ten years older than my own thirty, red hair just starting to gray at the temples. "I know what was written on the report but I'd like to hear it from you, Ashley."

My response was immediate and the distaste crawled across my face as I spoke. "It's Ash, just Ash."

Sarah nodded. "Very well, Ash."

I knew the answer well enough. The words seemed so simple, innocuous even. But could I tell her? They prompted deeper analysis and introspection, and I felt myself sliding to a darker and much older place. As quickly as I could, I put a halt to my train of thought and slammed the door to my past. No, I could not truly tell her why I was there. I could only give her the official reason. The most recent reason. "I had to make a choice when all my options were bad. Someone was going to live, and someone was going to die, and I was responsible for the outcome either way."

"You make it sound so impersonal."

I shrugged. "It's my job."

She glanced down at her notes and looked sympathetic so I looked elsewhere. "Tell me about Derek Smith. Who was he to you?"

Derek. My memories collapsed over each other, flickering like the frames of old moving pictures. Derek with his laughing brown eyes and crooked smile, his muscles flexing as he picked me up in a fireman's carry and spun me around before dropping me back onto my bunk at the station. Derek holding me in his arms when my first girlfriend broke my heart in college. We had been friends since elementary school. Both of us needed someone who understood our hearts and kept the rest of the kids off our backs. Derek holding my hands in the cafeteria in high school and refusing to let them go.

"Let them think we're dating, it doesn't matter and it makes it easier."

I went along with it because he was my best friend. I thought about Derek's excitement when I said I wanted to be an EMT and firefighter after we graduated. He enthusiastically followed me into my profession because we had become family, siblings. Then back to the present with Derek lying on the floor, pinned beneath fallen debris in a burning warehouse, telling me to go with his mouth as much as he begged me to stay with his eyes. Derek in the closed casket with me imagining those brown eyes unseeing and unsmiling.

I could feel the emotions coming up, the building pressure in my head and the persistent watering of my eyes that prompted me to shut it all down. There was a technique I learned years ago that involved visualizing a steel wall between me and my pain. I reached for that wall with Sarah's words and pushed it firmly into place. I was ice, I was empty, and I didn't care. "Derek is dead." My right hand started to tremble. I shoved it beneath my leg to still the tremors and to prevent me from reaching for the only thing that brought calm. There was no way I could do that while she was looking at me. The lump in my pocket was a distraction. I could see the rectangular outline as I sat with my legs stretched out in front of me, crossed at the ankles. It was a habit, maybe even a nervous tic, and psychologists were canny. No, the lighter would have to stay where it was.

"Are you okay?"

My head jerked up, my own brown eyes meeting her blue ones. Was I okay? Of course not. I wasn't sure if I'd ever been okay, but especially not since the night of the warehouse fire. The one she didn't know about. "I'm fine. I just don't want to talk about Derek right now. Please."

Our eyes held as uncomfortable seconds ticked by. I was aware that as far as she knew, the reason I was here was because of Derek's death. To not talk about it was like going to the horse race and not placing a bet. What was the point? I should have realized that my request to avoid one uncomfortable subject would just deflect her onto another. She gave me a small smile. "I understand. We can move on to something else." With another glance at the file, she began speaking again. "What about your friend Brandon James? He was with you that night."

I sighed because I didn't want to talk about Brandon either. I didn't want to talk about *anything* but the sessions were non-negotiable where my chief, Dave Bagley, was concerned. I saved two men and left another to die. I broke my arm at the same time. Those were hard things to deal with. But that wasn't what earned me a trip to the shrink. I'm pretty sure it was the bottle of Vicodin that I washed down with a fifth of vodka. Yeah, that could be why I had my ass in such a comfy leather seat.

She waited me out and I let my eyes wander around the room. I only had to be there for an hour but there were no clocks visible for me to check. I discretely pulled my hand out from under my leg and checked the watch. I still had more than half an hour to go. When I got fitted for the cast I was forced to wear the watch on the opposite hand. It had been a gift from my landlady and adopted grandmother, Mary. I did the math in my head and was startled to realize that I'd lived with her for thirteen years. My thoughts were interrupted by Sarah's voice again.

"Ash?"

I swallowed the lump in my throat. "Derek, Brandon, and I were all best friends. We were family both at work and outside of work. All the guys on the truck used to call us the Three Musketeers." A small smile stole across my lips when I remembered back to the time we all sat around in lawn chairs in Derek and Brandon's backyard, arguing about who was which character. Beer featured very prominently in the argument. The discussion ended when I suggested that Brandon, the relative newcomer to the group and Derek's lover, was more like Milady de Winter. He picked me up and threw me into the kiddie pool, not caring a bit if my freshly opened brew was wasted in the process.

My shrink rustled some paper at her desk, pulling me out of my past. "It says here that Brandon suffered two cracked ribs and a concussion during the collapse. It also mentions that he has requested a transfer when he returns to active duty."

"I know."

"Do you also know why?" I nodded. I definitely knew why. "Would you care to share?"

The anger was slow to rise, but it always seemed to simmer just below the surface. I met her eyes and felt my lip curl into a snarl. "And how much of what I say to you gets funneled directly into Bagley's ear? That is private and I think I'll keep it that way, thanks."

"None of it." Her words surprised me and for a second I didn't understand what she was saying. She seemed to sense my confusion and elaborated. "None of what you say leaves my files. This is a doctor-patient privilege and will remain confidential. The only way I would be required to break that confidence would be if you confessed to a crime, or became a danger to yourself or someone else."

I gave her a mirthless laugh. "Well I did try to off myself once already."

She just shook her head and fixed me with a serious gaze, looking further inside than I cared for. "I don't think you'll do than again. I think that was a response to deep emotional trauma and you simply gave up in the weakness that followed. You strike me as someone who is strong, emotionally and physically. Am I wrong?"

She waited, and I waited, stringing the words together in my mind. Finally I sighed at the truth she had pulled from me in so short a time. "No, you're not wrong. I've never done anything like that before and I highly doubt I'd do it again. That was..." I trailed off into silence and I strolled through hazy memory of the night Derek was buried. I could still see Mary's out-of-focus face as she begged God not to take me. Then the disjointed ride to the hospital in the back of an ambulance with people I'd known for years and the embarrassed heartbreak I felt after. "It wasn't me."

Sarah sat there with hands clasped on top of her desk. She was patient with me, I'd give her that. "Now that we've established that you're not a danger to yourself or anyone else, and that your secrets are safe with me, tell me about Brandon."

It wasn't my secret to tell, but clearly she thought it was necessary and I needed to get through this bullshit therapy to move on with my job. My internal struggle raged for about thirty seconds before I finally gave in. "Brandon and Derek were lovers. They lived together and had been in a relationship for a little over a year." Her eyes widened imperceptibly and she glanced back down at her file notes. I knew what she was looking for and it pissed me off. "What? Queers look just like everyone else, Doc. You can't judge a book by its cover!"

Her head jerked up at my outburst. The words sounding loud in the room, ringing in my ears. "I'm sorry, that is not what I was looking for. There is no mention at all of either man being gay or in a relationship. I was just curious is all."

I growled, frustrated by her question. "Of course there was no mention of it! I was out because let's face it, I'm pretty obvious." I waved a hand at myself. I was nothing if not the epitome of a tough Detroit dyke. I had dark hair that was clipped into an undercut, short on the sides and back. It was longer on top and I styled it up or slicked back when I wanted to go out, otherwise it fell into a tangled mop that tickled the tops of my ears and fell into my eyes when I forgot to get it cut. I was wearing jeans with two cuffs at the bottom and a slim fitting button down shirt with sleeves rolled up my forearms. Only a small percentage of my tattoos were visible below the softly rolled cotton.

"There is no way I'd ever be mistaken for anything other than what I am, and I've taken a lot of grief for it in this profession. But Derek was the all American kid, the high school football player and golden boy of the department. Homophobia is real and alive. Especially in what they all consider a 'man's profession.' No, they were very careful about their interaction at the station and when they were out at functions where they'd be recognized."

"You say that neither man was out at the station, did being their friend help buffer you from some of that homophobia where the rest of your coworkers were concerned?"

I just stared at her. Could she really be so clueless? "Of course it helped! Because they accepted me, the rest just kind of fell it line. But I still have to prove myself every single day that I'm on the job."

Sarah glanced at the papers again and I was pretty sure that she didn't need them. She seemed like the type that would memorize a file before the first session. "I see you've received two commendations before, and you're up for a third. You've got a handful of medals to your name, and earlier this year you broke the previous record for climbing the Detroit Renaissance Center in that charity event. Thirteen minutes twenty-seven seconds?"

"Twenty-eight seconds." I thought about the fundraiser back in March. Even now looking back it seemed almost surreal that I didn't just break the previous record set by a woman, but I came in twenty-ninth out of three hundred and forty-seven firefighters. I beat both Derek and Brandon that day and everyone in the firehouse came together to congratulate me. I also won our money pool for the person who posted the best time. I bought pizza for the entire team and donated the rest. The guys razzed me about donating my winnings but it was all for a good cause and it was my money to do with as I pleased. Hoofing it up seventy floors carrying seventy pounds of gear in record time meant that I earned every single penny. I looked at her curiously, wondering why that would have made it in my file. "Does it really mention the American Lung Association event in there?"

She shook her head. "No, I just remember reading about it in the paper and recognized your name."

I didn't really know what to say to that. "Oh."

Sarah started again. "We seem to have gotten off track a bit. Why is Brandon requesting a transfer? Does it have to do with the fact that Derek died?"

The wall slipped and my eyes filled again, faster this time. I knew why Brandon wanted nothing to do with me, because I let his lover die and saved him instead. But admitting it out loud was hard, because it meant saying the words that were burned into my brain. It meant speaking aloud what I had done, and not done. I let my best friend die and saved Brandon instead. And Brandon would never forgive me, nor could I forgive myself. My control was fading and I hated the way I felt. I didn't want to break down in front of this woman, this stranger. She didn't know us and she didn't know me. Before she could prompt again I heard a faint beeping. When I pulled my wrist out from under my leg, the digital sound got louder. My session was done for the day. Instead of answering her question I simply shook my head. "I'm sorry, but I have to go."

The doctor wanted to protest, wanted to stretch time until she could wrap it back around and pull me into its fold. I could see it in her eyes. Instead, Sarah was forced to nod her head. "Yes, our time is up for the day. I will see you Wednesday though, right? I have you down as three times a week."

I stood from the couch and fumbled to get the truck keys out of my left pocket with my right hand and transferred them to the left once they were free. Then with a single glance, I headed for the door, calling over my shoulder on my way out. "Yes, Wednesday. Thank you."

I jogged down the stairs at the end of the hall and in less than a minute I was outside the building on the sidewalk. I quickly dug the old silver Zippo out of my pocket and began opening and closing it as I walked to my truck. The distinctive *ching-clp* calmed my nerves and brought me back from the emotional edge. I knew one thing for certain, I wasn't looking forward to Wednesday. It was still early, only three in the afternoon and I needed a few things from the grocery store before I could head home. I made a quick trip inside and returned with the essentials — milk, eggs, bread, lighter fluid, and cigarette rolling papers.

When I pulled into the drive at home, my attention was caught and held by the moving truck on the street in front of the house next door. It had been on the market for a while, one of the city specials that were going for cheap. The sold sign finally went up two months ago, and that's when the construction traffic started. They replaced the roof and front porch, and did who knows what kind of work inside the place. I didn't ask and I didn't peek. My hours at the station are regular but atypical from the average person with me working twenty-four hours on and seventy-two off. We could switch out or trade days with others on the team but for the most part that was what I worked. Or, what I used to work before the fire that left me with broken bones and a broken heart. It also left the team down three people.

I had just gotten out of the Wrangler with that thought and I paused. I looked at the Jeep that I'd owned since shortly after graduating high school. It took working two jobs the summer before starting college and it was half rust when I brought it home to Mary's house. It would have stayed that way if not for Derek. The pain of loss took me by surprise and left me shaking. I leaned against the front fender and slowly slid to the ground, resting my back against the large off-road tire.

Derek's pop owned a garage over on Eight Mile and Derek learned everything he knew about cars from the old man. His pop hated me though for taking his son away from the family business. He probably hated me more now. Derek and I rebuilt the Jeep from the ground up. Well, Derek was the brains, I just handed him the tools and bought the parts. It was pretty sad that a Detroit girl knew squat about engines. The Wrangler was old and I never stopped having problems with it but I always had Derek. I *always* had Derek. An overwhelming sense of loss washed over me and my eyes started to burn with the unshed tears of earlier. I felt the heat of the concrete driveway through my jeans and I knew that I had to get my groceries out of the Jeep and inside but the will to care was fast slipping away.

"Excuse me?" My head jerked up as panic cleared out the pain. A woman stood in the driveway next door holding an envelope in her hand. She was maybe my height or an inch shorter. It was hard to tell while I was sitting on the ground. With black hair pulled back into a bun, light brown skin, and a smile that would put toothpaste models to shame, I couldn't help noticing her beauty despite my misery. Was she the new homeowner? The collar of her pale yellow sleeveless shirt ruffled in the summer breeze and she wore form fitting dress pants that accentuated her slim figure. "Are you okay?"

I jerked my head away from her shoes and moved my gaze up to hers. Brown eyes with an exotic tilt and an epicanthic fold. So maybe not completely African American. I flushed when I realized why she was showing such concern and I awkwardly stood, using my good hand to pull myself up. I dusted off the back of my dark jeans and couldn't bring myself to meet her eyes again. "I'm fine, thank you."

She cocked her head and I refused to be drawn to the cuteness of the gesture. "Do you always sit in your driveway at..." She glanced at the smart watch on her slim wrist. Homeowner, nice clothes, and an expensive watch screamed money. "Three forty-five in the afternoon?"

I still felt raw after the session with Sarah and my new neighbor's questions seemed a little abrasive to my abused psyche. She wasn't getting any more from me than anyone else. "No. Is there something you needed?"

A tendril of guilt crept in when the look on her face fell at my abrupt response. She sighed and held up the letter. "I was just wondering when the mail came around each day. I need to know if I could leave this in the box now, or if I should drop it at the post office so it will go out first thing in the morning." She hesitated a few seconds then spoke again. "I'm sorry to have disturbed you."

I ran a hand through my hair and turned away to walk around and grab my groceries out of the back. "It's fine. I'm sorry for being such a dick. The mail lady comes by around five, so you still have time." With all the grocery bags loaded on my one good arm, I hip checked the back door shut and turned toward her again. I pulled up short at the look on her face, surprised despite all that had happened. She had been checking me out. Stranger yet, the look on her face clearly said that she liked what she saw. That was curious, and more than a little distracting. Unlike some of my acquaintances of the past, I had no will or energy to be messing with a girl from the other side of the tracks. Stuff like that burned hot at first but it never lasted. Nothing ever lasted. I'd do better to find someone worse...or no one at all.

She smiled that smile again but nothing was going to penetrate the pain with Derek gone. "Thank you for the information. I just moved in next door." She held out her hand. "I'm Mia Thomas." I looked down at her hand, then back at my own. One in a cast and the other loaded with Kroger bags. I couldn't see the blush with her skin tone but assumed it was there. "Oh, sorry. I'm such an idiot! Bad Mia, no biscuit!"

I don't know what it was about Mia Thomas but in that very moment I forgot all about my pain, about my guilt, and about my broken arm. The laugh that tumbled from my lips was the first to pass since before Derek died. I said the first inane thing that came to mind. "You should never keep yourself from biscuits, especially if they're homemade buttermilk ones."

"Oh I know it! My grandma Letty used to make the best ones. It's actually her house that I bought." Mia shrugged. "I guess I just thought it should stay in the family."

The name sparked my memory. "Oh! Loretta Thomas! Yes, I remember her, Mary used to have dinner with her twice a week. I haven't seen her here in the past few years though."

"Well, she couldn't live in this big house by herself once she broke her hip. So my dad had her moved into a home right after I graduated from college and hired an agency to rent out the place."

I remembered the old woman next door. She was the sweetest person you ever could meet. Always bought Girl Scout cookies from the kids, always offered them to me if she was outside on her porch when I came home. Sometimes I mowed her lawn after I mowed ours. It just seemed the neighborly thing to do and the lawns weren't that big. "How is your grandma?"

Sadness replaced the beautiful smile. "She actually passed away about a month ago." Mia shrugged and I suddenly felt uncomfortable.

I nodded my head at her. "I'm sorry to hear that, she was a wonderful woman. Always had a million stories and at least a couple cookies."

My new neighbor graced me with a melancholy look. "Yeah, she did." She glanced down then and got a guilty look on her face when she noticed my grocery bags. "Oh, I didn't mean to keep you so long. You should probably get that milk inside in this heat."

I followed her gaze to the sweating milk jug and realized she was right. "Yeah. I doubt it would kill me but I don't want lumps in my cereal either." I shifted the bags slightly and turned to walk up to the house. "It was nice meeting you, Mia. Good luck with your renovations."

"Hey, wait!" She called out when I was on the first step of the porch and I turned to look back at her over my shoulder. "Do I get a name?"

Even from nearly twenty feet away I could see the humor in her eyes, shining in the summer sun. She had definitely been checking me out. "Name's Ash Hayes. Catch you later, Mia." I continued up the steps and inside the house. I was confident that she would still live next door tomorrow, but the freshness of my groceries had no such guarantee.

Chapter Two

"ASH?"

I CALLED out to the worried voice as I made my way to the kitchen. "Just me, Mary!" After putting away the groceries I grabbed a beer and took it out to the back porch where my landlady sat in a rocker with her eBook. I bought it for her more than a year ago when she kept complaining that the print in books was too hard for her to read. Now the books were cheaper and she could make the text whatever size she wanted. Problem solved...if only they were all so easy.

Mary narrowed her eyes as I sat in another chair and kicked my feet up on the stool. Her gaze took in the beer then flickered down to my cast. "You s'posed to be drinkin' that?"

"Chill, Grams. I stopped taking the pain pills yesterday and besides, one beer won't kill me."

She snorted. "That swill might!"

I glanced at the bottle of Bud and shrugged. "What can I say, I'm simple and I have simple tastes. I don't need anything fancy, you know that."

The woman, who was old enough to be my grandmother and had acted as such since I met her, muttered under her breath. "Well, you got the first part right..."

For the second time in less than an hour laughter tickled its way past my throat. "You're feisty today."

"How was your session?"

And just as fast the laughter froze. I took another swig of beer then held the sweating bottle against my head to avoid answering. The oscillating fan felt good against the condensation left behind. Detroit was a hot city in July. Since I wasn't going to open up when I didn't have to, I gave her the only answer left. "It was fine."

She nodded and took a sip of her iced tea. "Mmm hmm." Then she changed the subject. "You see the new girl moving in next door? She's certainly a pretty sight around this old neighborhood."

The image of Mia Thomas checking out my ass flashed in my head and I smirked. "I saw."

Mary grunted at my bare bones answers, possibly knowing me better than I knew myself after all these years. "You know she's Letty's granddaughter? I was sad to hear she passed."

"I do know. Mia seems nice, though I'm not sure why she'd want to move to this neighborhood."

The old woman riled up instantly, just like I knew she would. "This is a beautiful neighborhood, you ungrateful child! Why, back in the day we had neighborhood barbecues and..."

I mimicked a puppet talking with my hand and interrupted her. "And then we carved the Ten Commandments into some stone tablets we found in my backyard —"

"Oh you!" Rather than say any more she fished an ice cube out of her tea glass and threw it at me. Her aim was surprisingly accurate where it bounced off my head.

"Hey! I'm injured here and can't defend myself."

Chocolate brown eyes and a deeply wrinkled face morphed into something tender with my words. "Babydoll, I will always defend you."

Her words tore down the wall I had built and left me feeling bereft. I whispered to her as she held my eyes. "I know." Then I shut my own and leaned my head back against the chair. The tears had come again and I didn't want her to see. I heard the creaking sound first, then the air stilled as she stepped between me and the fan. I was forced to open my eyes again when tender fingers wiped the moisture from my cheeks.

"It's okay to cry, darlin'. God's gonna cradle you in his hands and not let go. Cryin' won't change that."

I turned my eyes away again. "You know I don't hold to all that, Mary. And I don't like to cry."

She gave me a kiss on the forehead and went back to her chair. "No, you never have." Once she was seated, she picked her eBook again and spoke without making eye contact. "I got us a chicken all done up, can you pop it in the oven at three-fifty for me? I was thinkin' about makin' some fried green tomatoes too. Picked them from the garden just this morning."

I nodded though she wasn't watching me. "Sure, I'm going back inside in a few minutes, you want it in now? Anything I can do for dinner later?"

She finally broke away from the words on her screen and gave me a sly smile. "Now is fine. And I may have some of that fancy risotto in the cupboard and a package of mushrooms in the fridge."

Mary had the most eclectic taste of anyone I'd ever met, and I don't think there was a food that existed that she didn't like. And between the two of us, we could cook just about anything. I just shook my head and gave her another smile. "You're a funny old woman."

"And you're a somber young one. Maybe we can help each other, hmm?"

I stood and drained the rest of my beer then saluted her with the bottle. "Maybe we can."

Just before the screen door shut behind me I heard her call out. "And it wouldn't kill you to put on some shorts and show off those white chicken legs of yours. At near ninety, you're likely to stroke out!"

She was talking about the temperature but laughter burst out of my mouth as I stopped in my tracks and looked back at her. I ignored her reference to the high heat and came back with a dig about her age. "Shouldn't that be my line?"

I got another ice cube to the head for my smart mouth. "I ain't ninety!"

Dinner that evening was amazing but I still couldn't resist getting up to my room as soon as possible afterward. Mary had stopped using the upstairs years before and gave me free run of the place. I had a room I used for my exercise equipment and another for my bedroom. I also had a full bathroom at my disposal. Downstairs she had her bedroom and the master bath, as well as the kitchen and a living room. The washing machine and dryer were in the basement. I did both our laundry every week so she didn't have to go up and down the stairs.

I'm not sure what I would have done had she not taken me in during my senior year of high school. I lived here while I was in school, working sometimes two or three jobs just to pay my way at first. I did all the odd jobs and fix-it work around the house in exchange for a fairly low rent after high school. Mary's place was paid off back in the nineties but I know she didn't have a big monthly income after retiring from the hospital fifteen years ago. Once her partner Marge passed away, it became too much for Mary to handle.

But she was more than someone who rented me a room. Like Derek and Brandon, she had become family. She knew more about me than my coworkers, my absentee father, and my own mother who sat rotting in jail. But she didn't know everything. No one did.

I had a recliner in the weight room and a small folding table with an ashtray. I set my newly opened bottle of beer on the table where rings had stained the cheap wood over the years. Then I pulled one of the packages of rolling papers from the grocery bag at my feet and dug the Zippo out of my pocket. The metal was warm from my own body heat and just the feel of the smooth surface in the palm of my hand comforted me. I opened the rolling paper pack and pulled out one of small rectangles. My breathing increased with the distinctive *click* sound of the lighter cover opening, then the *tschhick* as the wheel spun over flint and threw sparks into a stable blue flame.

I savored the heat and flickering light for about thirty seconds before holding the paper closer and watching it catch. I stared intently while it burned down nearly to my fingertips, then dropped it into the glass ashtray. I lit another while the lighter was still warm. The fire was pure and beautiful. The fire was my greatest shame. Three beers and almost an entire pack of papers later, I finally went to bed. Nightmares of the past chased me into the next day.

"WHEN WE LEFT off on Monday, you mentioned that you knew why your friend Brandon requested a transfer from your station." Tuesday went by in a blur. Mary kept me busy all day, fixing the knob on the back door, the gate to the backyard, and a piece of trim that had come off in the living room. I also did laundry, then made a trip to the store for another six-pack of beer and to pick up a prescription for Mary. But Wednesday had arrived and I did nothing since waking this morning, dreading my appointment with Sarah.

I sighed. "Do we have to talk about Brandon? What relevance does this have to my mental health?"

Sarah gave me an infuriating know-it-all smile that all the TV shrinks seem to have and cocked her head. "Why don't you tell me? Clearly, Derek and Brandon are two people who have impacted your life greatly. From the outside looking in, I see that you didn't just lose one friend in that warehouse fire, you seem to have lost two. Most people come together to grieve over a loved one, but you and Brandon did the opposite. Why did he request a transfer?"

Her questions were giving me a headache and I'd been on the couch less than five minutes. I thought about the reason I was there and cursed my captain under my breath. "Bagley can suck my dick—"

"Did you say something?"

"No, it was nothing."

Sarah seemed to let it go but continued on with her questioning. "You were going to tell me about Brandon."

"I wasn't—" I paused and she continued to stare at me, which drew a sigh from my lips. "But you're not going to let this go, are you?" Sarah merely smiled again as a response. Finally giving in, I leaned forward on the couch and rested my elbows on my knees where I could look away from those knowing eyes. "Brandon requested a transfer because he can't forgive me."

"Forgive you for what, Ash? Didn't you save his life?"

Tears pricked my eyes. "Yes. But I let Derek die."

She sat back in her own chair, I could hear the creak of it. After a minute of silence she prodded again. "And do you think he should? Do you blame him for his lack of forgiveness?"

I shook my head slowly, and had to swallow the lump in my throat to speak. "How can I when I can't even forgive myself?" I looked up, maybe hoping to see condemnation in her eyes at my next words. "I let my best friend die!" But there was nothing on her face to suggest my guilt, to justify it in a stranger's eyes.

She glanced down at a page in my ever-present file. "The report says the fire had gone out of control. You were in the process of bringing a civilian out and made it to the door with the unconscious man when the distress call came over the radio. You heard Derek request aid and left the civilian outside with paramedics then ran back into the building despite the risk."

She didn't understand what it was like and I shook my head to deny the risk. "I had to go."

"What did you see inside, Ash?"

I squeezed my eyes shut in order to get the words out. "They weren't very far inside the west entrance, but Derek was pinned below a beam where part of the roof had collapsed. Brandon was unconscious nearby and his breather mask had been knocked off. I tried lifting the beam but it wouldn't budge and I could see Derek was in pain, probably from broken ribs where it pinned him at the chest. He..." The pain overwhelmed me again and a shudder ran through my body as I dug the heels of my hands into my eyes to hold back the tears. "He told me to get Brandon out and come back for him with help. But we both knew that the fire was too far gone and that no one would be coming back in."

Memory of that night blazed back into my mind with the flames of my pain.

The heat was intense when I ran back in to the last place I had seen them. My first thought was that both men were dead when I saw their bodies on the floor. The ceiling above us was on fire, as were the walls around. The only way out was the way I had come in, and it was rapidly closing off. Relief coursed through me when I saw Derek staring at me through his own SCBA mask but it rapidly turned to dismay when I realized that I couldn't move the beam that had him pinned. I'll never forget the moment his gaze looked past where I crouched at his side and landed on Brandon. "Take him...please."

I dug heavy gloved fingers into his shoulders and screamed through the mask and smoke. "No! I'll get you out!"

His words were fading with the pain, but he managed a few more. "Ash, please...his kids...I love them. I love him!" Precious seconds went by before I finally nodded my head, and he closed his eyes as he struggled to breathe. Brandon had two kids from his previous marriage and after a year, Derek loved those kids as much as he loved Brandon. I knew I couldn't let them lose their father. His voice cut through the roar of fire and burned me. "...love you, Ashley."

An ominous cracking sound above me warned of imminent disaster and I spun in place to grab Brandon from where he lay prone on the floor. I had to do a power squat to get him up over my shoulders then made my way as fast as possible toward the exit. Just before we got out, the ceiling gave way above us and one of the beams struck my left arm. I held on through the pain and pushed through the doorway and onto the asphalt beyond. We were swarmed by firefighters that pulled us back just as the roof gave out and the entire place exploded. "Derek!" Even with a broken arm, it took four of my fellow firefighters to keep me from running toward the engulfed building. I fought weakly after that, even when my gear was removed and I was forced into the ambulance. Everything went dark with a prick of the paramedic's needle.

"Ash...Ashley..."

I jerked my head up at the sound of Sarah's voice and realized with shame that tears were coursing down my cheeks. I hastily wiped my face with the arm of my sleeve. "I'm sorry."

She stood and grabbed a tissue box from her shelf and walked it over to me. "It's all right, take the time you need."

After blowing my nose, I took a few extra seconds to lean over and deposit the used tissue in the nearby trash. Then without looking at her I tried to explain Derek. "He was always the hero, you know? If he saw someone with car trouble, he would always stop. Even if it were two in the morning or in the worst neighborhood, he'd do what he could to help. He skipped classes to sit in court with me when I went through the emancipation process, and again when my mom was put in jail. He was my best friend, my family."

"How old were you when you went through emancipation?"

"The proceedings were started when I was sixteen, the court approved me when I was seventeen."

Pale eyebrows rose in surprised when I hazarded a look at my shrink. "That's young. I know you finished high school, did you live with Derek and his family?"

"No, his pop never really liked me. He wanted Derek to go into the family business and work at the garage. But from the moment I said I wanted to be a firefighter, Derek did too. I think his family blamed me for that, probably more so now."

"Ash..." I met Sarah's eyes and they held nothing but compassion. "You know that you can't take responsibility for someone else's actions. Derek made his own choices in life. From the way you speak of him, saving people was just his calling. Even if you hadn't put the initial career idea in his head, he may have gone into something similar. I think the first step for you to move beyond the tragedy of that night is to accept that Derek's death wasn't your fault. You physically couldn't save him and you were not responsible for his being there in the first place."

I ran a hand through my disheveled dark hair, sending it further into disarray. The sessions were just as hard on my tough dyke image as they were on my psyche. "That's easier said than done. The guilt...eats at me. And..." I took a deep breath and admitted a little more. "And you're right, it hurts that I lost not one friend in that fire, but two."

She made a few notes on her pad of yellow-lined paper and I wondered why she didn't just use a laptop. "Have you reached out to Brandon since the fire?"

"They kept me overnight for observation, but I didn't suffer from smoke inhalation like Brandon did. I stopped by the next morning, on my way out, but his kids were in the room visiting and I didn't want to intrude. But he met my eyes while I was in the doorway and then he turned away. He couldn't even look at me."

"What about the funeral? Did you speak to him then?"

I gave her an incredulous look. "And what was I supposed to say? The funeral was packed with friends, family, and our fellow firefighters. Was I supposed to walk up to him and say, oh, hey, sorry I let your boyfriend and my best friend die? It was bad enough that every time I looked at him he turned away. That was when I knew I'd lost them both."

Sarah cocked her head to study me and I waited, knowing what she would ask next. "Is that why you tried to take your own life that night?"

My bottom lip began to quiver and I covered it with the fingers of my right hand. Grief, anger, and guilt filled me when I remembered waking the next day to see Mary sobbing at my bedside. My one word answer was a whisper. "Yes."

I drove home later in my Jeep and flashed back to the words she left me with as my session ended.

"Have you considered the possibility that Brandon feels just as much guilt for Derek's death as you?"

I looked at her with confusion. "No, why would he feel guilty? He did nothing wrong."

Sarah sat back in her chair and gave me another one of those "shrink" looks. "What if he feels guilt over the fact that you saved him instead of Derek? What if he can't look you in the eye because he is afraid you'll hate him for the choice you made? Everyone reacts differently to emotional trauma."

I shook my head in denial. "But that makes no sense."

"Doesn't it? He knew how much Derek meant to you, right?" I nodded. "Then it stands to reason he would know what Derek's loss would do, and feels survivor's guilt because of it. I'm going to give you some papers before you go, as something to review before our next session. They are about dealing with grief, and about survivor's guilt. I think it would help you to read both." I nodded my head dumbly because it wasn't like I had anything else to do with my life until our next meeting.

Chapter Three

WHEN I GOT home I grabbed the printed pages from my passenger's seat and carefully folded them in half. I was surprised to see Mia outside mowing our lawn. She stopped when she spied me getting out of the Jeep and I froze as she wiped the sweat from her brow with the bandana she had tied around her wrist. She met my eyes with a smile. "Hey, Ash."

"What are you doing?"

My gruff tone gave her pause for a moment and I immediately regretted it. But she answered anyway. "I came over to borrow your push mower since I haven't had a chance to get one yet. I lived in a condo before moving here, so..." She shrugged. "Didn't have to mow. Anyway, I told Mary I'd give your yard a trim while I was at it, as a way to say thanks. I figured the vibration wouldn't be good on that healing arm."

I tried to protest her help. "That really isn't necessary. I can finish up and pay you for what you've already completed..."

She waved me off with a smile. "Nonsense. Even if I hadn't needed to borrow your machine, Mary has promised a payment worth more than gold in my book."

"What—" My question was cut off before I could ask.

Mary stuck her head out the screen door and yelled. "Ash, quit buggin' that poor girl and get your backside in here! I need you to take the biscuits out of the oven."

Realization dawned on me then and I turned back to Mia with a smirk. "Ah, I see now. Buttermilk biscuits."

She grinned back. "She promised me they'd be as good as my grammy used to make, plus I'd get an ice cold glass of Vernors to go with."

I opened my mouth to respond, only to hear Mary again. "Dagum it, Ash! Get in here before they burn!"

I gave Mia a salute with my papers. "Whoop, gotta go! Don't want your payment to burn." Then I jogged off toward the house.

Mia had been almost finished mowing when I got home so she knocked on the front door about ten minutes after I took the biscuits out of the oven. They were still piping hot, but then so was everything else in the house. With another nearly ninety degree day and the oven having run, the three of us took the plate of food and our drinks to the porch. After receiving the evil eye from my landlady-turned-grandmother, I bypassed my usual beer and grabbed a can of Vernors for myself as well.

Mary and Mia got along like two peas in a pod so I settled into one of the porch chairs and let the conversation happen around me. I held the first biscuit awkwardly in my left hand while I slathered butter with the knife in my right. The way the cast came up across my palm made it difficult to close my thumb and fingers together. I gave up after the biscuit broke a second time and just crammed the delicious bits into my mouth, then wiped my hand on one of the paper towels that Mary had set out. Rather than risk more mess, I sat back and sipped my ginger ale and regretted not filling a glass with ice like the other two had done. The can was rapidly warming in the heat.

"Ash, honey, is that all you're gonna eat? I can normally count on you for at least four."

I looked up into two pairs of brown eyes. Mary's were a dark chocolate color, and Mia's were a much lighter brown in the slanting light of the sun. I stared at the plate of fluffy baked goods hungrily before shrugging, denying both my taste buds and my belly. "Eh, I'm not that hungry." Even as I said the words, Mia's hands were already in motion. She deftly cut a biscuit in half and slathered butter on both sides before putting the halves together again and handing it over to me. I stared at it for a second, before moving my gaze up to her.

"Please?"

I couldn't say no to those eyes, especially when my stomach was threatening me with mutiny if I did. So I took the biscuit. "Thanks."

Mary continued on as if Mia and I hadn't just experienced a moment. "So Mia, I was tellin' my granddaughter here that I'm sure glad you moved in. We need more permanent residents in the neighborhood. It just hasn't been the same since my Margie passed."

Mia stopped chewing and looked from my pale face to Mary's significantly darker one. "Granddaughter?"

It always confused people when Mary called me that. "May as well be. I've lived with her for thirteen years now and she's the closest thing to family I have."

"Oh, okay." My new neighbor turned back to Mary. "And who is Margie?"

The old woman across from me smiled and sighed. "Oh, my Margie..."

I couldn't help laughing at the torch she still carried for her long deceased partner. It made me sad that not only did Marge Jensen die before I could meet her, but that Mary had to spend so many years without the love of her life. I was also a little jealous that their bond had lasted even beyond death. "Now you've done it, she's going launch into the story of how they met—" My words cut off when an ice cube bounced off my head.

"You hush over there!" Mary turned to a laughing Mia and began the story that I had heard so many times before. "I was serving as a nurse in the Army in the Eighth Field Hospital in Nha Trang. There weren't many of us women back then, and hardly any black women. It was pretty hard goin' for me but God put me on this earth for a reason, and healing people is my callin'. I'm sure of it."

Mia clapped her hands together once. "Oh, you're a nurse too! I'm a Clinical Nurse Leader at the Detroit Medical Center."

Mary cackled and looked at Ash, while pointing toward their new neighbor. "Oh, I like this one! And a CLN? She's smart too!"

Though I tried to remain separate and aloof from the conversation, I was drawn into Mary's tale of love once again. Something about the story touched me every time, though I would never admit it. My tough butch image would be in shreds. Rather than encourage her antics, I waved a hand to stop Mary's not so subtle matchmaking and prompted her to continue. "Get on with it, old woman! Tell Mia what you thought of Marge when you first met her."

I smiled as Mary slapped her palms on her capris covered thighs. "Oh, well the first day Marge arrived at the MASH unit, it was right after two platoons were ambushed by Charlies and we had been seeing a steady influx of wounded. Nothin' but blood and screaming for days and in she walks with her flaming red hair and freckled face, lookin' like the girl incarnation of that Howdy Doody! Her hair was short for a woman and it just sort of...curled just so around her face. Right there in the middle of the tent, with death all around us, I couldn't help but laugh out loud." Mary took a sip of her ginger ale and continued. "And oh, the look on her face when this twenty-five year old black woman was laughing at her...you have not seen a temper until you laugh at a redhead with a serious face." She sighed again. "She was magnificent!"

Mia had buttered another biscuit and set it in front of me,

then buttered another for herself. She didn't acknowledge my motion when I hesitantly picked it up and began chewing. Instead she leaned forward as if she were truly into Mary's story. "What happened then?"

"Well you wouldn't think it possible for such different people to become friends in the middle of a war zone, but we did. She made it so that I no longer cared about the way the white doctors and nurses treated me, she was my light. And as luck would have it, we were both set to discharge at the same time. When it was time to come back to the States, she followed me to Detroit instead of returning to her family back in Kansas. We both found jobs here at the Hutzel Women's Hospital. And that's where we both retired and would have happily lived out our days if Margie had made it that long."

It was when Mia leaned closer and placed her hand over Mary's that I saw a similarity between the two. They were healers, both. Mary never stopped trying to take away people's pain, and I got the same impression from our new neighbor. Maybe it was a nurse thing. But either way, they shared a look of understanding before Mia spoke. "If you don't mind my asking, what happened?"

The tear that had been sitting on the precipice of Mary's lashes broke free to paint a shiny line down her weathered cheek. "Marge was older than me by some five years. One day she just started feelin' poor like, with some back pain and digestion problems. Then she started losin' weight and I told her she better get to the doc! She was diagnosed with pancreatic cancer and the doc said that by the time the symptoms show it's already spread too far. She didn't want to leave me with a lot of medical debt so..." Mary paused and took a shuddering breath. Even after fifteen years, it still affected her deeply. "She opted not to take the chemo treatments. Said they'd just make her feel worse and wouldn't do any good in the end. She was my best friend and love of my life."

"I'm so sorry for your loss, Mary. I can only hope to find a love like the one you two shared. It was obviously deep."

Mary gave her a watery smile. "Oh, it was the best. I'm not gonna' lie, I cursed God for a long time for taking my Margie from me. But then I realized that not only did he bring us together in the first place, but we got forty beautiful years together." She wiped her face and turned that sweet "Mary" smile my way. "Not only that but just when I was feelin' loneliest, he sent me my Ash."

Throughout the time that Mary was talking, whenever I'd finish a biscuit, Mia would butter me another. I had just finished the fourth and was licking the butter from my fingers when Mia turned my way. I froze at the way those light brown eyes darkened with a look I hadn't seen in a while. Then the moment passed and she turned back to my grandma. "That was a beautiful story, Mary. Thank you for sharing that and the wonderful biscuits with me." She turned her curious gaze my way and I began to sweat even more, if that was possible in the heat of the late afternoon. Interacting with new people meant shared stories, questions, and answers. And I was so very tired of questions. "So how did you break your arm?"

Mary immediately shot me a warning glance at the look on my face. She had known me a long time and knew that I could get pissy when uncomfortable. And there wasn't much that didn't make me uncomfortable lately. Instead of giving a gruff answer like I'd done a few times with Mia, I tried to be casual. "I broke it on the job."

She cocked her head in that curiously cute way. "What do you do? Oh, wait, you're a firefighter aren't you?"

I looked at her in surprise. "How did you know that?"

She grinned. "You have a decal on the back window of your Jeep." She paused for a second as some thought flitted across her face. "Did you know the firefighter that died a few weeks ago?"

Despite the heat of the fading afternoon, coldness washed through me with her words. My thoughts whirled in the silence that followed her question. Did I know him? No, he knew me. He was my brother and I let him die. Before she could ask another question I stood and walked back into the house. On my way through the kitchen I grabbed a beer from the fridge and went straight upstairs to find solace in the only thing that remained. As I sat in my recliner, burning little papers, I could hear their voices down below my open window.

"He was her best friend. She broke her arm saving their other friend in that same fire."

I stopped burning and got up to turn on the fan to drown out their voices. When I sat back down I stared at the silver rectangle in my hand. Then I focused on opening and closing the lighter, letting the familiar *ching-clp* take me back to the day it came into my possession.

Yelling came through the thin wall that separated my bedroom from the living room. Mom was yelling at another boy-friend. She was always yelling about something. But this time I knew what it was about, this time it was my fault. From the moment I saw the gleaming silver lighter in his hand, listened to the sound it made as he opened and closed the lid, I was entranced. And the flame from it was so beautiful and pure, I knew it had to be mine. So last night when mom was working at the gas station and Dave was passed out on the couch, I snuck out of my room and took it. In all eleven years of my life, I had never owned anything so amazing. I startled when the doorknob jig-gled. Then I nearly dropped the lighter when she started pound-ing on my door. As quick as I could, I stashed it into the little hole in the corner of my mattress. "Ashley, open this damn door, now!"

"Just a second, Mom!" I rushed to the door and pulled the butter knife out of the doorjamb that prevented my door from easily being opened. I started doing that when her last boyfriend slipped into my room one night. I never liked him because he always gave me the creeps. But when he came in and started jerk-ing off next to my bed, I got really scared. When I told my mom, she slapped me for making shit up. But he was gone less than two weeks later. I was never sure if she believed me or if he did some-thing else to piss her off.

Desi Hayes pushed into my room with a cloud of stinking cigarette smoke. She was never up this early unless she had to work the overnight. That's how I knew to watch my tongue because she was probably tired and madder than normal. She walked in and looked at me like I was nothing more than a bur-den. I knew what the look meant because she's told me often enough in actual words. "Did you take Dave's lighter?"

My life was nothing but lies and I looked at her in confusion. "His lighter? I've been in my room since dinner last night. I was studying because I have a test today. Is that all you want? Because I'm going to be late for school if I don't finish getting ready."

She popped me upside the head and the sting of it only made me more resolute to keep my secrets. "Don't be a smart ass!" She looked around one last time and frowned. "And clean up this fucking room tonight, it looks like a pig sty!" Then she walked out and I blew out a sigh of relief.

The theft of the lighter never really mattered since Dave was out of our lives a month later. But the lighter…my lighter, it has been the longest relationship that either me or my mother ever had. With Derek gone now, no one had been with me as long, nor comforted me more. People were overrated.

A little while later a knock sounded on my weight room door and I knew immediately it was Mia. I didn't want to answer the door or more questions, I just wanted to be alone. But my hopes were dashed when another knock sounded, and her voice came through slightly muffled. "Ash?" With a final *clp*, I crammed the lighter back in the right front pocket of my jeans and hid the ashtray and papers in the top drawer of the end table. Then I got up and opened the door before she could knock again. I must have startled her because she leaned back slightly when the door whisked open in front of her upraised fist. "Oh!"

"Is there something you needed, Mia?" I tried to convey my displeasure at being interrupted with the look on my face. I didn't want to say anything to offend her but I didn't want to become bff's either.

She looked unsure, but pressed on anyway. "I just came up to see if you're okay. Mary told me which room you'd be in and…" She trailed off and shrugged.

My life was nothing but lies. "I'm fine."

Delicate black brows drew down into a look of displeasure and I watched Mia purse her lips. "I'm going to go ahead and call you on your bullshit right now, Ash. Sometimes it helps us work through our grief if we talk to someone—"

My broken laughter interrupted whatever words were left to pass her lips and I abruptly walked away from the door. Then I grabbed the bottle of beer from my folding table and drained the rest before it could get too warm. I felt the air in the room change and I knew she had followed me in. "Good to know Mary didn't show you all my skeletons."

Mia ignored my snarky remark and walked over to stand in front of the fan. I was immediately bathed in the scent of her perfume. "Goddamn but it's hot in here. How do you stand it?" She turned back to look at me for an answer. They were always looking for answers.

"I don't know, I guess I'm just used to the heat. Compared to a four alarm fire in full turnout gear, this is pretty mild."

She walked over to look at my weight machine, running her hand along the plates and up the cable, and I couldn't take my eyes off her fingertips. "I suppose you have a point there. Do you mind?" She gestured toward the equipment and I nodded for her to go ahead and sat back on the edge of the recliner. It wasn't like I would be using it anytime soon. At least not until the arm healed.

Mia was wearing a tank top and running shorts and I took a minute to appreciate the length of smooth muscle tone displayed as she lay back on the bench. The machine was currently set up for bench press. It was less than my regular amount but still set at a weight I assumed would be too heavy for her. I was wrong. She pressed out half a dozen rapid reps and I said the first thing that came to mind. "You're stronger than you look."

She sat up and the soft skin of her stomach that was on display during her weight demonstration was covered once again when her tank top dropped back down to the top of her shorts. She caught me staring and I turned my eyes away, ignoring her smirk. Mia shrugged. "It comes from my years working as a nurse on the floor, before I got my current position." She paused for a moment and continued with what I knew to be her reason for coming upstairs. "I'm sorry, Ash. I know how hard it is to lose someone—"

Anger flared at her words and I stood up from my chair again, pacing in front of her. "What do you know about it? I've known Derek for more than twenty years, he was my best friend! How could you remotely understand his loss to me, huh?" I stopped in front of where she sat on the bench, panting from the sudden release of pent up anger and grief. I reached for that emotional wall but couldn't find it, and my eyes watered with pain.

Mia stood and moved right in front of me. Then she reached down and delicately took the clenched fist of my good hand into both of hers. "I lost my best friend to a drunk driver the night we graduated high school. Tanie and I grew up together and we had plans to be roommates in college. She had a full-ride basketball scholarship to U of M and all of that potential was just...gone."

And just like that, my own anger and grief receded into the background. She *did* know. I had no control left when my bottom lip began to tremble, nor when the tears came. Mia, a complete stranger to me, took me into her arms and held me while I sobbed on her shoulder.

It was as if I only owned five words in my vocabulary, like my entire life was boiled down to that one thing. "I miss him so much." I repeated the words again and again like a mantra, and she held me through it all. I pulled away when I was finally calm again and my hot and swollen eyes lit on the face of someone Mary would have called an angel. In that moment I knew that Mia Thomas was more dangerous than any fire. I looked away from her face, anywhere but her eyes. "Um...I have to go clean up. Thank you for listening." Then before she could speak again, I backed out of the doorway and retreated to my bedroom. Weakness was best dealt with in solitude and silence.

Chapter Four

IT WAS FRIDAY and the city had finally cooled off. High seventies were predicted for the entire weekend and I was glad, if only for Mary's sake. It didn't make me any more comfortable while I sat on that leather couch though. I rubbed the lump in my right pocket with the second and third finger of my right hand and waited for Sarah to begin.

She made a few notes on the ever-present notepad then looked up. "I want to go back and discuss something we touched on in the last session." I didn't acknowledge her request and she continued. "The topic of your emancipation came up briefly and you mentioned that the proceedings started at sixteen, then completed at seventeen. Why did you go through the emancipation process?"

I clenched my jaw when the familiar anger rose, as it did every single time I thought of my mother. "Is this really relevant to my leave from the department?"

Sarah sighed and sat back in her chair, hands resting shoulder distance apart on the desk in front of her. I could see her searching for the right words to say and wondered why a shrink would struggle to answer so simple a question. I didn't have to wonder long. "Ash, I'm going to be frank with you, just as I hope you display nothing but honesty to me in return for as long as we continue with our sessions. Working our way back through the reason why you're here, I'm seeing a pattern in your behavior that I don't think started with the death of Derek Smith. The mind is not something you can simply slap a Band-Aid on and have everything be one hundred percent. Here is where my honesty comes in. You cannot return to the fire department as long as you display this emotionally at-risk behavior. While I may not believe that you are a danger to yourself right now, I do believe that another deep substantive blow to your psyche would send you out of control again. As a paramedic, you of all people should know that you have to heal the deeper hurts as much as the ones on the surface. And for that, you'll need help from others."

My breaths came faster the more she spoke. I thought the sessions would be easy, would be quick affirmation of my sincere regret at trying to take my own life. But her words were like fingers digging deep into the soil of my past. I wanted her to help me with the grief of Derek's death but I didn't want her to know any more. I stood abruptly and had to give her credit for not flinching. My mother made me angry, restless, and I couldn't talk about her without something to distract that anger. My lighter wasn't an option. I didn't want to talk about her at all but I could see in Sarah's eyes that the uncommunicative path was a no-go. "I don't like talking about my mom. She's in prison for a reason, and I'm glad."

She made another note. "When did she go to prison, and what was the charge?"

Her words echoed in my head. What was the charge? More like, what *wasn't* the charge. My mind reeled back eighteen years, a year after I stole the lighter. I was twelve.

"Fuck you, ya fuckin' bitch! I wasn't starin' at your whore daughter and I'm sick of your accusations!" I heard a crash from the living room and Damon's voice yelled again. "Keep breaking your own shit, psycho, I'm outta here!" A door slammed but I stayed where I was. I sat on my bed with knees drawn up under my chin, trying to block out another one of my mom's relationship implosions. Another crash sounded and I glanced up to make sure the butter knife was in the doorjamb.

Footsteps grew louder outside my door and pounding began shortly after. "Get your ass out here and clean up this mess! Fucking useless kid..." Her voice trailed off and the footsteps receded again. There was no way I was going out there when she was drunk and in a mood. The really fucked up thing was that Damon wasn't even one of the bad ones. He was a good guy, or at least not a sleaze like the rest. Probably why he didn't last, no decent guy is gonna put up with my mom's shit for long. Before I could debate what to do any longer I heard her keys jingle and the front door slammed as she left the apartment. I took my first deep breath since getting home from school earlier. I wanted to call Derek but the phone was shut off again. Instead I finished up my last bit of homework and tugged my coat on. My key was on my key ring and I shoved it in my left jeans pocket, my lighter was in the right. The pants were baggy but that's just what's cool, no matter what my mom said. Besides, half her loser boyfriends wore theirs the same way.

The warehouse was close, just two blocks away from our

apartment building. The whole neighborhood was nothing but boarded up businesses and gutted warehouses. There were two apartment buildings but neither one was any good. I go to the big warehouse sometimes, my mom's flavor of the months can't touch me there. She can't hit me either. I keep a stash of newspapers to burn in a barrel, it makes me feel better. Something about the fire as the flames cycled between colors of blue, red, yellow, and orange soothed me. The flames were pure and they burned the words of man. We're studying history right now and every time I light newspaper on fire I feel like it's my own protest of society. I don't like my home but I can't change it. And I don't like being different but I can't change that either. At least I have Derek. Last week he told me he felt the same as me, that we were both different. I wish Derek was my real family.

Before pushing through the rotted wood door, I peered in the broken windows to make sure no one was around. Voices sounded from somewhere nearby so I ducked down behind a stack of pallets and waited.

"Did you bring the stuff?"

"What do you think, fucker? I want the cash first!"

Clearly there was a deal going on so I stayed as still as possible, hoping they'd finish and leave soon. Less than a minute later I could hear the transaction come to an end. Unlucky for me a stray cat jumped from one of the stacks of pallets to another nearby and sent it crashing to the ground. I knew they'd come investigate rather than chance a witness to the exchange of drugs. I had no choice but to bolt. It was chilly outside and with my knit hat low, there's no way they could recognize me. They didn't see where I was, I was able to weave around the stacks of pallets in the warehouse parking lot and crawl through the fence that was supposed to keep looters out. I ran two blocks as fast as I could and didn't slow down until I was on the third floor outside our apartment. I bent over gasping with a cramp in my side, in pain from that as much as I was afraid of being caught by the gang bangers. I'm going to have to find another warehouse to do my burning in.

As soon as I walked through the door, hands grabbed my jacket and threw me to the ground. I hit my head on the corner of the coffee table, knocking the bottle of Popov vodka onto the floor. Pain flared in the back of my head and when I moved my hand back to the spot to touch it, my fingers came away bloody. "Where the fuck have you been? Did you follow Damon out, you little whore!"

She was drunker than when she left and I wondered how that was possible until I glanced at the capped bottle rolling around on its side. It was half empty. Rather than deny her words I used the same excuse that I'd used many times before. "I went to see Derek but he wasn't home."

She looked like she wanted to spew at me some more but she didn't. Instead she stubbed out the cigarette that had been stuck to her bottom lip and walked over to light another. She waved her hand toward my bedroom and leaned down to pick up the vodka from where it had rolled under the coffee table. "Go on, get out of my fucking face!" I scrambled up from the floor and didn't stop moving until I was safe again inside my bedroom with the door as locked as I could make it.

"Ash?"

Shit, I had fallen into my memories again. I hated it there. I tried to remember what she had asked me before the memories hit. "She went to prison when I was seventeen."

The sound of Sarah's pencil scratching across the paper was loud in the quiet room. "And the charge?"

I rubbed the lighter harder through the denim of my jeans. "Charges." I recited the words like I wasn't the one that had been on the receiving end of each. "Felony child endangerment, felony child abuse, drug trafficking, child trafficking, driving while intoxicated."

The pencil stopped and my shrink looked up in surprise. "All of that?"

I stopped rubbing and leaned forward to put my elbows on my knees. The bottom of the cast was hard and uncomfortable where it rested on the top of my left knee. She wanted answers from me and she was going to get them. "The abuse was systematic, proven by my own testimony, and with pictures taken by CPS the night she was arrested. They also pulled the past records of my medical care at the walk-in clinic near our apartment."

"What happened the night she was arrested?"

I thought back to that night and I had to fight to keep from being sucked into my memories again. "She was drunk, like usual, and mad that I'd filed the emancipation papers. If I wasn't living with her anymore, she wouldn't get food stamps or rent and heat assistance anymore. I didn't know how mad she was at the time. She told me we were going to Kroger for groceries and made me get in the back seat of the car. Once I was there she locked the doors so I couldn't get out." Sarah gave me a curious look so I explained. "Our doors had those child locks so you couldn't open them from the back seat." I stopped talking because the pain of that night was overwhelming. It was one thing for a parent to tell you over and over how little you meant to them, but when they actually show you, it was something altogether different.

"Take your time, Ash. Just go on when you're ready."

While I appreciated her concern, I didn't need it. "I grew up in a rundown apartment building off Connor and Eight Mile. I didn't realize she was drunk when I got in the car, but it was pretty obvious when she started driving. I tried to get her to stop, I leaned over the front seat and she just kind of...punched backward. She hit me so hard she broke my nose and it wouldn't stop bleeding. It hurt though and I didn't want her to hit me again so I sat back and put my seatbelt on. She had a hard time staying between the lines and cars were honking at us. I don't know why a cop didn't get her then, but we went for about five minutes like that. Then she pulled around the back of a closed-up movie place where there was another car waiting. Three men got out and I got this sick feeling in my stomach. When she told me to get out I refused and started crying. I tried to run when she opened the door but one of the guys caught me and I...I wasn't strong enough to get away."

Sarah gave me a look of sympathy. "What happened next?"

"The big man, a blond, he continued to hold me while another one gave my mom a paper bag. She pulled out baggies of drugs. I know what they were because I'd seen them before in some of the street deals in the neighborhood. Then she pulled out a wad of money, more than I'd ever seen in my life. And..." I swallowed as the anger abruptly left me and tears took their place. "She said, 'she's all yours, get her out of my face!' then she got in her car to drive away. Only, she didn't drive away. Things got crazy after that. A minute later one of the men pulled out a gun and told the other two guys and my mom to freeze, that he was a cop. Mom tried to run, but ended up hitting the building and stalling her car. The guy that was holding me let go and pulled out a gun. As soon as I was free I ran behind the dealer's car and hid. The guns sounded loud echoing off the buildings, then the sirens came and drowned out the gun fire." I took a shuddering breath, remembering how scared I was that night and it happened thirteen years ago. Some things just stay with you. I looked up at Sarah and sensing my eyes, she stopped writing.

"You asked about the charges, well she was driving drunk, driving me around drunk, and she sold me for fucking drugs and money. And as soon as she got in her car, she was already snorting some of the dope that she'd been given, so she had illegal substance in her system at the time she was taken in. After they dug into the clinic records and recorded the marks I had on my body, cigarette burns, bruises, and other lacerations, they nailed her with the child abuse charge. My mother got life in prison for what she did to me, but with good behavior she'll probably be out in a few more years."

Sarah cocked her head to stare at me intently. It reminded me so much of Mia's curious look that I had to glance away. Her voice was quiet, barely loud enough to hear over the rumble of the sound machine that masked our sessions to others in the building. "There's more, isn't there?"

I glanced up and away again just as fast. She would never get more out of me. That was a shame that was mine alone to bear. I could never tell another soul about the first fire, if I did I'd lose everything. "What more could there be than the fact that my mother was a homicidal addict who hated my guts? Isn't that enough?"

She opened her mouth to speak and shut it again as my watch began to beep. Our time was up and I drew in a great breath of relief. I stood and met her eyes. "I'll see you Monday, Doc."

"Wait, before you go..." I paused with one hand on the doorknob and looked back at her. "Did you read the papers about survivor's guilt?" I nodded. "And have you given any more thought to contacting Brandon?"

"You don't think further rejection by him would send me over the edge?"

"I think that knowing either way will do more good than harm and I think you need a clear path forward at this point. Maybe something to think about this weekend?"

My sigh was resigned and her words filled me with anxiety. But after reading the papers she sent home, I had to admit that there was a possibility she was right. "I'll think about it."

She nodded once. "Okay, thank you. Have a good weekend, Ash."

"You too." Then I was out the door and digging into my pocket. I wasn't sure how this weekend would be any better than the last. Derek was still dead.

A PART OF me was disappointed that I didn't see Mia's car when I got home. I don't know why, it wasn't something I could explain. She probably had to work so it made sense that I wouldn't see her around all the time. But there was something about dredging up the memories of the night my mother sold me that left me feeling...bereft. It was probably good that I didn't see her, after my breakdown in the spare room. Mary's car was gone from the driveway so I assumed she'd be at the community center. She donated her time every Tuesday and Friday, sometimes more, and I suspected it was one of bright spots of her week. That and the weekly euchre game she attended with her three delinquent friends from the Baptist church. I smiled at the memory of the last time they came to our place. Those women could get rowdy!

It was too early for the mail so I made my way up to the front porch. Before I could get the key in the lock I heard a vehicle pull into the drive next door. Mia was home. She exited the new looking white SUV and I thought she either made a lot of money as a Clinical Nurse Leader, or her parents were pretty comfortable. Of course the other possibility was that one of her parents worked for Ford and got a nice discount. "Hey, Ash!"

Her smile didn't falter, and she never hesitated to give it. Even after my cowardly display from two days before. Rather than unlocking the door like I had planned, I found my feet walking down the steps of the porch and heading next door. Mia looked surprised but continued to smile as she leaned into the passenger seat and grabbed her purse. When she shut the door I said what was at the top of my head. "I'm sorry."

Mia gave me a curious look, like she didn't remember my actions from the other night. Her hair was pulled back into a tight bun and she looked as put together as always. "Whatever do you have to be sorry about?"

I sighed and rubbed the lighter in my pocket, then quickly pulled my fingers away when she followed the motion of my hand. "I'm sorry for being a dick the other day. I..." I what? What was I going to tell her? Or rather, why would I tell her anything? Then the reason clicked. I felt comfortable with Mia, and she comforted me in a way that I'd only ever felt with Mary. There was something about her that made me feel like it was okay to...feel.

"Ash?" Fingers grazed my forearm and I shivered at her touch.

I had to give myself a mental shake to prompt the words. "Yeah, sorry. I just don't normally open up like that. I don't break down and I didn't want you to see me that way."

She smiled and I watched as little lines crinkled at the corners of her eyes. Her teeth seemed very white against the dark caramel of her skin. Then I realized that she was watching me stare at the shape of her cheekbones and I flushed with embarrassment. Her voice was quieter than normal, and just a little huskier. "And how do you want me to see you?"

I looked up into her honest eyes and took a chance. "Not weak."

Mia shook her head. "I don't think I could ever see you as weak."

And right there was an opening, just one more if I were brave enough to take it. "Not broken then."

"All breaks can be mended with time." Then she threaded her left arm through my right and turned me toward her house. "Come on, let me show you what I've done with the place." I followed her willingly into the light colored house.

Chapter Five

I DON'T KNOW what I was expecting when I walked into Mia's house, but I was genuinely surprised. It was a two-story like Mary's, but the downstairs seemed much more open. Maybe I thought that with her obvious signs of money, Mia's house would be more…extravagant. It wasn't over the top though, it was comfortable. It had been ten years at least since I'd been in the house, back when I'd help out Letty with odd jobs now and then.

When I first moved in with Mary, I was always looking for ways to make money. A few of the older folks in the neighborhood would hire me to mow their lawns in the summer and shovel snow in the winter. Letty's health was never as good as Mary's, so I'd come over and give her a hand with odd projects around her house and some light house cleaning. She even bought me a silly apron and begged me to wear it while cleaning. Here I was, this tough Detroit dyke and a teenager, humoring an old woman because it made her laugh. I liked Letty, she was good people. While I let her pay me for the outside work, I never charged her for the rest.

Everything had a fresh coat of pale green paint, and the floors had all been pulled up and replaced with a rich dark hardwood. The leather furniture was a soft butterscotch color and her end tables looked like they came out of a magazine. My eye was caught by the big screen TV hanging on the far wall then flickered like flame back and forth along the speakers mounted all around the room. I whistled and she grinned at me. "You like?"

I nodded and smiled back at her. "That is my dream set up, right there!" She started leading me through the living room into the area that used to be Letty's dining room. However, instead of the dark closed off space I remembered, the entire back of the first floor had been opened up. The kitchen was state of the art and it melded smoothly into a casual seating space. New French doors looked out over the back deck and I fell even more in love with the changes made to the old place.

My admiration was interrupted by a voice that held a tinge of pride. "This is my favorite part of the house. I love to cook so I wanted to make sure I had plenty of space. What about you, do you like to cook?"

I slowly ran my hand over the treated butcher block island. "Mary and I both do, and we take turns on meals throughout the week when I'm not on duty. Sometimes we each pick dishes for the other to cook and make dinner together."

"That's really sweet. I like Mary, she reminds me a lot of my own grandma. Come on, I'll show you the upstairs."

I followed her up and did my best to keep my eyes off the perfect shape of her pants in front of me. I felt a little heated by the time she took me through the guest room and master bedroom. Besides the renovations on the first floor, she'd also had the master bath gutted and refinished. I ran a finger over the soaker tub. "Nice." The bathroom was colored in earth tones of pale yellow, greens, and browns. The bedroom featured dark wood furniture complimented with white and a variety of blues.

When we went downstairs I followed her back into the kitchen. "The basement is finished too. I just have some exercise equipment down there and my laundry room. No frills. You want something to drink?"

"Sure, whatever you're having is fine."

Mia smirked. "You like prune juice?"

"What?" I stared at her with confusion and no small amount of disgust.

Then Mia started laughing and I knew she was pulling my leg. "Just kidding. I have a pitcher of fresh lemonade. It's refreshing on its own, even better with a little cherry vodka."

I grimaced at the thought of vodka. It wasn't that I didn't like the liquor, but it made me remember my recent session with Sarah. It also made me think of the night of Derek's funeral. "I'll just have the lemonade, thanks."

That curious look stole over her face again and I knew she'd ask. "Not a fan of liquor?"

"I...I like it just fine. But right now it just reminds me of things I'd rather not think about."

"Fair enough." She filled two glasses of ice and poured the lemonade. My gaze was caught by the slices of lemons and limes floating in the top of the pitcher, then of the smooth dark skin of her hand and neatly trimmed nails. She caught me staring but gave me a mild smile as she handed over the tall glass. "We can drink it in here or take it out on the deck. We won't melt since the heat wave finally broke but it's definitely cooler in here."

My own laughter took me by surprise. "Yeah, I noticed that

you had central air and I'm jealous about that too. It's a beautiful day though, so let's take it outside." She glanced down at my denim covered legs and short sleeve button up shirt and I felt the need to reassure her. "It's fine, I'm used to the heat."

I don't know what happened but as soon as we took seats on her cool stone patio, I felt...free. I was lighter somehow. We talked about our jobs and compared schedules. While I worked twenty-four hours on and seventy-two hours off, Mia worked twelve hour shifts every Tuesday, Wednesday, and Friday. The reason she'd been home all week was because she took the time off to move. She talked about growing up in Troy. I asked about her parents and she said her mother, Lucy, was a second-generation Japanese American working as an HR administrator at a big insurance company downtown. Apparently her dad, Robert Thomas, fell in love with Lucy when they were both attending Wayne State, and they got married right after graduation. Robert was an engineer at Ford, which was how Mia got her Edge at such a sick price. I laughed because you couldn't spit in Detroit without hitting someone that either worked for an auto manufacturer or was an employee's family member.

"So you said my living room was your dream setup. What do you like to watch? Oh, and I should ask, Lions, Tigers, or Wings?"

I smiled back at her and my jaw hurt. I hadn't smiled so much in a long time. "Well..." I didn't want to seem stupid with my answer.

Mia curled a finger toward her. "Come on, I promise not to laugh."

"Musicals!" I blurted the word out, then was mortified when I realized that I couldn't take it back again. In my mortification, I didn't tell her that I didn't see my first one until coming to live with Mary. We barely had a TV that would pick up the local stations, we definitely didn't have anything like movies or a DVD player. Well we did, but my mom sold them. The only reason she didn't sell the television too was because she liked to watch it late at night. So it was the sound of the musicals and all the bright colors, they reminded me of the first safe place I'd ever really known. Mary Poppins was my very first. I guess I liked them as much for the sense of nostalgia as I did for actually liking them.

Rather than mocking, her face took on a look of shock and delight. "Really? Oh my God, I love musicals! Seriously, none of my friends ever want to attend so I rarely go to live events."

I blushed because I hadn't been able to go to many live shows

unless they were put on by the colleges or local community the-
aters. "I haven't seen many live events, the tickets are pretty
pricey. But I'll watch them on TV when I can."

"Disney animated movies too?"

My face warmed again as I admitted a bit of silliness. "Yeah.
Mary had an entire collection and I kind of plowed through them
in the first six months after I moved in. Now I buy every new one
that comes out." Mia shook her head, looking like she was trying
to hold back a laugh. "What?" I challenged. "Surprised?"

My eyes tripped over her smile, caught in the symmetry of
her face as it lit from within. Her lips had my full attention as a
single word slipped out. "Pleasantly."

My attraction caught like a flame on dry tinder and our
moment stretched into a minute or more. Reluctantly I looked
away and cleared my throat. Mia Thomas was not so easy to resist
and I could read her interest as easily as I could the colors of a
flame. I acknowledged my own interest as well, but not aloud.
Desperate to change the subject, I went with something basic. "So
it looks like you're pretty much done moving. You've clearly been
busy with your week off."

"Damn straight! And now I get to kick up my heels and relax
a bit before I head back to work on Tuesday. What about you,
how long until that cast comes off?"

I held the cast up and gave it a dirty look. "Fractured ulna
and the doc said that average time in a cast for adults is four to
six weeks."

Mia shot me a sympathetic look. "Well that sucks. Are you
off work the entire time until it heals?"

Her words stirred my memories and Sarah's statement bubbled up to the surface.

*"You cannot return to the fire department as long as you display
this emotionally at-risk behavior. While I may not believe that you are a
danger to yourself right now, I do believe that another deep substantive
blow to your psyche would send you out of control again. As a paramedic, you of all people should know that you have to heal the deeper
hurts as much as the ones on the surface. And for that, you'll need help
from others."*

I shook my head. "No, it's...not that." I looked into Mia's
eyes and they radiated compassion in a way I'd only seen from
one other person. Mary. "After Derek died, I didn't handle things
well. I was there in the building with him and Brandon, but Derek
was pinned. Our other good friend and fellow firefighter, Bran-

don, was unconscious and Derek told me to save him then come back with help. I knew he was right and I had no choice but to leave him there and carry Brandon out. But as soon as we cleared the building it..." I stopped because the pain was still so heavy.

She covered my hand with her own and the gentle softness pulled me from my spiraling despair. "Hey, it's going to be okay. I know you hurt right now and it's okay to hurt. But you'll get through this."

My knee started jiggling and I took a moment to wipe the tears that had fallen with just the short retelling. "That's not all. I haven't spoken with Brandon since the accident. The three of us were like...we were best friends. But worst of all, Brandon and Derek were together, and they loved each other so much. No one in the department knew but me. To the rest of them, we were all best friends. They called us the Three Musketeers. But now I think he hates me. Be...because of that I came home the night of Derek's funeral and drank a fifth of vodka. Used it to wash down the pain pills they'd given me for my broken arm. So I'm off work until a shrink clears me to come back."

"Oh, Ash..."

I looked up at the tone of her voice, expecting judgement or pity. I saw neither, just a woman who sympathized with my pain, a face that understood exactly what I felt and did. "You know, don't you? You understand it?"

Mia nodded. "While I didn't attempt suicide after Tanie died, I started cutting. It wasn't anything really serious, and I've only got one scar from it today. It was my college girlfriend, nearly a year after Tanie, that made me see what I was doing and face up to the survivor's guilt that I felt."

I'd never even heard the term until my shrink had mentioned it and suddenly here it was again. "Why would you feel survivor's guilt?"

Mia sighed. "I was in the car. I lived, and she didn't. The other car struck the driver's side and she never had a chance."

I made a sound low in my throat, the only thing I could get out in the face of her past sorrow that was so similar to what I was going through now. "I'm really sorry for your loss. My...um, psychiatrist is covering survivor's guilt with me now, as well as a ton of other shit about my past that I'd rather not discuss." I grimaced and took a sip of my lemonade.

"Listen to the doctor and I guarantee things will get better."

I smiled shyly at her, aware that her hand still rested on

mine. "They already are."

With a light squeeze she pulled away and took a drink of her own lemonade. "Enough of this maudlin stuff. What are your plans tonight?"

"I haven't really had any plans since the fire. Derek, Brandon, and I used to hang out together all the time. We'd grill over at Brandon's house, sometimes catch a Tiger's game...we were family, you know?"

"Well shit, I didn't mean to bring that up again."

I couldn't help smiling at her curse. She seemed too...proper for swearing. Too put together. "It's okay. I don't do a lot on my own. I either watch Netflix, or let Mary beat me at scrabble. That woman is a fiend!"

Mia's eyes twinkled and perfectly matched her beautiful smile. "Do you shoot pool?"

My shrug was nonchalant. "I played a little back in the day. You?"

"Oh, I played back in the day too. But I also play now, I love it actually."

The snort came out before I could sensor myself. "Oh, back in the day huh? And just how old are you, Mia Thomas?"

She shot back just as fast. "How old are *you*, Ash...what is your last name again?"

"Hayes."

"Well how old are you, Ash Hayes?"

I smirked at her youthful attitude and good looks. "I'm thirty, as of last month. And? Tit for tat, young lady!"

Mia rolled her eyes. "Pshh, who are you calling young lady? I've got nearly five years on you!" She shot her fist into the air in victory. "Yes!"

Not in a million years would I have guessed her age. She looked barely out of college. "Wow! Not bad, Thomas. Not bad at all."

Mia swirled the ice in her glass and took another healthy swallow. "Not bad yourself, Hayes. But anyway, we got off topic, youngster. Would you be interested in shooting some pool with me tonight?"

Thoughts and feelings tumbled through my head and I tested the sore spots of my mind that had been opened with Sarah's session earlier. Did I feel like being social? Being around a lot of other people? "That depends, where are you thinking?"

"Do you mind going out a little farther? I like Gears, up in

Royal Oak."

I thought about the bar that was an old converted mechanic's garage. It was bigger than it looked from the front because it expanded into a two story brick building that sat directly behind it in the lot. It had a nice industrial vibe, with all manner of black painted gears and sprockets adorning the walls. The guys and I would go up that way a few times a year but it had been a while since our last night out. The brick building's second floor had four pool tables, a foosball table, two air hockey tables, and a variety of arcade style games. The clientele had a lot of LGBTQ flavor but really was a little of everyone. Royal Oak was a fairly open place. I finished my drink. "I wouldn't mind hanging out for a few hours."

She got a mischievous glint in her eyes. "Are you sure you can play with that plaster on your arm?"

I raised an eyebrow and grinned at her. "The left hand is just a stick rest anyway. You shouldn't taunt the pool masters, Mia Thomas! Mess with the best, cry like the rest." The moment suddenly became too ridiculous and we both cracked up laughing. I hadn't laughed so hard since the last game night at Derek and Brandon's house. But the thought of my loss didn't pull the smile from my face like I expected. Instead, that constrictive band around my chest eased just a bit.

"What are you thinking about?" Mia's question pulled me from my thoughts and she tilted her head curiously, cutely at me.

"Nothing much."

Mia finished her own drink and set it back on the patio table. "You look lighter, Ash. I like your smile."

My lips turned up more with her words. "I like your smile too." Then, thinking I had admitted too much, I stood. "I should probably go. I promised Mary I'd start my pasta sauce for dinner tonight." At her questioning look I elaborated. "I make it from scratch from our garden tomatoes so it takes a bit."

"Ooh! I've got leftovers for dinner tonight but next time you make something like that, you better invite me over."

"Deal." I lifted my empty glass. "You want me to take care of this?"

"No, I'll get it on my way in. How does eight tonight sound? I'll drive up if you like, or do you have to drive everywhere?"

A light blush crawled up my cheeks. "I'm not that controlling. You can drive if you want. See you in a few hours, Mia." Then I trotted down the stairs and walked around the side of her house that butted up against Mary's yard. I still had to pick some tomatoes.

SURPRISINGLY, MARY DIDN'T say anything when I told her that Mia and I were going out to shoot pool later. She just kept giving me her sly smile in between bites of spaghetti. I figured that since Mia was driving I could do the nice thing and walk next door so she didn't have to come fetch me. I wore a tight white V-neck t-shirt that highlighted my colorful half sleeve of tattoos. The shirt itself was the softest one I owned and I loved the way it felt against my skin. I never did much with my hair, just added a little pomade and pushed it back and to the side. Derek used to tell me that my hair and pouty lips were guaranteed to drive the ladies wild. I wasn't sure I missed his advice but I missed him. Beyond the top half, the bottom was the same as always—dark denim with cuffs at the bottoms, and my black steel toe boots. With my belt threaded through the leather strap of my wallet chain, I was ready. I debated grabbing a jacket but the temp wasn't dropping as fast as I thought and I knew I'd be fine. It wasn't like it was winter.

Mia was just closing and locking her front door when I wandered across from Mary's yard to hers. She hadn't noticed me so I paused just to take in her look. She had a black baby doll tee paired with light-colored denim capris pants and black sandals. While I wasn't normally the type to care about clothes, she certainly wore hers well. When she looked up and met my gaze, we both froze for a moment until words poured from her mouth. "Wow, you look great!"

Panic nearly made me pass out because I didn't want to ruin whatever new friendship we had going. I didn't want her to know exactly how attracted to her I was. A desperate mantra began rolling through my head as soon as I caught the barest hint of cleavage peeking out of her shirt. More than a little freaked, the words came out of my mouth when they were supposed to remain thought and nothing more. "This isn't a date!" Oh shit. This and a million other reasons were why I was still single. This was why I needed a wingman. And that familiar, persistent thought creeped back in. I miss Derek. "I'm so sorry, I don't know why I just said that."

Laughter and a waved hand cut me off mid-apology. "Oh my God, the look on your face just now. You are so funny!"

I breathed a sigh of relief and kicked the heel of my right boot against the toe of my left. "So you're not mad?"

Mia had already made her way down the porch steps but my words caused her to step uncomfortably close to me. She made eye contact as she ran an index finger along the vee of my shirt collar, all the way down to the point then back up again. Her voice was sultry but her mouth was all smirk. "Just so you know, Ash Hayes, while I will hang out with new friends that I've only known a week, I won't go on a date with them after so short a time." She paused for a second. "Even the hot ones." Then she winked and turned to head around her white SUV. I remained frozen until she was on the other side. "Get in the car, Ash!" Her laughter cut off with the slam of the driver's door and I started to sweat.

Chapter Six

I WAS ACTUALLY relieved that Mia drove because my Jeep had never been completely reliable, and I no longer had a friend to call if I had trouble. Given the track record of my old Jeep, it wouldn't last much longer without my best friend's TLC. Besides, her Edge was a sweet ride.

"What are you thinking so hard about over there?"

I glanced to the left and watched Mia navigate multiple lanes of traffic. The sun was low but not down quite yet, and I took a moment to study her face without sunglasses to obstruct the view. "Nothing important. Just deciding what I want to do when my Jeep finally dies. It turned over hard today when I was leaving to go to my appointment. Der...Derek was my guy. The man knew anything and everything about cars. I'm certain that was one of the reasons why his pop hated my guts when Derek followed me to become a paramedic and later a firefighter." She looked at me curiously and I realized that I'd never told her about Derek's family, or about Derek really. "His pop owns a garage near Eight Mile where we grew up. With two older brothers already working at the shop, Derek figured it wouldn't be a big deal if he didn't join the family business." I blew out a breath. "Anyway, they hate me more than ever now."

"That seems unlikely. They lost their son, you lost your best friend."

"Mia, all they know is that I went back into the building and brought a man out, but that man wasn't their son. It wasn't Derek and they'll never forgive me. His oldest brother told me so at the funeral."

"Ash..." Her eyes remained on the busy expressway but she reached her hand across and covered mine where it lay on the center console. "You said Derek was pinned. If you had a crowbar or axe on you, would you have been able to bring him out?"

My voice was quiet, barely louder than the air conditioner that was running on low. "No. The beam was huge. It would have taken at least four of us to lift it. Or we would have had to cut through it."

Even though my head was down, staring at the way she held

my hand with hers, I still saw her glance my way out of the corner of my eye. "And was there time for any of that?"

I swallowed the lump in my throat. "The collapse happened so fast. They were around a corner, maybe ten feet from the door, and I just barely made it out with Brandon. There would have been no time to free him. We would have all died too. I know the facts, Mia, but that doesn't make it easy to just wash away the guilt. The moment I looked into his eyes, we both knew he wasn't going to make it out. It's hard to take."

She squeezed my hand. "It is hard to take, but there was nothing you could do. You can and will feel bad for surviving when someone you love didn't. But you are in no way responsible, by direct or indirect action, for his death."

I nodded but couldn't speak to answer. The drive to Royal Oak took about half an hour total. It wasn't that it was a long drive, just that traffic was a zoo on northbound I-75 on a Friday night. We exited 75 and turned left onto Eleven Mile, which took us all the way down to Woodward. Gears wasn't on the main strip, but on a side street not far from all the action. The silence between us continued until we hit the downtown area of Royal Oak proper and I hated thinking that I'd ruined what promised to be a fun night. When she pulled into the parking lot for Gears, I tried to make it right. "I'm sorry."

Mia shut off the car and stashed the keyless fob in her front pants pocket. "What are you sorry for?"

"Being such a downer I guess..."

Her words cut my self-pity off at the knees. "Don't! Derek's death was just as much a wound as that broken arm. You wouldn't apologize for wearing a cast and you shouldn't apologize for missing your best friend. Wounds take time to heal, and you can't force them to heal faster just because it may be inconvenient to the people around you." She turned in her seat to face me properly. The streetlights started flicking on when she spoke again. "You're a good person who's suffered tragedy but I think you'll find in the end that you're also a strong person too. And you will get through this."

I smiled at her then, and it was both real and honest. It wasn't born of the fake expectation of a stranger, nor was it the result of some found humor between us. It was the smile I gave to my friends. Without even realizing it was happening, Mia Thomas had snuck over my emotional wall and hugged me with her optimism. We had become friends. I took a deep breath and nodded

to her, feeling more resolute than I had since Derek's funeral. "I
will get through this. Thank you."

"Any time. Now, I believe I owe a certain younger woman an
ass-whoopin'."

I snorted at her words and pushed open the car door. She had
found my laughter again too.

IT WAS EARLY so the bar wasn't very crowded yet and cover
was only five bucks each to get in. It just seemed natural to pull a
ten out of my wallet for the both of us, and to give Mia credit, she
didn't hesitate or give the gesture a second glance. But inside my
head my conscience was screaming at me. *This isn't a fucking date,
you asshole!* I shut it down but still felt better when she bought my
first beer. At least until I looked at the bottle. "What's this?"

Mia wagged her finger at me. "I'm sorry, but nuh uh, I will
not watch my friends drink rat piss if I can help it."

My dark brows rose. "Well, well, such language Miss
Thomas! And exactly what is wrong with Budweiser?"

She snorted. "I'm going to go out on a limb and say the tap
water northwest of here probably tastes better."

I pushed her finger out of the way with my own. "You are a
beer snob!"

"I have taste!"

Leaning close, I slowly enunciated each consonant. "Beer
snob."

She rolled her eyes as she started up the stairs in the back of
the bar. "Oh please! The increased alcohol content and flavor of a
good beer make the dollar extra a bottle well worth the cost. It's
not like we're here to get drunk. That's what I have a house for."
She suddenly stopped and caught me staring at her ass.

My face grew warm with embarrassment in the dim lights
but I met her eyes anyway. I wanted to dismiss my obvious
ogling as something else, to make some excuse for my inappropri-
ate action. But sadly my brain to mouth filter was clogged. My
throat made a strange noise but no words actually came out in my
defense. "Uhh..."

Mia smirked. "Bad Ash, no biscuit!" I wasn't sure I liked this
new lack of control I had around the woman two steps above me.
Before I could try to explain away my wandering gaze, she continued with her tirade. "It's summer—live a little."

Her words seemed like a challenge so I lifted the bottle to

peer at the familiar orange and blue label. Just because I'd never had it didn't mean that an Oberon wasn't immediately recognizable. You couldn't live in Michigan and not know what an Oberon was. Standing halfway up the stairs, I maintained eye contact and raised the bottle to my lips. My first impression was that it was thicker and more...wheaty than Bud. The second thing I noticed was the hint of citrus in the aftertaste, from the trademark orange slice slipped in by the bartender. As much as I hated to admit it, the beer was good. "Hmm..."

"*Well?*"

"You're pretty damn impatient, you know that?"

"Ash." Her voice had a low warning quality to it and I was starting to recognize that glint in her light brown eyes.

"Fine, you win. It's really fucking good."

She gave me an impish smile and spun around to start up the stairs again. "Thank you." I kept my eyes on the treads the rest of the way up.

After playing two games of pool, we each had one win under our belt and we were getting ready to play a tiebreaker. I grabbed my second empty beer bottle to take back to the bar and called out as she was racking the balls. "You want another beer?"

"No, I'm good. Thank you, though."

I looked at her curiously. She didn't *look* like she was having a bad time. "Is everything okay?"

Mia shrugged, looking almost apologetic. "It's no big deal. I just don't drink much when I'm driving. The rest of my friends all have their own individual limits, but mine's always been pretty low."

I wondered about her low limit for a second then the reason behind it dawned on me. Her best friend had been killed by a drunk driver. "Oh shit, I'm so sorry! I didn't even stop to think." I immediately set the bottle down but she stopped racking and walked over to me.

Mia's smile was genuine as she rested a hand on my good arm. "Seriously, it's all right. Have another one. I'll get you home safe. I promise." She winked at me and a stupid grin magically appeared on my face. Right in the middle of my damn face. What was it about Mia that had me reacting so far outside my normal self? I didn't know and there was no way I was going to analyze it at that moment. Instead, I came back from the bar with another Oberon for me and a bottle of water for her. The look she gave me had my stomach doing little flips but the way she ran me around the pool table afterward calmed things back down again.

After she beat me a second time, we decided to grab a table and take a break from the competitive sports for a bit. Well, *I* decided. "Why are you so damn good at pool? Seriously, I used to make money in college by hitting the douche bars and betting college bros."

Mia smirked and sipped her water. "Oh really? Bros aren't really known for being good losers."

"No, just losers." She cracked up laughing and I shrugged. "Well they always had money, and enough bravado to not back down from a challenge. But they rarely had any game. Of course, once they started throwing around names like 'dyke' and 'fag' I never stayed long. I'd take my winnings and bolt for someplace with better clientele."

"Do you get that a lot?"

"What?" I gestured at my Detroit meets rockabilly style. "Because I'm not oh-so-femme and pretty, like a lot of other girls?"

She smiled mischievously. "Oh, you're pretty all right. But you've got this veneer of...toughness."

Her comment took me off guard. "Oh...well, um, sure...I get called dyke a lot. But I guess I'm used to it by now. I just live simply and I try to be as comfortable as possible. I like jeans, I like boots, and I like fresh shirts. I prefer my hair not to be in my way and if that means shaved short on the sides and slicked back..." I shrugged again. I was just me.

Mia winked. "It's a good look and you wear it well. Tell me about your tattoos."

I had been very aware throughout our many conversations that while she talked about her family, and some of her friends, she let me bring up the things I wanted to discuss about me. It didn't take me long to figure out that Mia Thomas was a very empathetic soul. She must have sensed that friends weren't my only sore spot. I raised the soft white sleeve of my tee to show her the tattoo on my shoulder. It was a colorful Japanese tiger that came down from shoulder to bicep. It was part of a much larger tapestry that went up to wrap around my shoulder blade and covered part of my left pectoral muscle and came down to just above my elbow. "This was my first tattoo. I got it after my emancipation process was complete. Derek actually had a matching one on his opposite shoulder."

"Emancipation?"

Shit. I'd never told Mia about my emancipation. I don't know what it was about her but it seemed as though we'd known each other for a lot longer. She was...familiar, she was comfortable. I hadn't felt so at ease with someone new since meeting Mary. "I uh...I didn't have the best home life when I was a kid. When I was sixteen I read something on the internet in the library about kids being able to go through emancipation from their parents so I filed the papers myself. I didn't want to run away because I wanted to go to college and be a firefighter."

"You knew even then?"

I thought about the lighter in my pocket but didn't allow my fingers to rub across it. "Yeah, I've known since I was thirteen. Anyway, a few months after I filed the paperwork, not long after my seventeenth birthday, my mom found out. She was pissed at first. Then she got all weird but didn't say anything more about it. I knew she would be freaked out because without me she'd lose her welfare assistance. We were poor and she got food stamps and money from the state for taking care of her own damn kid." I stopped to finish off my beer. I didn't want to get into detail but I could still give her the basics. "Well, just when I thought she was over it, some shit went down. It was...bad. Long story short, she went to prison and I was awarded not only my emancipation, but a cash settlement from the court as part of a much larger federal case that was going on at the time."

Her eyes grew wide and she sat back in her chair. "Holy fuck. Did that have anything to do with the Charles Greene trafficking case about thirteen years ago? The Federal one? It was all over the papers back then. I believe I was in my last year of college."

I nodded slowly and cleared my suddenly dry throat. "Yeah, though I was at the tail of it. No actual trafficking went on." The look in Mia's eyes was one that I'd never seen before. I hadn't known the woman long at all, but she had a very expressive face. "What are you thinking?"

"Your life...damn but you've had it rough, haven't you? And now your best friend?"

I looked away from those compassionate eyes and started peeling the label off my empty bottle. "Yeah, I suppose."

"You know, I always thought my granny was strong for what she went through back in the sixties. But none of her stories were personal. They were just about a hard life made harder by the color of her skin. But your story...Ash Hayes, you are the strongest woman I've ever met. And I've met some powerhouses, believe me."

I looked in bewilderment. A beautiful and successful, half-black and half-Japanese woman, who probably had her own struggles making her way in the world...she was calling me strong. "But I'm not strong. I told you about my moment of greatest weakness."

She leaned forward, elbows on the table, and pointed a finger at me. "Listen here, it's not the fall that defines you, it's the way you get back up and keep going. Don't be so hard on yourself. You're moving again and that's what counts."

"How do you live with such...optimism?"

Mia laughed. "I don't know, it's just a gift I guess. Now, are you ready for me to trounce you at some air hockey?"

I thought about the air hockey table in Derek and Brandon's basement...well, just Brandon's now. I was the undisputed champion on game nights. The grin I gave Mia was positively feral. I could feel it in the curve of my lips and in the way my eyes narrowed. I knew that look on my own face. "Game on."

We walked over to claim one of the two empty tables but Mia stopped just before we got there. "You need another beer?"

I smiled back at her, feeling just a little bit freer from my painful memories. Perhaps Sarah was right. *Sometimes it helps to share those painful memories and you'll find that the more you share the easier it will get.* While Sarah had unlocked the closet to my past, at least some of it, Mia was gently and cautiously pushing it open. And much to my surprise, I didn't find the monsters inside that I'd always feared. I found cobwebs and some old pictures of the kid I used to be. And *that* Ash didn't recognize the woman I was now.

All that was left was to deal with that old guilt that ate at me from the inside, from a memory much older than Derek's death and more traumatizing than the actions of a useless mother. That deeper memory was from a guilt that was all my own, from things that I alone was responsible for. I just needed to find a time and a place to pay restitution for my own murderous deeds. But I was determined to get through this too.

Chapter Seven

WE KILLED A few more hours at Gears and found ourselves back home a little after midnight. Sitting in Mia's driveway, she reached down to cut the engine with the keyless start button. I was still trying to process the sheer quantity of different emotions that had gone through me over the course of the night. There was something about Mia that made me feel safe and comfortable, and it seemed like a real friendship was developing between us. Unfortunately, there was also something about Mia that left me with sweating palms and a racing heart, and it had nothing to do with friendship. The attraction was beyond anything I had previously felt and I wondered if it was because I felt so easy in her presence. And there were moments throughout the night when I thought she might return my attraction but I was notoriously bad at reading people.

"So…" Startled, I jumped and turned to Mia in the streetlamp lit darkness of the vehicle. "I'm really glad we did this, I had a blast tonight."

I blurted the first thing that came to mind. "My face hurts."

She looked confused, for good reason. "I'm sorry?"

The smile that came with the cute tilt of her head left my cheeks aching even more. "From smiling. I had a great time and I don't think I can remember the last time I smiled so much. It was nice to get out and, I don't know, just lose myself for a while." I swallowed to keep from admitting deeper feelings. "It was nice to be happy again."

Her hand touched my knee and I trembled. "Ash, it's okay to be happy. If you can't find anything good or light in the world, even when things seem darkest, that is when you need to worry. But you can still see and appreciate all the laughter and light that life has to offer. You're healing, and it's a good thing."

I smiled again. I couldn't help it. "I am healing, and I think with the help of my friends both old and new, I could be better than I was before. I mean, I will always miss Derek, but he wouldn't want me to wallow forever."

"No, he wouldn't."

I covered her hand with my right one because I knew the cast on my left would be uncomfortable. "Thank you for understanding, and for caring." I looked up from our hands and met Mia's eyes and found that same look I'd seen multiple times. I knew the look, the one that said it would be the most natural thing in the world to just lean forward and close the space between us. And I was right. Mia met me halfway, over the awkward expanse of the center console and her lips were so soft and sweet. I lightly caressed them with my own at first, letting my tongue graze her bottom lip lightly after a few seconds and she opened to me the same amount, following my lead. In that instant, when our tongues met between the confines of our lips and teeth, it was as if an accelerant had been thrown on the fire. Mia moaned and fisted a handful of hair at the crown of my head where there was length enough to grab. We pressed together even more around the bulky cast on the center console and I was surprised at how fast my arousal came to the forefront. Eventually things slowed and we pulled away, our breaths coming in shallow pants.

Mia abruptly realized that her hand was still in my hair and she let go to allow me to sit back in my seat. "I'm sorry."

I blew out a breath and ran my right hand through the tousled strands, slicking it back again. "Don't apologize. That was probably the singular most amazing kiss I've ever had."

Mia's face lit up with a smile, then just as quickly flickered out again like a dying flame. I felt a sinking feeling in the pit of my stomach. "No, I'm sorry because I shouldn't start something that neither one of us are ready for. I like you a lot Ash, but..."

I didn't want to hear her reasons why a Detroit ghetto girl wasn't good enough. I had heard the kiss off enough times that I just wanted to go home and go to bed at that point. "You don't have to say anymore, I get it." I started to open the door but she grabbed my arm, strong fingers curled around my left bicep, and I was forced to stop.

Mia tilted her head curiously and I didn't expect it. It was that look that constantly caught my attention. My stomach flipped again at her nearness, and the remembered kiss. Her perfume in the closed car was like warm vanilla. "I don't think you *do* get it so I'm going to go out on a limb here. I *do* like you, and I don't think I've been so instantly attracted to anyone before. But I know that you're still healing from some major emotional trauma and I've learned the hard way that if you don't give yourself time to grieve, the stress of that trauma will tear apart any relationship you have. You can't give your heart to someone when it's still broken."

Shock must have shown on my face at her words. "Whoa, heart?"

She smiled and shrugged. "I don't do casual, Ash. If I'm going to date someone, I'm going to make sure they have potential for something serious."

My mind went stupid, and the response that fell from my lips reflected it. "Oh. I just thought it was — "

"You thought what?"

I pointed back and forth between us. "Look at us. I figured it was because we come from such different backgrounds. I'm not exactly someone you bring home to your parents, Mia. I'm a diesel dyke from the wrong end of Eight Mile."

Mia suddenly let go of my arm and brought her hand up to caress my cheek. It wasn't something that had been done to me before and it felt strangely intimate. "You sell yourself short. My grandma Letty used to say that it doesn't matter where you start in life, it's where you end up that counts. You have everything to offer someone and if they don't see that then they're not worth your time. A woman just needs to be patient and wait out some of the pain you've got inside."

I swallowed the lump in my throat. "And how would that be fair to any woman that is worth my time? I...I have a lot of pain."

She smiled and I didn't need much light in the car to see how it transformed her face from beautiful to radiant. "Well, a person would get the benefit of your friendship until you were ready for more. And speaking as someone who's only just met you over the past week, you'll be a pretty great friend."

"But how do you know?" My voice was a whisper.

Mia shrugged and gave me an impish smile. "You're smart, funny, loyal, and you care deeply about Mary. That says a lot right there. You'd help anyone out in a pinch. Whether you want to admit it or not, you're a hero, Ash."

"I'm not a hero." Her words stabbed at me.

She put her hand back over mine. "You are. You save people's lives and property, and you help guarantee the safety of thousands of people all over the city. You risk your life every time you go into a burning building, and you have the scars to prove it. Perhaps you can only see the shadow of yourself that is cast by the flames you battle. But for those of us who are really looking, we see so much more."

"I, um, thank you." I didn't know what to say to her. "And you're right, I don't want to rush into anything with anyone just yet. I really like you too but I know I'm not ready." I looked up into her eyes. They were barely illuminated by the streetlight outside yet I still remained caught in her gaze. "But until I am ready, I can always use a friend." As I waited I could feel that familiar tension rise between us again and I knew I had to get out of the car. Our new friendship was worth it. I started to pull the door handle and stopped again at the sound of her voice.

"Ash, I was going to ask you earlier but I forgot. I'm having a housewarming party tomorrow. It's just a barbecue with my parents and some friends. I'd like it if you and Mary came." She paused for a second. "I mean, if you don't have plans."

That face-aching grin returned. "I don't have plans, and I'll pass on your invite to Mary in the morning. Is there anything I can bring?"

"Just yourselves, and whatever you like to drink. I'll have Oberon and vodka lemonade to share around but if Mary wants something else, or you have a craving for that beer piss, then you're on your own."

I rolled my eyes. "You're hilarious. What about food?"

She shook her head. "Nope, got it covered. It's just going to be some good barbecue food and all the sides."

"Fine, fine, I'll be there and drag Mary with me. Though I don't have to drag too hard because she loves good barbecue. What time?"

She smiled triumphantly. "It starts at noon, so any time after."

I smiled back. "All right, I'll see you then."

We both got out of her car and she locked the doors. I went across the small lawn into my own yard and watched while she went up the steps and opened her front door. Just before going in, she gave a little wave. "Good night, Ash."

I waved back. "Good night, Mia

I SLEPT IN the next morning then worked out for an hour or so, as much as I was able with a cast on my arm. I knew Mary would be outside puttering in her garden so I could turn up my music to a decent level. She preferred mornings and evenings to do stuff outside since it was coolest then. Once I was showered, I went downstairs to start a pan of scrambled eggs for breakfast burritos. The screen door on the back of the house squealed and I remembered another thing I had to do. "Ooh child! Somethin' sure smells good in here." She peered around me to look at the pan full of eggs, peppers, onions, and jalapenos. "You haven't cooked that in a while!"

I was busy chopping cilantro while the eggs were cooking. "It just sounded good this morning." Before she could answer, I gingerly flipped the ten-inch soft taco shell that was warming on the oiled griddle on the back burner. "Can you grab the shredded cheese from the fridge?"

When I turned to look, Mary already had two bags in hand. I raised my eyebrows and she just shrugged. "I wanted pepper jack and cheddar."

I shook my head and spooned a healthy amount of eggs onto the shell, added cheese, then quickly folded it up and let it sear on the bottom for a minute. Then I removed it from the griddle and started a new shell. "Your breakfast is served!"

We sat on the back deck with our breakfast since it was still cool out and the day was looking to be a nice one. "You're in a good mood this mornin'."

I looked up at Mary between bites. "Sure, I guess."

"It's good to see you smile again, child. I sure missed it."

"Yeah." I sighed, then continued eating.

Mary made a little *MmmHmm* sound and took another bite. After a couple more minutes of eating and listening to the birds, she finally spoke again. "So how was your date with Mia?"

That aching smile came back. "It was great!" I quickly amended my statement. "I mean—it wasn't a date. We're just friends, Mary."

"Friends, huh?"

My food nearly finished, I set my fork down and gave her a stern look. Mary hated every woman I ever brought home, not that the number was very high. I just wasn't good at relationships. My past always interfered and inevitably I'd ether break it off out of fear, or they'd break it off because I wasn't as open as they'd like…or wasn't good enough. But I couldn't be too open, I couldn't let anyone find out what I'd done. "Of course we're only friends. She just moved in for Christ's sake!"

"*Ash!*"

While I wasn't very religious, Mary had her share of faith. And she hated it when I took the Lord's name in vain. I took a breath and looked away from those serious eyes. "I'm sorry. I don't know what's wrong with me this morning, I feel, uh, all over the place."

Mary sat back in her chair and smiled. "You like her."

I nodded stupidly. "Yeah."

The burrito I'd just eaten sat like a lump in my belly so I just watched the old woman across from me finish off her own breakfast. When she was done eating, she set down her fork and picked up the cup of cooling coffee. "I think she likes you too."

Another sigh slipped from my lips. "She said as much last night. But it's not that simple. We barely know each other and..." I hesitated. There were things I didn't like admitting aloud to anyone. The very same things that I'd only started coming to terms with during my sessions with Sarah. But Mary was Mary, and I knew that she was already aware of more than I'd ever told her. "I'm just a little too broken right now. It's because I like her that I want to wait until I'm feeling better, feeling more like me."

Soft wrinkled fingers covered my hand and my eyes met Mary's where she leaned across the small porch table. "I think that's one of the wisest things you've ever said. Now, what are your plans today? I'm thinking somethin' on the grill for dinner tonight, you up for working it?"

"Oh, I almost forgot to tell you! Mia invited us both over for her housewarming party. It's going to be a barbecue so you'll get your craving for grilled food satisfied. We just need to bring something to drink."

Mary looked at me in consternation. "No dish to pass? And we can't show up without a housewarming present!"

"But she said—"

She wagged a finger at me. "No ma'am! Ashley Hayes, you may be thirty years young but you know nothin' about women or a proper housewarmin'. The first thing you need to learn is that sometimes what's right outweighs what's requested. Come on now and finish your coffee. You're gonna take me shopping!"

I grinned and did as told. "Yes, ma'am!" Who was I to argue with age and wisdom?

At a little past noon Mary and I wandered up the steps to Mia's front door and rang the bell. There were numerous cars in her driveway and along the street. I wasn't sure I liked the idea of being around so many strangers at once but I figured I could always escape next door if I needed space. I held a six-pack of wine coolers for Mary in my left hand and had a case of Oberon tucked under my right arm. I could hear faint music from the backyard but louder yet were the footsteps that approached the front door from the other side. The door opened and Mia met us with a happy smile. "Hey, Mary! I'm so glad you could come." Then she spied the casserole dish in Mary's hands and scowled at me. "Didn't Ash tell you that I had all the food covered?"

"Oh hey, Mia, I'm glad I could come too." I was being sarcastic at her lack of acknowledgement to the fact that I was also there, and I got an eye roll for my tone. "And I did tell her that we just needed drinks but she forced me to go shopping anyway."

Mia stepped back to let us in and Mary held the dish out to her. "Well my momma raised me proper and that means you always bring a dish to a barbecue and a gift to a housewarmin'. It's just my famous cheesy potatoes recipe, nothin' much."

Mia's face lit up. "Cheesy potatoes? My grandma Letty used to make that!"

Mary winked at her. "Where do you think she got the recipe?"

"And what do you mean, gift?"

Mia led the way into the kitchen and Mary took the opportunity to look around and gave a whistle. "You done this up real nice. Ol' Letty would sure be proud of her house now if she could see it! And I left your gift over on our porch. It's not anything big, just one of those patio tomato plants. It even has fruit on it, little tiny cherry tomatoes!"

Mia clapped delightedly. "Oh, you shouldn't have, but that sounds perfect! Thank you, Grandma Mary!" She bent down and hugged the older woman and I felt a little pang in my chest at the way Mary leaned into her embrace. I realized then that maybe Mary was lonely with just me around. Being the kind of couple they were back in the day, she and Margie never had children themselves but they'd always wanted them.

Mary patted her back and gave her a watery smile when they pulled away from each other. "Oh, it was no problem at all, my dear. Now I'll just grab one of those wine coolers and wander out back so you two can say hello."

And with that, Mary snagged a bottle out of the six-pack, twisted the cap off, and dropped it into her smock pocket. I just shook my head as she went out the patio doors. "Spry and feisty, I tell you what!"

"What was that all about?" Mia raised her eyebrows and I gestured toward the alcohol I'd brought. "Oh, you can slip Mary's coolers in the fridge up here and I've got a fridge in the basement that we can put the beer in. You can just drink the Oberon that's upstairs for now. Glad to see you brought the good stuff!"

She led me through the basement door into pitch-blackness, then stopped in front of me so fast that I collided with her from behind. Afraid I'd knock her down the stairs, I immediately wrapped my casted arm around her waist. I had the case of Oberon tucked beneath the other arm and cursed it. The light suddenly came on and I felt foolish when I saw the stairs down were still a few feet away from us. I quickly removed my arm and blushed. "Um…sorry. It was dark and I didn't want to knock you down…"

Mia turned to face me and we were less than eight inches apart. "No, my bad. I should have warned you that I'd have to stop and feel for the switch." Rather than step back, or continue down the stairs, we stared at each other in the harsh overhead light. It was a simple hundred watt incandescent bulb mounted to the ceiling above us but I was afraid it would show how my pulse jumped at my throat. We heard the door and window alarm beep, letting us know someone had come inside and she pointed farther down the stairs. "We should…um, the fridge is down here. Follow me." Mia met my eyes with a smirk and a wink. "Just not too close because we're at the stairs now."

As she moved off the wood steps and onto the concrete basement floor, I rolled my eyes at her, unseen from behind. "You're hilarious, Mia Thompson."

She strode up to the old refrigerator directly in front of us and pulled it open. Then with disturbing honesty, countered my remark. "And you're incredibly easy to read."

The only thing I could do was apologize again. I quickly slid the case of beer into the fridge then turned back to her as she shut the door again. "I'm sorry —"

She stilled my words with a slim finger to the lips. "Don't apologize for honest emotion. It's reassuring to know you feel this pull between us as strongly as I do. I guess I've never met someone that I felt so immediately comfortable with. Especially not someone I was also insanely attracted to."

"Insanely, hmm?" I smirked but didn't admit any more feelings to her. I wasn't ready to give over that bit of control just yet. We were friends and I liked having Mia as a friend. But I was nothing more than a slow moving train wreck and no matter how much I liked her, I wasn't about to tangle her in my mess. While a week of shrink appointments didn't cure me of all my demons, it allowed me a better view of what they were. It also gave me hope that they could be vanquished with time. Most of them at least.

My teasing allowed the moment to pass like water through a fire hose. She swatted my good arm and started up the stairs. I kept my eyes on the steps to avoid any more embarrassing reactions. "Number one rule of housewarming club—"

"Don't talk about housewarming club?"

She got to the top of the stairs and smiled at me. "Nope, don't piss off the hostess or she'll leave you in the dark. And with that she shut off the light.

I was looking up at the exact moment she hit the switch. Watching that single bulb flicker out, leaving me with nothing but the childhood terror of sudden sensory deprivation made the panic swiftly rise. I couldn't say anything at all through the fear that coated the back of my throat. I was a child again, scared and alone.

I don't like living with Jeff, he always has people over when Mom is gone. I shut my eyes and listen to the music and laughter. The air smelled like weed and cigarettes and someone threw up in the bathroom next to the closet. The retching carried through the thin walls. Jeff always locked me in when he had parties but I don't like this one. He and Mom were fighting earlier before she left for work. Once she was out the door he didn't even let me finish my macaroni and cheese, just grabbed me by the arm and shoved me toward the closet that was between the front door and the bathroom. I learned weeks ago not to argue or fight him because his belt hurt. He was way worse than Dave. As soon as I heard the click of the knob lock, I pulled my old winter coat off the hanger above me and tried to get comfortable on the floor. Fear made my belly sick and I didn't like it. Normally I'm not afraid in the closet but my lighter was out of fluid and no matter how many times I flicked the wheel, no flame would come.

It was only a matter of time before he'd turn the light off. He always turned the light off. To take my mind off what I knew would happen, I practiced opening and closing the lighter with one hand. *Ching-clp...ching-clp...* Despite the music that flooded the apartment, the sound of Jeff's boots outside the door stilled my fingers and I held my breath as I stared blindly into the bare bulb above. Then the light went out.

"Ash!"

My eyes popped open and Mia stared down at me worriedly. She was standing at the top of the stairs and I stood two steps below with my lighter in hand. I don't even remember pulling it out. "Are you okay?" I nodded but remained mute, the horror of my flashback still with me. "Are you afraid of the dark?"

The words would have sounded absurd between any other adults, but coming from Mia there was no judgement. And answering her didn't leave me feeling awkward. I cleared the rest of the panic from my throat. "No. Just the bare bulb going off and the small space reminded me of something from a long time ago. From when I was a kid."

I forced my feet to move up the last few steps as the strength in my legs returned and Mia engulfed me in a hug. "I'm so sorry, hun. I didn't know."

Rather than fight the intimacy of the moment, I let her hug soothe away that last bit of fear. "It's okay, I didn't know either. That took me by surprise as much as you." When we pulled back, I could see the concern in her eyes, and I had to give one last warning. "I told you before, I'm pretty broken. I would understand if you didn't want to hang out, I'm a mess, Mia."

She smiled and patted my cheek. "Bullshit! You're a scratch and dent, and I love old furniture."

"Just who are you calling old?"

Mia laughed and turned the knob to let us out of the basement stairwell. "Come along, Hayes. I'll introduce you around."

Chapter Eight

AS SOON AS we walked into the kitchen, a short-haired blonde called out to Mia. "I just searched the whole house for you, where have you been?"

Mia jerked her thumb in my direction. "I was showing Ash where to put the beer downstairs. Ash, this annoying person is my best friend, Gail. Gail, this is Ash Hayes. She lives next door with Mary, who I'm sure you've met already."

Gail started laughing. "Oh my God, that woman is hilarious! Everyone has met her. She's talking to your mom and dad right now."

I did the polite thing and held out my hand to greet Mia's friend. Her handshake was firm but not overbearing. But her eyes never stopped moving as they took me in, analyzing me. I worked closely with Detroit's finest and it was hard to mistake them for any other occupation. "Cop?"

She gave a smile that was less than friendly. "Detective." She glanced at the tattoos on my arms. "What's the matter, do cops make you nervous?"

"Gail! Don't be an ass. Ash is a firefighter. Now play nice ladies, I'm going to go pee." Mia walked out and I grabbed a beer out of the fridge. It was cold and just as delicious as the night before, maybe slightly less so without the orange slice.

"Ash Hayes...your name sounds familiar." She snapped her fingers. "The big fire about three weeks ago?" I felt my eyes shutter and she immediately put a hand on my shoulder. "I'm sorry, sometimes I don't think before I speak." She moved her hand when I gave it a pointed look. "We heard about what you did in there and who you lost. Your crew had one of the best records in the city. It was just a shame that it went up like it did. I heard there's an investigation team on it...suspected arson."

Her words tripped some sort of signal inside my head and all the old guilt and shame washed through me in a cold wave. I abruptly set the beer down on the counter. "I'm sorry, I should go check on Mary."

As I was walking out the door onto the upper deck of the patio, I could hear Mia berate her friend inside. "What did you say to her?" But Gail's reply was cut off with the closing door.

"Ash! Come meet Mia's parents!" Mary was waving me over to where an older couple sat at a table on the lower part of the deck. I wasn't ready to socialize yet but I would never say no to Mary. Mia's dad was a well-built man with skin as dark as Mary's, a graying mustache, and a little bit of gray at his close-cropped temples. He was wearing transition-tinted glasses, a tan short-sleeved shirt, and brown shorts, looking completely comfortable in the summer heat. Mia's mom was quite small in comparison. Her black hair was cut in a short bob with a side part. She wore a burgundy blouse, with white shorts and strappy sandals. I could see Mia in the tilt of her eyes and those high cheekbones. Mary gestured toward the couple. "This is her father, Robert, and her mother, Lucy."

Her mother held out her hand so I shook it first, then turned and shook her dad's. "It's a pleasure to meet you, Mr. and Mrs. Thomas." It wasn't my mom that raised me right, it was Mary. I wasn't sure what to say beyond that so I fell silent.

"We were just talking about Robert's mama, Letty. Such a sweet woman, I sure do miss her."

Robert nodded. "She's gone back to God and my daddy now, so at least she's not suffering." I liked his voice, it was deep and soothing.

Lucy turned to me with a welcoming smile. "Mia says you've lived with Mary for more than a decade. You must have known Loretta too."

"I did. She was one of the sweetest people I've ever met. I was sad to hear that she passed away."

"Hey Ash, can you come here a minute?" Mia called me from the open patio door so I excused myself and made my way back up the stairs and into the house. I already knew what it would be about. When I walked in, Mia was scowling at Gail but before I could say anything she turned to me. "Gail has something to say." Then she abruptly went outside, leaving us alone.

For her part, Gail looked equal parts annoyed and chastised. I just shook my head at her. "I already know what you're going to say. Don't worry about it."

She held up her hand. "No, Mia was right to tear into me. Sometimes I don't think before I speak. I've known quite a few firefighters and you all are a close-knit group. Not like cops. Sure we work in pairs, but nothing like what you do, watching each other's backs day in and day out. I'm sorry about Derek, he was much too young." She held out her hand and I could tell she was trying to start over with me. I took it and let her shake with me again.

Finally I pulled back. "He was much too young and his loss affected a lot of people, not just me."

"But still..."

I looked down, wanting to be anyplace but Mia's kitchen. "Yeah."

The sound of the fridge opening and the distinctive *tssst* of a beer cap twisting off drew my eyes upward. Gail held out a fresh bottle to me. I looked around but didn't see my other one, just a small cutting board with orange slices on it. "Mia claimed yours, said she didn't want it to go to waste."

I took it from her and she grabbed her own from the fridge. After opening it, she held her bottle out for a tap. "Cheers."

The bottles made a dull *clink* and I repeated her word. "Cheers." Something in her eyes told me that I wasn't the only one who had lost someone close in the line of duty. And I was left with the feeling that maybe she wasn't so bad after all.

"Come on, I'll introduce you to my beautiful and crazy wife, and the rest of Mia's insane crew."

We stopped to grab orange slices for our bottles, then Gail opened the door. I grinned at her. "Does she know you call her that?"

Gail laughed. "She calls herself that!"

Outside, Mia was busy talking with a group of women that were hanging out by the yard games. She had cornhole set up, as well as ladder ball. While I was stellar at the first one, having played many times with Derek, Brandon, and their friend Josh, I never quite got the hang of the second. "Ash, come meet my cousin." The woman she referred to was a curvy African American woman with thick natural curls. She had a wrap on her head and wore a colorful sundress. As I got closer, Mia grabbed my hand and pulled me to her side. "This is my cousin, Jenn. She and the rest of the group rode over together from St. Seren."

I thought for a second. "St. Seren, isn't that north of Ann Arbor?"

Jenn nodded and gave me a smile that was vaguely similar to Mia's. "That's us!"

Mia continued around the group of women, which paused their game for introductions. She pointed at the couple who stood at the boards closest to us. "The tall nerdy brunette is Jaime, and the curvy goddess next to her is her girlfriend, Kelsey. On the opposite end is Tam—" Mia paused while the short butch woman waved "—and her wife, Shell." An equally short redhead waved too.

I waved back at all of them. "Hello, nice to meet you all."

Mia looked around at the drinks in everyone's hands. "Hey, which one of you delinquents is driving home?"

Four people pointed at the redhead, who had started to walk toward the group with her wife. Jenn threw an arm around Mia's shoulders. "Don't worry, mama bear...Shell's our DD today."

There was a bottle of Snapple in Shell's hand. Knowing the feisty redhead liked to drink as much as the rest, Mia laughed. "You draw the short straw this time?"

"Actually..." Shell stopped and turned to share a gaze with Tam. I watched as her wife nodded before they both turned back to the group. The redhead looked at Jenn and smiled. "How do you feel about a new patient in the next year or so?"

"Holy fuck!"

Jamie elbowed her girlfriend. "Kels!"

Kelsey looked like she had a little Latina in her. "What?" Then she leveled a gaze at Tam. "Dude, you're my best and longest friend, I can't believe you never even told me you were trying!"

Tam grinned unrepentantly. "We were trying. Seriously though, we didn't have a ton of money to throw into it so we weren't sure if it would take." Tam wrapped her arms around Shell with a happy smile on her face. "She will be three months along tomorrow."

"Oh my fucking God, I can't believe it! How exciting is this, I love babies!" Jenn's response was exuberant to the extreme.

Mia snorted and turned her head toward Jenn. "Then why in the world did you become a pediatrician, instead of say...OB-GYN?"

Jenn shot back. "I like patients better when they're post-diaper and pre-puberty." Even I had to laugh at that. Mia's cousin was funny.

As the five St. Seren residents walked away, Gail and another woman that I assumed was her wife, joined us. "Hey Ash, this is my beautiful wife, Frankie."

Frankie had dark hair and even darker eyes. I met her hand with my own and turned a grin back to Gail. "You left off one of the words in your description from earlier."

"Let me guess, crazy, right?" Frankie just rolled her eyes, even as she slapped Gail's shoulder.

"Hey, Ash, you play cornhole?"

I nodded at Gail. "Sure. I'm up for a game if we can get two others.

She pointed at Mia and Frankie. "The four of us right here." Then the detective called out to the previously departed clown crew. "Hey, we have next cornhole game!"

Tam yelled back with a sour look on her face as Kelsey pumped her fist a few feet away. "You want to play the winners?"

Mia started laughing. "Hell no, Kelsey's a sore winner. You cats can go play the other games for a while." Then she turned back to the three of us. "Ash, you're playing with me."

A few minutes later found me at the far end of the yard next to Frankie, waiting for Gail to throw her bags. Mia had handy little drink holder poles stuck in the yard by the games. At waist high, they were perfect for the backyard. "So Mia tells us you're a firefighter?"

I nodded as the first beanbag hit the board and continued sliding until it went safely off the end. "Yeah. Been with the department ten years now. Two as a paramedic and eight as a firefighter." I turned to glance at her after watching Gail's fourth bag land and stick for a point. "What about you?"

She took a drink of her beer. "ER nurse at the Detroit Medical Center."

"Same place Mia works at, right?"

She nodded. "Yeah, we've been friends for years. Mia was actually the one that introduced me to Gail, a few years after they broke up."

My dark eyebrows shot up. "They're exes?"

Frankie snorted. "Lesbians. They either love each other forever when they split, or they hate each other forever." I knew exactly what she was talking about and I laughed as Mia's second bag stayed on the board, cancelling out Gail's point.

As she was getting ready to throw her third bag I glanced from Frankie, to Mia, then back to Frankie. Both of them were girl-next-door pretty, sporty femmes with dark ethnic looks, and nurses. I commented with a smirk. "Gail has a type."

Laughing, Frankie looked back and forth between me and Gail. "Apparently so does Mia."

Mia finished her turn before I could respond. I called out

gleefully across the grass that separated us. "One to nothin', us!" Mia crowed and Gail scowled. And suddenly I felt a little of Kelsey's competitive spirit from earlier. I wanted to keep that smile on Mia's face and to do that we needed to win. As we both picked up our bags, I turned to Frankie with a grin. "Sorry, but I'm about to take you to school."

She raised an eyebrow. "Oh really?"

Instead of answering, I started tossing my bags. I had first throw since we scored last and I made all four bags count. I dropped two in the hole for 6 points and the other two on the board for 2 more points. Then I gestured toward the other end. "Your turn."

Smile gone, Frankie groaned. "Well shit." Before tossing her own, she called to her wife, "You better pick up the slack down there, love. Mia brought in a ringer!"

Everyone settled into their groove after that and I was surprised to discover that Mia easily matched my skill at cornhole. We pretty much destroyed Gail and Frankie. Gail tried to protest the outcome. "It's not exactly fair that the two best players were on one team!"

"Don't be a sore loser, G!"

Gail finished her beer and flipped off Mia. "Says the woman who owns the damn game!"

Mia put her hands up. "Hey, I had no idea that Ash could play so well. I claimed her on my team just in case she couldn't. I figured it would balance out the teams."

Frankie snorted and held up her empty bottle to Gail. "You want another beer, babe?"

"Sure, but I'll come with you because I have to pee."

I watched them walk away and Mia approached me smiling. "We kicked their asses!"

"We did."

She tilted her head at me and I melted. "So, are you having fun?"

"I am. I like your friends, they're funny."

Mia glanced to where the five St. Seren ladies had taken over the ladder ball game. Surprisingly, Kelsey was watching from a camp chair near Jaime, laughing at the antics of the four players. "I actually met them all through Jenn. She's got the cutest boy, though I'm guessing he's with his dad this weekend. Every so often I go over there and stay the night so I can hang with the girls."

"Really?"

Mia tilted her head back and forth. "Jenn is...she likes all types, though I think she prefers women. However, she will tell anyone that listens that Malcom is the best thing that's ever happened to her."

I sighed and it came out more wistful than I would have liked. When Mia gave me a curious look, I let a little more private information slip. "If only all parents were like that."

"Your mom?" I just nodded. She didn't say anything more about it but changed the subject instead. "Come on, I'm getting hungry, which means everyone else probably is too."

Mary's cheesy cubed potatoes went great with the barbecue chicken, corn bread, and macaroni salad. Probably the thing that surprised me most was that Jamie and Kelsey brought a big tray of cake pops. Well, Kelsey made them and apparently Jamie taste-tested them ahead of time.

Mary cracked everyone up after she ate her first bite. "Kelsey, child...if you're looking for a place to stay over here I can move Ash out to the shed. I always wanted my own private baker and girl, you got some talented hands!"

"Hey!" I poked the old woman as everyone laughed around us.

They laughed even harder at Kelsey's response. "Sorry Abuela Mary, but I'm pretty sure Jamie likes my hands right where they are."

Mary winked at her and wagged a finger. "Oh, you sassy girl."

A few hours after dinner, Mary got tired and asked me to walk her home. Mia's parents left around the same time. The rest of the night was spent sitting in camp chairs around the portable fire pit in Mia's backyard. The St. Seren girls were the first of the younger generation to leave, just a little after midnight. They had an hour drive and Shell was getting tired. Everyone shared hugs but Jenn whispered in my ear when she leaned in to embrace me. "She really likes you. Treat her right and we're cool."

I never had a chance to reply because she moved on and I found myself hugging the next one in line. Gail and Frankie left soon after the others. Before they walked out the door, they elicited a promise from both of us to get together for euchre soon. At the time it struck me as strange because they all acted like Mia and I were dating. But we weren't. We couldn't.

At one in the morning, I found myself smiling at the irony as

I used Mia's hose to put out her fire. My mind was strange and I found it funny on so many different levels. I nearly wet myself when her voice came out of the dark behind me. "You know, that's kind of funny."

I continued soaking the coals but turned to look at her. It was dark in the backyard and the porch light was glaring into my eyes from behind her. "What's funny?"

"That you're standing here putting out my fire."

I squinted, trying to read the expression on her face but it was impossible. "Yeah?"

Mia sighed. "I wish you didn't have to."

I shook my head even as I shut off the hose. "Mia—"

She held up a hand. "I know, I know, trust me. I'm the one who said we should approach this slowly and I'm sorry that I keep sending you mixed signals." She followed me while I wound the hose back onto the reel and shut off the water. "You didn't have to do this you know, I'm perfectly capable of using my own hose."

The shrug came natural, as did the grin when I was near her. "I know, but it's not like my skills are getting used for anything else right now."

We walked out of the backyard through the side gate that was next to Mary's. "When do you see the doctor again about the arm?"

"This coming Friday. It will be four weeks since the break, and he wants to check the progress. He even said there would be a slim possibility I'd get the cast off then, and I hope I do."

Mary's front porch highlighted Mia's smile. "I bet it itches like crazy, doesn't it?"

"You know it!"

I took a step away but her hand on my arm stopped me. "I'm really glad you came over today."

My smile no longer took me by surprise in Mia's company, but I could feel this newest one come from somewhere deeper inside me. Somewhere honest. "I'm glad I did too. I had a great time and I like your friends and family."

She cocked her head. "Even Gail?"

I sighed and rolled my eyes with a smile. "Even her."

After that there was nothing left to say and we found ourselves in a lingering hug. Mia pulled away and snapped her fingers. "Shoot, what about your beer?"

She looked like she was going to go get it so I held her wrist lightly. "It's fine. Just keep it, I'm sure I'll be back over to drink some soon enough."

Her smile was sweet, and a little hesitant. "Yeah?"

"Absolutely. Goodnight, Mia."

"Goodnight, Ash." Then she turned and went back through the gate into the backyard and I walked up the front steps to Mary's house. I may have put Mia's fire out just minutes before, but it seemed as though the flames only grew higher. I needed more to offer, but more importantly, I needed to atone for my sins.

Chapter Nine

I RUSHED INTO Sarah's office, two minutes late for my appointment. My Jeep wouldn't start and I had to use Mary's old Buick to give it a jump. I also knew I would need new tires on it before winter and I had concerns that I was losing the very present battle between winter-salted roads and rust. Sarah was speaking with her receptionist when I finally made my appearance and she gave me a slight nod. "Good afternoon, Ash."

"Sorry I'm late!" I was sweating from jogging up the stairs after dashing in from the parking lot. It had gotten hot again Sunday night and Monday morning dawned already in the seventies with a high predicted of ninety-two. My Jeep also didn't have an air conditioner.

"No problem, come on in and have a seat."

I followed her into the private room and collapsed onto the leather couch. I was anything but calm, having stressed the rest of the weekend about this one appointment. I had managed to avoid thinking about my past for most of my adult life, but just in a span of weeks everything had been ripped apart. The fact that my flashbacks didn't seem to be limited to the shrink's office worried me. It was the one from Mia's basement that left me most afraid. Part of my job was going into those dark places, the tight ones. If I couldn't do that without a paralyzing flashback to my shitty childhood, I would never be able to work. I nervously ran my hand through my hair and decided to make an appointment for a cut after my session with Sarah. The stubble on the sides was getting long. Finally I looked up to where Sarah sat watching me. "I'm really sorry, my car wouldn't start and I had to give it a jump."

She smiled and waved a hand negligently through the air. Her hair was pulled back into a French braid today, gray and red all blended together. "It's quite all right, Ash. But you seem more on edge than normal, out of sorts. Is it just because you're late?"

I watched as she glanced to where my left leg was bouncing and I stilled it with her look. "I don't know. Things have been..." I paused, unsure how to answer her question. "All this talking with you has me thinking about stuff, remembering and...and I'm afraid there's something wrong with me!"

Sarah made a note in her notepad and leaned forward slightly. "Has something happened to you? Did something happen this weekend?"

"No." I picked at the edge of my cast, trying to figure out how to put into words what I was feeling. "I had a good weekend. Mary and I went to our new neighbor's house for a barbecue. Well, everything was good until..." I sighed and finally met Sarah's eyes. "You know how I've gotten stuck in my memories when you ask me questions?" She nodded. "Well that's happening more now, and not always here. It scares me. I can't just be out of it like that at any time." My frustration rose. "They'll never fucking allow me back to work!"

"Okay, let's talk about these flashback episodes. Are they always about your mother?"

I heaved a long sigh and leaned forward to rest my elbows on my knees. "No, sometimes they're about her boyfriends, or both."

She made a note. "And are they only about your childhood, or have you had more flashbacks to the fire?"

I froze for a second, until I realized she was talking about the fire that killed Derek. Then I felt guilt for a different reason. "No, I haven't had any more flashbacks to the day of Derek's death, at least not since your office. It's almost like...all those things that I hated from my childhood are just bubbling up." I glanced at Sarah and she gave me a gentle smile.

"In a way, that's exactly what's happening here. As you talk about your past, you're dredging up all those old memories that have gotten buried with grief and time. Now, I want you to answer me honestly, okay?" I nodded. "Were you ever sexually abused as a child?"

I thought back to my childhood and willed myself not to fall in. All my mom's creepy friends, and boyfriends. The man who'd stand over my bed and jerk off...the one who tried to touch me once when I was sleeping. My mom was home that time and I screamed as loud as I could when I woke to a hand on my small breast. He snuck out of the room and I told her I had a nightmare. She slapped me for waking her up. It was right after that I learned about shoving a butter knife in the doorjamb to keep people out. I was only eleven.

There was a guy from high school that cornered me at someone's party once. It was Derek that walked in to see me struggling against him. The stupid douche was so startled by Derek that I was able to knee him in the balls. That's when the wonderful nickname of 'ball-busting dyke' started going around. At least until Derek began holding my hand at school, then it was just ball-buster. Or Buster for short. They didn't like my clothes, they didn't like my attitude, and I didn't care. I fucking hated that school. I finally looked up at Sarah with her answer. "No, not like what you're talking about. Mostly just harassment stuff. Some of my mom's boyfriends probably would have tried but..."

She cocked her head curiously. "But?"

"I learned how to wedge my bedroom door shut with a butter knife. And sometimes I'd just sneak out the window and go..." I stopped and my body broke out in a sweat. How could she ask just one word yet lead me back to that place? The place that no one was allowed to go, not even Derek.

"Go where, Ash. Where did you go when you snuck out?"

My head moved back and forth and no matter how much I tried, I couldn't stop the slide into the pit of my worst memory.

Pounding on my bedroom door brought me out of a sound sleep. "Open the fucking door, you little brat!"

I called out to Dougie, mom's latest. "You're going to wake up Mom and she'll be mad!" He didn't have a job and was living with us for free so I assumed he wouldn't want to piss off my mom.

The pounding stopped and he did lower his voice a little, but he didn't stop talking. He sounded drunk. "Like I fucking care! The bitch is passed out and she promised me some action tonight." I shrank against the covers, terrified of the man. He was the worst of all of them. He'd sit on the couch and stare at me while I was doing my homework. Dougie scared me because even when my mom was around, he would just wait until she turned her back, then he'd smile at me and stroke his dick through his basketball shorts. The guy was a sleazy creep. "Open the damn door, I wanna see if you fuck as good as your mama..."

My heart was racing and I knew I had to get out of there because he was really going to do it. I'd snuck out of my room before, just to burn stuff in the warehouse nearby. I got dressed as fast as possible and looked at my clock. It was almost eleven at night but I couldn't stay in my room. At least it was spring so I wouldn't completely freeze to death. The doorknob rattled as I grabbed my jacket and slipped the lighter in my jeans pocket. Then I quietly raised my window. "Go to bed Dougie, I'm..." I struggled to think of something, anything that would put him off. "I'm on my period."

A single slam of his fist against the door made me jump. "Listen you little fuck, the only thing I want you on is my dick!" The knob turned and I watched in horror as the knife started to bend inward. And that was all it took to send me out the bedroom window in a panic.

I heard mom's voice as I was shutting it behind me. "What the fuck are you doing by my daughter's room?" I didn't stick around to hear any more. Instead I tried to be as quiet as possible as I scampered down the fire escape, then jumped off the bottom rung onto a dumpster that was below.

After that I stuck to the sides of the buildings as I made my way toward my favorite warehouse. I was only thirteen and I knew if the cops caught me I'd be up shit creek. Wary since witnessing the drug deal that time, I always waited about five minutes to make sure no one was around before going inside. The place was massive, just another abandoned building, a page in the story about Detroit's decline. Sometimes there were homeless people inside, but not often. We were too far from the shelters and the free food handouts. Usually I only had to worry about druggies. The main part of the warehouse was a large open concrete floor. Crates, trash, barrels, and other things I didn't recognize were littered throughout. The concrete was cracked and pitted in places. On the far end of the two story structure, there were upper and lower offices built in with broken windows that overlooked the warehouse itself.

There was a big barrel in the corner farthest from the steps leading up to the second floor office. I had made it into my own private place. I kicked in a trash can and used it as a seat when I first found the place. I also broke up as many pallets as I could for small bits of dry wood to burn. But wood made a lot of smoke and I was always afraid of being caught, so I usually just used old magazines and newspapers I found. Once my heart calmed, I ripped off a piece of the Detroit Free Press sports section and dug my lighter out of my pocket.

Ching-clp. Ching-clp. I opened and shut it a few times to calm me further, then rolled my thumb over the wheel and watched the flame catch. It flickered and danced and I stared at it as I held the silver lighter between my thumb and forefinger. Then I brought it to the paper and watched the flame catch and expand. It burned nearly to my fingers before I dropped it into the barrel and grabbed another piece. The thing with Dougie had freaked me out, and the more scared I was, the more I liked the flames. The temperature had dropped and eventually I even threw some of the pieces of pallet in the barrel to get a nice fire going. It made kind of a muffled roar when I stood near. I was sweating with my jacket on and I could feel the heat burning my face because I was so close. I lost track of time as I stood there watching it, feeding it like it was alive. But the moment I stopped watching was abrupt, like ice water down my back.

"Fucking asshole, someone's in here! You told me this place was empty!"

"Ouch! I don't know man, nobody comes here. I'm sure it's nothin', just some bum. Here, tie this for me, my hand won't stop shakin'..."

I stepped away from the barrel as I heard one of them moan up above. "Fuck dude! You said this was some good shit but..."

Laughter came through the broken windows above me and I panicked. If I was caught, my mom would really be pissed. I looked around for a trash can lid or something I could put out the fire with. Then I remembered the demonstration that one of the local firefighters had given at school. They came in and told us what to do if we were ever on fire, something every kid learns by the age of ten—stop, drop, and roll. But they also said we could smother a fire with a blanket or something. I cast my eyes around and they landed on a stained pad of some sort.

"Should we check out the lights?"

"No, man. Just gonna chill for..."

"I'm not feelin' nuthin'...gonna hit again."

"G-Man? Hey dude, come on...fuck!"

They could see my flames! I ran for the blanket as fast as I could and grabbed it off the floor. It smelled strong, like cleaner, but I didn't care. I threw it over the flaming barrel, exactly as I had been taught in school. I may as well have thrown more newspaper on it because the blanket went up in flames so fast. "Shit!" With one last look at the upstairs office, I did the only thing I could think to do. I ran. I ran back to our apartment building and used the dumpster to reach the fire escape ladder. Then I made my way quietly up to my window but didn't go inside. I had a perfect view of the inferno that stole my safe place. I peeked in my window and saw that my door was still shut, with the bent knife in the doorjamb, but waited a little longer to go in, just watching the glowing sky. It was the most amazing fire I'd ever seen.

I woke the next morning, earlier than I thought I would. I dressed, grabbed some bread, and sliced a chunk of rubbery cheese we got as part of my mom's welfare allotment. Her door was shut and I assumed they were passed out inside so I grabbed my keys and jacket and left to go over to Derek's house. I knew he'd be up and his mom would probably let me eat breakfast there. Derek's pop never said anything when I ate with them, just grunted and read his paper. As I walked along, I caught sight of the newspaper box outside the Rite Aid and froze.

Two dead in warehouse fire near 8 Mile and MacArthur Blvd. Suspected arson.

I spun in place and looked behind me, feeling like someone was staring. But no one was. My hands started to shake and I began running through the streets until I found myself in front of that burnt-out shell of a building. Parts of it were still smoldering and there was police tape up around the perimeter. A patrol car was nearby and two officers stood outside talking. "Hey kid!"

My heart raced as I looked behind me. Another cop walked up and gestured toward the warehouse with his chin. "You see anything last night?" I shook my head but the terror must have been written all over my face. "Nuthin' huh? You sure about that?"

I cleared my throat. "I...I saw the fire from my bedroom window. It was really big."

"How old are you kid?"

"Th...thirteen, officer."

The man in blue sighed and took out a business card from his breast pocket and handed it to me. "Well if you hear anything about who mighta' been playin' around in there, you call and let us know, okay?"

I nodded, too afraid to say anything else. He walked away and I turned the card over to read it. It just had the words, "Tip line," and a toll free phone number. I stuffed it into my pants pocket where it rested next to the lighter. One thought kept pounding in my head, timed with the speed of my heart. That lighter had killed people. I had killed people.

A hand on my arm had me scrambling away and I found myself going over the arm of the couch. Luckily, the way I was sitting meant that I broke my fall with my good arm and not the one in the cast. "Ash! It's okay, it's just me...Sarah."

I suddenly felt stupid lying on the floor. I levered myself up.

"I'm sorry."

She offered her hand to help me up. Once I was back on the couch again, she backed up and sat on the edge of her desk. "Don't be sorry. Can you tell me what happened to cause that reaction? I'm assuming it was another flashback?"

My throat felt dry and I nodded, trying to work saliva onto my tongue. "Yea." Seeing my discomfort, Sarah walked over to mini fridge that sat against one wall, grabbed a water bottle, and handed it to me. "Thanks."

"Can you tell me what it was about?'

"No." I sat with my lips pressed together tightly. I would never tell anyone what a monster I was. Derek was the only one who could have understood and I had never even told him. No, that secret would stay with me.

Her voice was low, supportive, but at the same time holding some sort of warning. "Ash, if you can't work through these past memories, they will continue to resurface."

I remained stubbornly resolute. "Can we just talk about something else right now?"

She stared at me for another uncomfortable minute then stood and walked around to sit in her desk chair once again. "That's fine, I think we can let that one go today. Let's switch to the other important part of your grief recovery." She stopped to write on her notepad then looked up at me expectantly.

I relaxed with her words, though I should have known better. "Okay."

"I want to speak with you about Brandon James. Have you given any more thought to contacting him?"

My voice was practically a whisper. "No. Is this something I need to do? Are you going to force me to do this before you'll sign my release?"

Sarah gave me a sad look. "Ash, I'm not forcing you to do anything. However, in my professional opinion, you need to resolve your feelings about Brandon before you can fully allow yourself to grieve."

I exploded at her. "Are you *fucking* kidding me? Until this weekend I feel like I've done nothing but grieve!"

She cocked her head casually as if I hadn't just started yelling. "Oh? And what was so different about this weekend? You said you had fun..." Sarah trailed off, leading me and expecting me to answer.

I looked at my watch and saw we still had a half hour to go.

"I...the new neighbor that moved in is a few years older than me but really nice. We just kind of hit it off from the moment we met."

"And why do you think that is?"

"I don't know. Mia's really nice, and funny. I think she reminds me a little of Mary. They're both nurses. I guess I just feel really comfortable with her."

"That's a good thing, Ash. Just because you lose someone in your life doesn't mean you lose capacity to have more friends."

I looked at her in shock. "Of course you don't lose capacity for more friends! Do people really believe that?"

"Some people do. So what do you mean when you say you're comfortable with Mia?"

Mia's face flashed before my eyes and a smile came unbidden to my lips. "I don't know what it is about her, but with her I feel like I can talk about those things I don't even like to think about, let alone share. She doesn't judge, she just listens and gives me advice in return." I paused, remembering our shared experience. "She um...she lost her best friend too, when they were in high school. So she knows what it's like and understands what I'm going through."

More notes were written then she looked back up at me. "Making new friends is good, especially ones that have been through what you're going through. Those are the people that'll give you hope you'll eventually work past the pain. But I'm going to caution against deep attachment until you learn to work through some of your most traumatizing memories. Lean on your friends, but don't let them carry you. That can lead to unhealthy dependency. Does that make sense?"

I'll give Sarah one thing, she was certainly good at reading me. Just like that she picked up on the fact that I liked Mia as more than a friend. "Yeah. Actually, Mia and I have this crazy chemistry. We noticed it right off the bat. But she also knows what I've gone through and that I'm working through stuff. She understands that I'm still kind of broken. She said we should just remain friends until I'm ready for more, to see if that chemistry will lead someplace good."

"I think that's a very wise thing for both of you. Rushing into a relationship is never a good idea, no matter what other things are going on in your life." My handful of failed relationships immediately came to mind and I thought perhaps taking things slow wasn't always a guarantee either. My attention was pulled back toward the desk when she started to speak again. "So I think you're on the right track right now, Ash. I know that you still hurt inside, but you're also learning to have fun and socialize, yes?"

"Yeah, I met some really cool friends of Mia's, as well as her parents. They were all nice and I didn't once feel uncomfortable with them. Well, except for when I met her ex, Gail."

"Did it bother you that Gail was Mia's ex, or was there something else to the interaction?"

"No, she's a police detective and recognized my name from the news. I guess mentioning Derek's death and that they suspected it was arson just took me off guard."

I cursed myself internally as Sarah perked up at my words. "Why would the mention of arson bother you specifically?"

I backpedaled. "It doesn't, I mean...if it was arson then it would be like someone did it on purpose. Like his death wasn't just a random accident, there was someone at fault."

"Hmm..." She made more infuriating notes. When she looked up again, her face was a little too serious. "Tell me what you are most afraid of when it comes to seeing Brandon again."

Breath froze in my chest, then I exhaled. I knew I had to answer, she wasn't going to let me out of it again. "I...I guess I'm afraid that he hates me. I mean, I'm already afraid of that but if I go see him and he tells me that he hates me..." I stopped to rub my eyes. They were wet. "I don't think I could bear it."

"But what if he doesn't? Wouldn't it be good to share your grief with someone who knew Derek? Don't you think it would be nice to talk to someone about all that you remember and miss?"

I sighed. "Yeah."

Sarah flattened her palms against the desk. "I'm not going to tell you to contact Brandon, but I really think it would be good for you to find out either way. You strike me as someone who would rather know something, good or bad, than to not know."

"Yeah." She was completely right about me and I seriously thought about how I would go about contacting Brandon. I could send a text message, or call him. I could just stop by their house...his house. I started to speak again but stopped when the alarm on my phone went off. I looked down at my watch. "Time is up."

Sarah smiled. "I feel like we made some good progress today, but more importantly I feel like you're making good progress on your own. I just want to reiterate that the flashbacks are normal. They are your brain's way of dealing with trauma, both past and present. And I'm guessing you've never spoke with anyone about the things you dealt with as a young woman, correct?"

"No, I never have."

"Not even to your friends, or Mary?"

"A little bit with Mary, but mostly no."

Sarah tapped her desk. "But within the past week you've already been speaking with me about those events, but more importantly, you're speaking with someone who is practically a stranger. I think you *want* to dredge up those memories. Your mind is purging them from your system."

"Like poison." If my past was anything, it was certainly poisonous.

"You could look at it that way I suppose. But just like physical injuries, emotional trauma is much better dealt with than simply covered and forgotten." She stood and walked around the desk. "I think we're good for today. I'll see you on Wednesday, Ash."

I walked over and opened the door, then looked back at her. "Wednesday, yeah. Bye, Sarah."

Chapter Ten

I DIDN'T GO home right after my appointment. Instead I got a trim at the barbershop then drove around for a bit. I didn't like not having control over my memories. I suppose one of the worst things about childhood trauma is that you don't realize you were broken until much later. Without even comprehending it, my meandering took me by a place that was all too familiar. Brandon's Mustang was in the driveway but Derek's Ford pickup truck was gone. I assumed that his mom and pop probably got it. I didn't shut off my Jeep, but I idled across the street for a few minutes before moving on. I wasn't ready to see Brandon yet but I considered coming back a different time. It really depended on how much stock I put in what Sarah had said.

It was later than usual when I got home and I was a little disappointed that Mia's car was gone. She was supposed to return to work this week but her schedule was seven to seven on Tuesdays, Wednesdays, and Fridays. I considered the fact that she may have picked up an extra Monday shift then just let it go. If there was one thing I got out of my session earlier it was that I would never be fit for a decent relationship. It didn't matter how many fires I fought as an adult, that stupid kid that I was could never take back those deaths.

Mary had her book club meeting so I was on my own for dinner, which was fine because my stomach had been queasy since my session with Sarah. Rather than do anything productive, I sat for hours watching and re-watching a training video our department had made. I couldn't take my eyes off the television as I watched the three of us laughing and joking at the end. I sat rapt while our team went through the drills. We worked so well together. The entire time my hands hovered over the little glass ashtray, burning paper after paper. Every so often I'd take a break and just open and close the lighter, letting the sound lull me. *Ching-clp. Ching-clp.* I heard Mary come home around nine, then I heard her bedroom door shut. When I knew she was in for the night, I decided to take myself to bed. Staying awake made me nothing but sad, perhaps my dreams could soothe me instead.

TUESDAY CAME AND went without me leaving the house. I skipped breakfast and only came down for lunch and dinner. Mary knew me well and understood that sometimes I just didn't want to talk, so she left me alone. Wednesday was similar to Monday, with the exception of a quick stop at the grocery store for food and lighter fluid after my session with Sarah. I'd been burning a lot more lately. I thought maybe it was a side effect of my therapy and the flashbacks. I couldn't seem to block out the images of my childhood any longer. Every time something new would play through my head like a low budget movie, I'd take out my lighter. It had become habit, second nature.

Mia was home Thursday. I saw her car out the window of my weight room. But I didn't go say hello because throughout the course of the week, I had successfully sunk from the funk I was in all the way down to a piss poor mood. I managed to drag myself through the shower a little after five that evening and was standing in nothing but a towel when a knock sounded at my bedroom door. I felt guilty that Mary had come all the way upstairs but I was struggling to get the tape and plastic bag off my cast so I just called out to her. "Come in!"

I heard the door open then spun around at the sound of Mia's voice. "Oh shit! Sorry, Ash, I can come back." Unfortunately for me, between the struggle with the bag and the rapid turn, my towel came unwrapped, leaving me in nothing but an awkward smile. "Uh, hi...um..." Mia turned around but not until she'd given me a quick once over. "Sorry for the show, I'm just struggling with the bag today. I can't seem to get the tape off."

"Do you need a hand?"

I couldn't help smiling as I found my bad mood rapidly fading away. I bent down to pick up the towel and tried to re-wrap it. "Something tells me you're just going to peek."

Mia laughed with her back still facing me. "Am I obvious?"

"Kinda."

She laughed again. "As obvious as you were when you followed me up the steps at Gears?"

"Heh, no comment." I was able to halfway tuck the towel around myself and I'd just about given up on getting the bag off. "Okay, this is going to take a little longer. I asked Mary to tape me up but I didn't realize she was going to make sure I could do a deep dive in the Detroit River. The tape isn't coming off."

Mia sighed. "Are you decent?"

I smirked, unseen by my guest. "Rarely."

Without asking again she turned around and walked over to where I fought a losing battle with plastic and duct tape. "Duct tape, really?"

"I ran out of the other stuff."

Her sigh caressed my damp skin. "I have some at home I can bring over later. Don't you have any scissors?"

As her words hit my ears, I wanted to slap myself upside the head because it never even occurred to me to use scissors. "Now I just feel stupid."

Mia put a hand on my free one and looked me straight in the eyes. "Don't. This is as natural to me as fighting fires is to you. Just tell me where they are."

"I can get them—"

"Ash." She stopped me with a word.

"Yeah?" Mia pointed at my towel and the blush took me by surprise. "As much as I'm thoroughly enjoying the view, you may not want to move unless you want that little scrap of fabric to slip any farther."

I did my best to pull it up again and explained why I was using such a small towel to begin with. "My bath towels are in the dryer and I haven't felt like going down to the basement to get them."

I pointed through the bathroom doorway. "Scissors are in the top right drawer of the vanity." After she walked through the doorway I tried once again to get the towel wrapped better but it was simply too small. "Dammit." The word slipped from my mouth and she chuckled as she walked back into my bedroom.

"You're really riding the struggle bus today, aren't you?"

I rolled my eyes and held out my arm so she could cut the bag free. Seconds later she had the damp tape and bag wadded up and stuffed into my bathroom trash and the scissors were returned to the drawer. I stood there watching Mia's smooth efficiency and the way her ass moved in her tight jeans. When she turned around and caught me staring, I suffered from a sudden lack of words. "I...um..." I gripped my towel tighter. She seemed especially close and I couldn't help staring at her lips. "I should put some clothes on."

Mia's eyes roamed down the length of my body again, then back up. My body responded but I'm not sure if it was against my will or with full blessing. "You probably should. You're much too tempting like this."

I took a step forward, until we were nearly touching, just to see if she would back away. My grin was teasing and I knew it. "Oh really?"

But Mia didn't back away. She surprised me by stepping even closer, until our bodies were touching front to front. I quickly moved my hand out of the way then blushed as I realized that she was the only thing holding up my towel. When I looked into her eyes, I tried my hardest to remember that we were only friends. I tried to hold onto that advice that we should take things slow and get to know each other. I watched as words fell from Mia's lips and washed it all away. "I want to kiss you."

I stubbornly struggled for a response. "We don't always get what we want. Why do you want to kiss me?"

She sighed and I felt the rise and fall of her chest against my own. It was titillating. "Maybe want isn't a strong enough word then."

"No?"

Mia bit her lip. "No. Need...I need to kiss you."

I wasn't going to be told twice. I could no more ignore the feel of the rough towel rubbing against my breasts than I could ignore the way her breath came faster as it puffed against my face. So I kissed her. And when she moaned into my mouth I reached my good arm around her and pulled us even closer together. The kiss was everything I remembered from Mia's car and more. We drew it out and nurtured it, feeding the tiny tendrils of flame. At times slow and gentle, but then morphing into a thing of fire and consumption. Her tongue was hot and pulled a thirst from me that I'd never felt before. I whimpered when she gripped the back of my damp hair and pulled me hard to her lips. Her name fell in a whisper between desperate kisses. "Mia..."

Then, as quickly as it began, our mouths drifted apart. "We're not doing a good job at taking things slow, are we?" My heart was racing and I could only shake my head in response. Mia sighed. "Damn it, Ash, I have a habit of jumping into relationships with people who are broken. And obviously the fact that I'm single should tell you that it never works out."

I mourned our beginning before it had even begun. "So why are you here? Like this?"

She gave me a sad smile. "I seriously like you. It is unfathomable really that I could like someone so much that I barely know.

There is something about you that draws me like crazy."

My own lips turned to a grimace. I didn't need anyone's pity. "Why? To fix?"

"No, not to fix. To know. I want to know everything about you. I want to learn about those happy things that make you smile, and those sad ones that bring the tears. I feel so comfortable with you and I want to know why that is."

I smiled shyly back at her but it quickly faded. No one had ever said such things to me because deep down, how often did you meet someone that really wanted to know you? People want the image, they want the surface stuff and I had always been fine with that because only I knew what was underneath. But Mia in turns frightened and mesmerized me with her curiosity. "What if there's nothing worth knowing? I—" I stopped, afraid of the way words that I wanted to keep silent seemed to slip from my mouth lately. I shook my head slightly as we stood pressed tightly together. I would have backed away if I thought my towel would stay up. "I'm just...I'm not a good person. There is nothing inside worth sharing." Then before she could counter my statement I went on. "Mia, I've done things I'm not proud of."

"Is this about Derek?"

I looked away from her too intelligent brown eyes. "No."

She seemed somber, yet curious in her own special way. "Can you tell me?"

I whispered. "No." And just like that, the tears came. I couldn't tell anyone, I'd never told anyone. Not even Derek. He was my best friend and the one who understood me more than anyone else, and yet I kept secrets from him.

"Ash...I...I think I'm gay." We were sitting on the old swings outside the middle school. No one else was around. Derek's mom was at bingo, and his pop and older brothers were away at Michigan Speedway, racing one of the cars they rebuilt. Just me and him.

I thought about his words and wondered what they meant for the two of us. "Oh. Does that mean you don't want to be friends with me anymore?"

His look turned from fear to shock. "What? No, of course I want to be your friend. I was afraid that you wouldn't want to be mine."

"Naw man, I'm cool with it. How..." I trailed off, unsure how to ask him. He said it first so he was now the expert. "How did you know?"

"I guess I just know. I look at boys and I feel all those things that the guys talk about when they look at girls. Only I don't feel that way about girls. I never have."

I scuffed the toe of my tattered shoe in the dirt. "I guess I'm gay too then since I don't like boys."

"Really?"

When my eyes met his, he seemed excited for the first time since meeting me at the school. "Yeah."

Uncharacteristically sensitive, he asked what no one else would have known to ask. "Is it because of, you know, your mom and stuff. Her boyfriends?"

I gave him the truth. "I don't think so. I mean, they're always scummy assholes but no one's fucked around with me like that. But I'm scared sometimes that one of them will get in my room."

"You still use the knife, right?"

"Yeah, but it's not like it will hold up if someone pushes in like—" I stopped talking and sweat broke out on my upper lip.

He looked at me curiously. "Like what?"

"Oh, um, Dougie tried getting in about six months ago. Before she kicked him to the curb. He even bent the knife. I bent it back as best I could and got a better one out of the drawer. It wasn't like either knife would be missed in our mismatched yard sale set. Anyway, I slipped out my window to hide for a few hours."

"Why didn't you tell me when it happened?"

I tried to play it off like it was no big deal. "I don't know. It was the night of the big warehouse fire, I guess I got distracted."

Derek pulled a stick of gum out of his pocket and offered me half. "I heard some kids were playing around in there. I can't believe two people died though. That's just effed up."

The way he said the words, the way his face looked so disappointingly angry, I knew I'd never tell Derek. I would never tell anyone. "Yeah, effed up." I looked down at the ground. "So, we cool on the gay thing?"

He smiled and nodded. "Yeah. I don't want anyone to know though, so it has to be our secret. Maybe we can pretend like we're dating or something. You'll keep it a secret, right?"

I couldn't meet his eyes after that. "Yeah, man, of course. I'm good at keeping secrets."

"Ash?"

Fuck, I did it again. I stepped back, totally forgetting about the towel. "I'm sorry." Rather than bother with the towel, I turned around and yanked the drawer of my dresser and pulled on the first pair of boxer briefs I found. Then I grabbed a t-shirt and pair of sweats from the next drawer down.

The tears had streaked unabated throughout my flashback and I could hear the floor creak as Mia moved up behind me. "Hey..." Her hand felt warm on my back. "It's okay, I understand you're going through a lot right now and those memories sometimes take over. But I have faith that whatever demons are plaguing you will not last forever. And maybe someday you'll find someone you can share them with." I turned around and she gave me a tender smile before carefully wiping the tears away with her fingertips. "But I want you to know that I won't judge you. Whatever it is, I'll just listen if you need to talk."

There was something about Mia, something about us together that let me think maybe she was right. Then, not knowing what else to say, I pulled her into a hug. She seemed surprised at first, but quickly returned it. "Thank you."

When we pulled back again, she gave me that smile I had come to count on from her. "No problem, hon. I know the road is rough right now and I can't pretend to understand where you've come from or all that you've faced, but what I see before me is a strong woman. You will get through this."

"Or I'll die trying."

The attempt to lighten the mood failed miserably. Mia's face immediately looked pained, those light brown eyes dimming noticeably. "Don't you ever say that, not even as a joke. Just take things one step at a time, okay?"

"Okay." After a few seconds her presence really dawned on me. "Not to be rude, but why are you here?"

Mia smiled. "Oh, Mary invited me over for dinner. She said we were having biscuits and fried chicken. Of course if I eat all that I'll be working out twice as long tomorrow." She patted her trim stomach to emphasize her point.

"I think you'll be fine."

"Oh, so you think I'm fine, hmm?"

Rolling my eyes, I grabbed my forgotten towel from the floor and hung it up in the bathroom. As I came out and started for the door, I paused on my way by her. "I didn't say that."

She raised an eyebrow in challenge. "So you don't think I'm fine?"

My eyes searched her from head to toe, then lingered on her full lips. "Fuck yes I do."

"Good to know." She patted my cheek lightly and spun on her heels. As she led the way out of my room she called over her shoulder. "Come along, Ashley. I don't want to keep Grandma Mary waiting!"

I sighed. I could already tell they were going to team up on me all through dinner. Then I smiled at the thought as I made my way downstairs. "Yes, ma'am!"

FRIDAY MET ME with eyes wide open. I didn't get a lot of sleep the previous night because after Mia's visit for dinner I had come to a decision. I wanted to go see Brandon before my appointment. I thought I'd stop by and see if he was home after breakfast. There was no describing how nervous I was. Sometime near ten in the morning I drove the familiar route to his house. Brandon's name was on the title but I knew that Derek helped pay all the expenses and I wondered if Brandon would have to get a roommate now that he was gone. I sat in my Jeep opening and closing my lighter for nearly fifteen minutes after I parked across the street from his house. It was in another one of those revitalized neighborhoods that peppered the Detroit area. Finally, I couldn't wait any longer. I crammed the lighter in my pocket and got out. I didn't even bother locking the Jeep, secretly hoping someone would steal it so I could seriously look for something new. The sound of my knuckles rapping on the storm door momentarily drown out the hammering in my chest. There was too much noise in my head and I nearly passed out when the door opened and Brandon's broad chest filled the doorway. His boyish good looks were haggard and worn and I could see that he'd lost weight. My mind went blank and I said the only word that I could force out of my lips. "Hey."

Chapter Eleven

"OH GOD. ASH!" Before I knew it, the door was flung open and Brandon had me wrapped in his solid arms. We wept together standing on the porch as the sun climbed higher into the sky. We shook as the sobs took over both our bodies and I knew immediately that his pain matched my own. He didn't blame me, he grieved with me. Sarah was right. Once the crying slowed, we eased apart and he led me into the house. Nothing had changed and yet it felt so different without Derek's smiling face or laughter to fill the empty spaces. I sat in my favorite chair and he stood awkwardly for a second. "You want something to drink?" I shook my head and he finally sat down on the couch.

After nearly a minute of neither of us speaking, I couldn't bear the silence anymore. "I'm sorry."

Brandon looked genuinely surprised. "Sorry? Sorry for what? You saved my life, Ash! And I can never repay you for that." He stopped for a second and looked down, swallowing thickly. Then he met my eyes again. "My kids can never repay you for that."

I sighed. "I know. He knew too. He...Derek told me to take you. I think he knew we wouldn't get back in time to save him. And I tried so hard! We just..." I rubbed my eyes as tears started falling again. "I couldn't get him free and we just ran out of time. He said he loved you and the kids though. He wanted me to get you out for the kids."

His eyes watered. "I thought you hated me. I thought that's why you didn't come around, because I survived and he didn't. And when I heard about what happened, what you did the night of his funeral...I was certain you'd never want to see me again."

I gave him a sad smile. "It's funny, but I thought the exact same thing. I thought that you'd hate me for not saving him. My shrink said that it's called survivor's guilt. That we feel guilty for being alive when someone else is dead."

We sat in silence for a long moment until Brandon cleared his throat and looked over at me. "So, um...are you back at the station yet? Or are you off because of your arm?"

It was hard to answer because doing so meant admitting to another failure on my part. Not only did I let Derek die on my watch, but I was barely keeping myself above water as well. Derek was always the one who'd nag me when I'd drink too much, or stay out too late before starting duty. He'd lecture me about taking care of myself. But now that he was gone... "No, I'm on medical leave because of what I did the night of the funeral. Bagley ordered me to see a shrink and I can't return to duty until she signs off. What about you?"

"Bagley gave me the same order. My concussion and lungs have healed enough to return, but for mental health reasons he ordered me to see a shrink too."

I looked up at him, sharply. He looked like shit, not at all like the beefcake that I knew and loved. "Why? Did something happen?"

Brandon picked at the frayed pocket of his cargo shorts. "Not like you. I told him, Ash."

Confusion stole over me. "Told who what?"

"Bagley. I've been so depressed, bad. And I guess I just wasn't performing so he called me into his office and I confessed everything. I told him that Derek and I had been together for about a year. I told him that you were one of my best friends and that I hadn't seen you since the funeral."

Shocked, I had no censor for my words. "You're shitting me! Did he blow a gasket?"

He chuckled mirthlessly. "He was surprisingly cool about it. I thought for sure he'd turn out to be a 'phobe. The department's lousy with them. But I kid you not, he just grunted and said he had a nephew who was queer and in the Marines. Said he was the toughest son of a bitch he'd ever met. But then he told me he was putting me on leave and that I had to see a shrink to work through my depression."

I ran my hand through my hair. "Jesus. What a fine pair we are, huh?"

"Yeah."

Now that we'd reconnected, I felt like I needed to see him more. He was my closest friend outside of Derek, and I missed him. I know that he had put in a transfer to another station house but I needed him to help me move on, just like he needed me. "Bran...I don't think I could bear it if you transferred." He made a pained face and I rushed to explain. "It's just that they're our family, you know? No one else would get what he meant to us, no one else could understand like our team. And you're my brother. If I lost both of you, I—I don't know if I can do it." I peered up at him through my dark lashes. "You know?"

Brandon went quiet and I held my breath dreading his answer. Finally he sighed. "You're right. Our station is our family and I don't think I could lose you either. As long as Bagley hasn't filled my position I'll stay."

A weight lifted from my heart with his words and I decided to change the subject to something a lighter. "Hey, you want to come over for dinner on Sunday? I'm sure Mary would love to see you."

"Can't. I've got Matt and Chloe this weekend. Jenny is bringing them over sometime before dinner tonight."

I thought about Brandon's kids. Matt was eleven, and a surprise that prompted the marriage to his high school steady, now ex-wife, Jenny. Chloe was eight and came along nearly three years later. Luckily for the kids, the divorce was amicable. Turns out that after having a long, frank discussion, Matt and Jenny discovered that they had something big in common, besides their kids. Brandon admitted he was bi and Jenny said that she was a lesbian. Both came out to each other, in a way, and decided to move on. "You can bring them, you know we always have enough."

Brandon smiled. "They were asking about you. They took Derek's death pretty hard. I think they loved him as much as he loved them. But they miss you too."

I sucked in a breath as I realized how selfish I'd been. Matt and Chloe had lost an anchor in their life. I never even stopped to think about what they'd gone through, or how it would feel to lose both Derek and me. "God, I'm such an asshole."

"Ash...don't. I think we've all been just...wrapped up in our grief. I'll bring the kids over, tell Mary that I'll stop at Big Boy and get a pie or something, so you guys don't have to worry about dessert."

I rubbed the back of my neck. "Okay. And thank you." I glanced at the wall of pictures that both men had added to over the past year. I immediately noticed that a couple were missing and figured that Brandon had given them to Derek's family. Derek hadn't come out to his folks until we were twenty-four, and it was rough for a bit. But eventually they moved past the fact that the youngest James boy was gay and even welcomed Brandon with open arms when they started dating. Brandon didn't just look like the boy next door, even into his thirties, he acted like it too. It was hard not to like the man, and Derek's family just fell under his spell. But me…me they continued to hate.

One of the pictures caught my eye and I stood and walked over to it. The picture showed me standing in the middle of both men, on a fully decked out float and surrounded by what looked like professional male strippers. "Do you remember that time the three of us went to Pride and you two got pulled up onto the float because you had on the cutest matching rainbow speedos?"

He stood as well and joined me, wrapping an arm solidly around my shoulder. I was tall at five-ten, but Brandon easily had six inches on me and the bulk to match. He looked at the picture that had prompted my memory. "If you recall, you were also sporting rainbow gear and we pulled you up onto that dance float with us. There you were in your multi-colored swim top and cargo shorts, surrounded by a bunch of dudes and you didn't give two shits about it. You just laughed and danced on the float with the rest of us. Derek laughed later at how many guys were grinding on you."

"It was probably the novelty of having a woman up there, even a dyke like me."

Brandon snorted. "Sweetie, you may think of yourself as just another Detroit queer girl but I'm gonna tell you that you'd make a hell of a cute gay boy! Gay men like two things…tits and cute boys. And when you put tits on a cute boi, they get all sorts of confused."

I cracked up laughing at him and felt an immediate release of tension. This was my Brandon, the man that I knew to be Derek's lover and best friend next to me. The man that was my best friend next to Derek. "And what about you? I mean, you've been on both sides of the fence. Are you more of a tits or a cute boys fan?"

He sighed because we'd had the same discussion many times between the three of us. Derek was just plain gay, no way around it, as was I. "You know me by now, Ash. I like it all."

Brandon got quiet after that and I knew why. It was hard to talk about things that we'd always discussed with Derek. While it was comforting to reminisce about those fun times, it was also sad too. No more Three Musketeers, no more Stooges acts at the firehouse. I felt the tears start and turned my head into his shoulder. I knew my voice was muffled in the fabric of his t-shirt but he understood me just fine. "I miss him so much."

He pulled me into his arms as the sob escaped my lips and held me tight. "I do too." I'm not sure how long we cried together, standing in the middle of Brandon's living room, but I know we had pretty much stopped when my phone alarm went off. I jumped and he let go of me so I could pull it out of my pocket. "Sorry, B." I knew what the alarm was for and cursed the timing of it. I wasn't ready to leave Brandon yet but I couldn't miss my appointment. "Shit, sorry man but I gotta go."

He looked worried. "You okay?"

"Yeah, but I have an appointment with the doc in twenty. I'm hoping to lose this cast today."

Brandon walked me to the door and gave me one last long hug. His smell was comforting because he smelled like Derek. His voice was rough, a little too emotional when he said goodbye. "All right, well good luck and we'll see you on Sunday. Text me with the time."

"Will do." My voice was tight as well. But life was going to move on with or without us so we had to try and keep up. Besides, I'd see him in a few days. After another sad smile, I made my way to the Jeep and took off.

I got good news at the doctor. She pronounced me healed and removed the annoying cast. Though after seeing my arm I wished it had stayed on. The previously toned skin looked sickly and diminished. I was cleared for light to moderate duty at the station for another two weeks, not that it mattered with my mandatory psych leave. After the doctor's office visit, I had to rush thirty minutes in the other direction to make my shrink appointment. At least I was on time.

As soon as I sat down, Sarah remarked about my arm. "I see you've got your cast off. How does that make you feel?"

I thought for a second. "I guess I feel a little free. I don't have to rely on Mary or Mia to help me wrap it, or for other stuff."

She looked at me curiously. "How have they been helping you?"

"Well, Mary has been wrapping it for me so I can shower, because it's hard to do one-handed. She's also been doing all the weeding and vegetable picking in our garden. I feel bad because I've always done stuff for Mary so it's been...hard."

"I see. And how has Mia been helping? You mentioned before that she is your neighbor, as well as someone you've been getting close to."

I rubbed the lighter in my pocket discretely with my thumb. "It's really crazy that even though we haven't known each other very long, it's exactly like you said, I feel very close to her."

"Does she feel the same way?"

My voice was quiet. "Yeah."

I watched as Sarah jotted a few notes on the lined paper before she looked up at me again. "Now back to how others have been helping you. How has Mia helped?"

"When she first moved in, she didn't have a mower because she was living in a condo before. So Mary let her borrow the mower and I guess as a repayment of sorts, she mowed our lawn too."

Sarah cocked her head and really looked at me. "I'm watching your face right now, Ash. That bothered you. Why?"

"I guess maybe it's because I've always taken care of our place. I know she was just helping us out for letting her borrow the mower, but she also mentioned something about how it would be hard for me to do it with my broken arm because it's a push mower. I guess I didn't like someone seeing me as..." I was at a loss for words.

But Sarah picked up perfectly. "Did you feel...helpless? Or less than capable?"

"Yes! That's it exactly. I didn't want to be seen as weak."

"Why don't you want to be seen as weak?"

I thought about it for a minute, really digging deep for answers to questions I'd never once thought about before. "Weak people are less. Weak people get taken advantage of and hurt. I don't ever want to be weak again."

Her eyes were full of empathy. "Are you talking about your childhood? Is that when you think you were weak?"

"Yeah."

"Ash..." I looked up at her after having turned away at the reference to my childhood. She continued. "The only one that can make us weak is ourselves. Even at your lowest point, you stood up for yourself and you never stopped fighting. I know you've gone through terrible things, but you went through it and came out the other side. Don't mistake powerlessness for weakness. What your mother did, what her boyfriends did, they took away your choices and your options, but they couldn't touch your will. You are *not* weak."

My mind whirled at her words. They flew in the face of everything I've always believed. "But..." I couldn't finish.

"But what?"

I rubbed the lighter again. "What about the night of Derek's funeral?"

She abruptly changed the subject but something told me that

there was a reason. "Have you done any pushups since you broke your arm?"

"No. But I don't see —"

"Bench press, boxing, anything like that?"

The same answer passed my lips. "No."

"Tell me Ash, are you a strong woman? Are you in shape? Can you do those things normally?"

She was crazy. My shrink was officially certifiable. "Of course I can do those things! It's just that my arm was broken, I was injured and it would have hurt a lot."

"Exactly!" I looked confused and she smiled. "Ash...Derek's death hurt you as much as the accident that broke your arm. But with your arm, it was only one small part of your body hurt. You could still breathe, you could still walk, and your life was normal for most things. But the death of Derek Smith affected your entire life. Yours and his were intertwined for decades and his absence left a hole that you didn't know how to fill. It wasn't just an arm that hurt, was it?"

"No. Everything hurt. Waking, walking, dreaming, breathing, thinking...and when I saw the picture on top of his coffin, when his family blamed and rejected me, it was like twisting the knife in a wound. I only wanted to take away the pain."

"If all you have is a hammer, everything looks like a nail."

I'd heard the saying before, but I wasn't sure how it applied to me and my situation. "What do you mean?"

Sarah cleared her throat. "You told me that you'd never spoke with anyone about your past, right?" I nodded. "So you've never had any formal counselling, you've never learned healthy ways to deal with pain or grief. You probably grew up watching people turn to drugs or alcohol to solve their problems and you fell into that thing that was familiar when the pain was greatest. Does that sound right to you?"

I thought about what she meant and my childhood. How had I always dealt with things that made me scared or afraid? I burned things. I turned to fire. Maybe it was because I told myself that I'd never be like my mom, I'd never take the same path she did. But I did drink too much on those occasions when things went sideways. Like the time I broke up with the one girlfriend I was going to move in with. Or when I received a letter from my mom saying she wanted to see me. Sure, I had Derek to lean on, but I also drank and hid in my room. I burned papers and I closed myself off. Finally I met Sarah's eyes. "You're right. I didn't know any other way to make the pain go away. The sleeping pills and vodka were things I had there at home, they were easy. I don't think I was even thinking beyond the pain. I certainly wasn't aware of the consequences of my actions."

Sarah gave me a sincere smile. "Which brings us back to our first session, and me saying that I didn't think attempting suicide was a natural or normal response for you. You're a fighter, Ash, and that's a good thing. Now, can we talk about Brandon James?"

My head shot up and I smiled, for probably the first time all session. "I talked to him today!"

She looked surprised. "You *did?* You've certainly had a busy day, haven't you?"

"Yeah. The more I thought about what you said, the more I just had to know. So I went over to his house this morning. Um...you were right."

Sarah jotted a note and looked back at me. "About?"

"He thought I hated him, the same way I thought he hated me. And when we started talking, it was like a little piece of me came home. I've missed him. But I feel terrible because I just dropped out of his life when Derek died. Not just his life, but his kids too. So they lost both Derek and me."

"And how did you leave things? Will you meet with him again?"

"It was fine. I realize how stupid and irresponsible I've been, how selfish. I may have saved their dad, but Matt and Chloe were still hurting and I added to that with my absence. They're good kids, they didn't deserve my abandonment, no matter how small a part I play in their lives. And uh...they're coming over for dinner on Sunday. We used to do it all the time, sometimes with Brandon's kids, sometimes without. But this one will be the first one without Derek."

She raised a pale eyebrow. "And?"

"I think we'll be sad...but I think we'll be fine too. We're a family and we'll get through this together. I forgot for a second that my family is more than blood, more than the useless woman I helped put in jail."

"Sometimes family is what we make it."

I gave her a sad smile. "Yeah. It is."

The session ended a little while later. I didn't have any flashbacks and she told me I only had to come back once a week after that so my next session wasn't until the following Friday. On one hand I was happy that I didn't have to see her as often. But on the other hand I was unhappy because I would have even more time on my hands to think and dredge up those memories. At least I no longer had a cast so I could pick up my normal duties around the house and get my fitness routine back on track. The arm really looked sad.

I WASN'T EXPECTING to see Mary's old Buick sitting in the driveway because she had told me before I left that morning that she'd be spending the day at the community center. But the car was in its usual spot and I suddenly got worried. I called out to her as I walked in the door, convinced that something bad had happened, like a fall or a stroke. "Mary...you home?"

"I'm in here, Ash! I'm just packing an overnight bag to take over to Gloria's house."

She was standing in her bedroom with the small rolling suitcase I had given her few years back. "You're staying at Gloria's house tonight? How come?"

She waved a hand through the air. "Oh, it's nothin' major. Her gout's acting up again so I'm going to stay the night and help her out with some stuff. She's getting up there in age you know."

Gloria was one of her oldest and dearest friends. I rolled my eyes at the thought of one little old woman helping another with things that little old women couldn't do. "Jesus, that's like the blind leading the blind."

Mary scowled at me. "Ashley Hayes! Don't you be taking the Lord's name in vain, you hear?"

I rolled my eyes again but not until I'd turned away from her knowing gaze. "Yes ma'am."

"Now there's leftover goulash in the fridge if you're hungry, and I should be home tomorrow afternoon sometime."

"Oh, I invited Brandon and the kids over for dinner on Sunday. That's not going to be a problem is it?"

Mary looked positively delighted. "Oh, you went to see him? How is he?"

"He's sad, his heart's broken like you'd imagine. But he doesn't hate me."

She walked over to me and wrapped me in a hug. "Of course he doesn't, child. You're both hurtin' the same way, and it will take the both of you together to get beyond this grief. And no one can tell you how long it will take. Grief doesn't have rules, it just is." Tears pricked my eyes and Mary ignored them, knowing how

I didn't like people to see me cry. "Now, about that dinner, why don't you take the pork roast out of the chest freezer? That should be fine for the six of us."

I pulled up short at her words. "Mary, it's just Brandon and the kids. It won't be six of us this time."

She laughed and patted my hand. "Oh my sweet girl, I invited Mia earlier."

She shocked me. "What do you mean you invited Mia? She's at work until seven. How could you possibly have invited her?"

"Why, I texted her, of course!"

What the hell? Mary didn't text. I tried to show her how the app worked but she didn't want anything to do with it. "Bullshit, you don't text, you crazy old woman!"

She *hrumfed* at me and gave me a poke in the side for good measure. "Shows what you know! I've been texting that pretty girl next door since she moved in. She gave me her number in case of emergencies. Esther showed me how to do that texting and told me about the emojis. Aren't they cute?"

I glowered at her. "They're freakin' adorable." I wanted to roll my eyes again but didn't dare. "Do you need help with your case?"

"Naw, it's light. I see you got your cast off though. How's it feel?"

"Puny!" I sighed and Mary chuckled at me.

"Don't worry mah girl, you'll be good as new in no time!"

"Your lips to God's ears, Mary."

"Ain't that how it always is? You get some rest tonight Ash...you look worn down." Then without another word she left the room, dragging her little wheeled case through the house.

I followed at a slower, surprised, pace. As I hit the living room, I heard the old Buick start up then she drove away. I muttered underneath my breath, even though there was no one in the house to hear. "Worn she says. Well, she's probably right because this day has been exhausting." It was exhausting and so much more. I was left with a lighter heart, a lighter arm, and a lot to think about. But I was moving forward and that was the important thing to remember.

Despite how worn I may have looked, I couldn't wait to actually do a full workout again, so I changed and went through an easy routine. The arm was sore, but it was so much better than having the cast on. After my workout I decided to push it further and go for a run. Out of frustration for everything that had been going on, I had let my endurance slide, and since the temperature dropped down to the upper sixties, I decided to chance heat stroke and put a few miles in. The neighborhood was quiet since it was around dinnertime. It was near seven by the time I got home and showered.

Unfortunately, the nervous energy I was hoping to burn off was still there. My mind continued to reel with everything I'd gone through earlier, everything I felt. I wandered into my weight room and the house felt empty around me. The normal creaks and sounds of traffic were momentarily drown out when I pulled the lighter out of my jeans pocket, then slid the drawer open that held my ashtray and papers. I stopped just as I reached my hand out and instead of pulling the items out of the drawer I abruptly shut it again.

Sarah mentioned unhealthy coping mechanisms and I wondered if my need to burn things was an addiction born of such coping mechanisms. I'd always thought that by limiting my burning to small things, to the ashtray, that I was being safe. But was it really? If I sat in my weight room every night and drank instead of lighting little fires, was that any different? Burning things, fire, they were both intimately connected to the shame of my past. Yet I turned to the action over and over again when things got hard, when I started to think or feel too much. I looked down at the lighter in my hand. It was just a standard Zippo, old and scratched in places. The silver showed every blemish, every fingerprint on its surface. I marveled at the simplicity of it. All it took was the right touch for all that heat to come out. Just a simple action to produce a spark and a fire.

Did I see myself in the lighter? I yearned to burn clean like the blue flame. It was with sober realization that I understood I had spent my entire life trying to turn my past to ashes, but it was only those that got closest to me who were burned. My hand shook and I wanted to open the lighter, to hear that familiar *ching-clp* sound that soothed me like no other. But I didn't. If I were to alter those coping mechanisms, it would have to start now. I stuffed the lighter back into my pocket before I could change my mind.

With that simple motion, my mind and my heart filled with purpose. Rather than overthink my actions, I left my room and clattered down the stairs. In the front room, I shoved my feet in a pair of unlaced boots and grabbed the house keys off the hook by the door. A minute later I was standing on Mia's porch. Her car was in the drive and her kitchen light was on so I knew she was home. I knocked on her door, both nervous and sure. She answered it before I could knock a second time and her face lit with a curious smile. "Ash?" When she stepped aside, I walked in and watched as she shut and locked the door behind me.

She turned back around and everything hit me at once. "Mia..."

She came to me then, stepping close and cradling the sides of my face with her hands. "Baby, what is it? What's wrong?"

Mia was real, she was so present in my system. And I felt that connection tighten as we looked into each other's eyes. When I brought my own hand up to her cheek, my skin seemed so pale next to hers. We were different but on some level we were exactly the same. It was that connection that drew me in and I kissed her. And rather than pull away or ask a million questions, she pulled me closer with her hands and kissed me back. Never stopping, I walked her backward until she was against the wall behind the door. All the feelings broke over me then. Grief, happiness, trust, and fear...I put every single one into my kisses, hoping she could understand. Praying that she could handle them. And she did, because Mia was real.

We never even made it upstairs until after midnight. We collapsed onto the couch, and eventually, painfully, ended up on the throw rug on the floor. It was only after the sweat and passion cooled that we wandered through the house, hand in hand. And it was Mia that drew me up the stairs behind her and down the hall into her room. I fell asleep feeling safer than I'd ever been. Her light was warm, but it didn't burn me. Mia's light would never burn. I hoped that I could say the same for my own.

Part Two: Ember

Chapter Twelve

I WOKE FROM a sound sleep, three tones blaring over the firehouse intercom. Fire! With a triple tone I knew it was bad, not that I'd be able to get ready any quicker than I already was. I didn't have to pee so I quickly exited my bunk and made my way to the lockers. I took a second to check on Gomez, the rookie, before donning my turnout pants and coat and grabbing the rest of my gear. The entire team raced to the trucks when they were ready. Fire waits for no one. My position was toward the back near Gomez, and I knew that Brandon was sitting up front with the First Whip, Haley. Dan Haley was the senior firefighter when Derek and I came on board, though I heard rumors that he was thinking about retiring.

Sarah cleared me for duty a little over four weeks ago but this was the first major fire either I or Brandon had seen since Derek died. Brandon started about a week before I did and he's the one that gave me a heads up that they'd filled Derek's slot with a rookie. I wasn't really surprised because the team was down a man. What did shock me though was finding out the replacement was another woman. Women just weren't that common in the field. It wasn't just that the work was hard, because a lot of careers were hard. But women were still discriminated against in certain industries and firefighting was one of them. Captains in fire departments would refuse to even consider a woman candidate, convinced they wouldn't be able to do the same work as a man. Even I was skeptical of women I'd seen on the force, at least until they proved themselves. I never wanted to see a woman start and then quit later because it was too hard, or the atmosphere wasn't the most welcoming. And while I would root for them and assist where I could, ultimately it was on them to win over the rest of the team. The thing that probably reflects the worst of me is that I didn't like seeing rookie women firefighters. The turnover rate was high and I always had this idea that if she were to fail, it would be a failure for our entire gender. It would give the sexist men and women a chance to say, "look, we were right!" and I didn't want that.

But Gomez was good. I'd seen her run the drills and I'd

worked with her out on calls. She had a level head, whether it was a burning vehicle or an engulfed residence, she kept her cool. Even as we listened to the call over the radio with the address and the vehicles requested, she didn't flinch. "Engine One, Engine Four, Engine Seven, Ladder One, Ladder Three, Rescue Three and Car Two."

"Shit." The word slipped out uncensored and Gomez looked at me as we bounced around in the truck.

She stared around, eyes wide. It was her first big fire, ever. "That's bad, ain't it?"

I nodded. "It's bad." And while she looked scared, she also looked excited. Firefighters loved three tone fires. It was the ultimate test of our skill and endurance. When your life is spent battling the beast, you get into the mindset that bigger is better. It's more exciting, more thrilling, and makes for a better story when it's done. You know there's risk to every burning building you enter, but the adrenaline rush makes up for it, pushes you beyond the fear.

Once we turned the last corner and saw the building, I knew we'd have our work cut out for us. It was a massive structure of old brick and mortar rising above the street. It was 2 a.m. and anyone's guess how the fire started to begin with. But the night to come would be a blazing inferno, the lurid orange turning firefighters into shadows within its depths. With hardly any windows, the ancient factory was going to be a bitch to bleed out the heat and smoke. And there would be no way to escape if we were trapped. It was a building that even the most seasoned of firefighters would be scared of, and we were going inside.

Once the ladder trucks were in position and jacks dropped for stability, men were going up to man the top hoses. Gomez and I went left around the building to the B side where the loading dock doors were located. We began the sweep of the first floor while others followed us in and went up the stairs to the floors above. Brandon was one of them and he called out to me over the radio. "Stay in the now." Though the entire team could hear, no one else knew what it meant but me. I had told him about the flashbacks I was having before returning to work. I hadn't had one since, but then I hadn't seen a fire that looked so much like that night either. This would be a test for both of us.

Every person going in carried hardware of some sort. I saw two with hoses and ropes looped over them. Brandon and I both had flat head axes and Gomez was carrying a Halligan tool, a rod of hardened steel that was flattened on one end and looked like a pry-bar with its two-pronged claw. The other end looked more like a hammer with a pointed side and another curved prying side. They were extremely useful when it came to prying door-jambs and the like. A message coming over the radio made me pause. "Be advised, homeless may be living in the building." The first floor was pitch black and filling fast with smoke.

"We'll never find anyone in here!" I didn't shine my light at Gomez but I still acknowledged her words.

"It's our job to try. Let's go." Assuming they wouldn't be sleeping out in the open, I pointed my light toward a section of offices along the back wall. I knew that outside would be a bee-hive of activity. While we were locating the fire and looking for any people inside, ladder crews would be opening the building in any way they could. They'd break windows, force doors, and even smash holes through the walls if they had to. The venting and holes made it so the engine crews could get their hoses in to best target the fire but they also served a much more serious pur-pose. It was imperative that they vent the building because flames generate a lot of smoke. That smoke in turn contained car-bon monoxide and other poisonous gasses that would be harmful to anybody inside. They rose up in a room and absorbed heat and once they reached a certain point they would explode.

The fire could go one of two ways during an explosion like that. A rollover, where the fire races toward you along the ceiling, then drops down the wall at your back, thus rolling over you like a wave. I'd been in the middle of a rollover once with Haley. I also survived it because I followed his lead and aimed my hose straight up at the ceiling. With each line pumping about two-hun-dred and fifty gallons a minute, the flames washed away. The other is what we call a flashover. That was infinitely worse. Much the same as a rollover, the gases spontaneously ignite. But unlike its less-dangerous cousin, a flashover happens everywhere at once and every object in the vicinity instantly turns to fire. You might survive if you were on the edge of a flashed room, but you were dead if you found yourself inside.

A call out over the radio let us know that the fire was on the third floor, D side, and I worried for Brandon. I caught a glimpse of an exit door, half blocked by debris, just as we reached the offices along the back of the building. Gomez took the nearest office door and I took the one ten feet down. The door was locked so I used my axe to get it open as quickly as possible. The smoke had gotten even thicker and I saw four people spread out in the room. Old mattresses, blankets, and other litter covered the floor and at least one pair of eyes looked back at me in the gloom. It was a child, not more than five or six by the look of her. I keyed the mic. "Gomez, we have a family over here, at least four."

"Roger that, Hayes. Got about six adults over here."

I cursed in my head but I knew we had to move fast. "Exit door ten feet from CD corner, on D wall. Clear it and push ambulatory that way." She was closer to the exit. I was going to have to move fast to get this family out. "Hi sweetheart, are those your parents?" The little girl coughed and nodded, clearly scared of me in my full gear and mask. I saw a bottle of water in her hand and took it, quickly dousing a bandana lying nearby. "Can you tie this around your face? It will help you breathe." While there was no visible fire on the first floor yet, I knew it was only a matter of time before it burned through the wood floors from above. As quickly as I could, I squatted down and grabbed a teenage boy and slung him over my shoulders. "I want you to hold on to my coat and stay with me, okay?" She looked at the two adults and I reassured her as best as I could. "I'll come back for them, I promise." We were running out of time.

I got her to hold my coat while we made our way to the exit door. We got out and I pointed toward the top of a hill where there were a few people sitting, away from the building. Paramedics were rounding the corner, alerted by my call. I yelled to one of the bigger guys on duty. "Jackson, take him, will ya? I have to go back in!" He grabbed the boy from my shoulders and I looked at the little girl and pointed at Jackson. "Follow him, I have to get the others." She nodded and I rushed back in, narrowly missing Gomez who was carrying an unconscious woman out. I rushed back to the office I found the little girl in and grabbed the body nearest to the door. Judging by the heft it was clearly the girl's father and I moved as fast as I could to clear him from the building.

Ten steps outside the back entrance a rumbling explosion blew out the top BC corner, the concussive force knocked me off my feet and I dropped the man gracelessly to the grass. "Shit!"

"Mama!" Even through the gear and darkness, despite the roar of the fire some forty yards up and over from my location, I could hear that little girl scream. I had to make one more trip in.

"Everyone out, building's coming down!" The call over the radio didn't even give me pause. Someone yelled as I rushed back in but I ignored them as well. Fire had started raining down from the ceiling and had engulfed the first floor, nearly to the end where the offices were located. The glow was ominous and I recognized it from the day we lost Derek. I was out of time. I slung the woman over my shoulders and forced my exhausted body to cover the thirty feet between the offices and the door in record time. When I cleared it paramedics were waiting.

"Where's Gomez?" It was Jackson asking and I quickly looked around.

I looked back at him. "What do you mean?"

He pointed. "She went back inside for the last one." I knew then that she only went back in because I did. When the call comes to evacuate a building, you listen. As a rookie she would have listened if she hadn't seen me bolt back in.

There was no hesitation. I spun in place and ran back inside in full gear. "Gomez!" The blaze had brought beams down. One was in front of the office that Gomez had been pulling people out of. Gomez was on the ground, her helmet lying next to her on the concrete. "Shit!" Another man was sprawled nearby, already engulfed in flames from the burning end of the beam. Memories threatened to overwhelm me but I drew from Brandon's words. *Stay in the now.* The man she'd been carrying was already lost but Gomez wasn't. I grabbed her by the boots to slide her away from the burning beam and squatted down to get her over my shoulder. As soon as I had her up, I could feel the rumbling start below my feet and I ran. I ran with the body of another person and twice the amount of gear pulling me down because our lives depended on it.

Five feet outside the door another explosion rocked the building, sending debris and other material outward. It knocked me to my knees but I managed to keep hold of Gomez, at least until I felt searing pain on the left side of my lower back. The inferno behind me lit the faces of the people standing up the hill in the grass. The thunder of boots sounded nearby as I ignored the pain in my back and stripped my gloves to check Gomez's pulse. It turned out to be unnecessary as she was just coming around when I pulled off her mask. "We have to move back from the building, are you all right to walk?"

Jackson tried to help me up but I yelled as the twisting motion only made the pain worse. "Something caught me in the back." I didn't recognize the other paramedic but he was already up under Gomez's arm and leading her to where the other teams were waiting.

"Damn, Hayes! Hold still." I was still on my knees as he checked out my back, my own mask off and dangling from my hand. "Shit, that can't come out here."

I turned my head to make eye contact. "What can't?"

"You've got about six inches of wood sticking out of you. I don't think it's hitting anything vital but I don't want to chance the bleeding. You're going to have to take a ride with us.

I squeezed my eyes shut with the pain and the knowledge that I'd been hurt enough for an ER trip. "Sonava—"

Jackson laughed. "Hey, it's not so bad. You can tell everyone that you finally got wood."

"That's the shittiest joke I've ever heard." I rolled my eyes as he laughed more.

He called out to his partner once he saw Gomez was in a secure location. "Drake, need the gurney for Hayes. I don't want to move her unless she's in a stable position." Everything seemed to go by in a flash after that. Someone told the captain that Gomez and I were being taken in, her for a concussion and me for the puncture. I learned one other firefighter from a different unit than ours was injured but nothing serious. And it wasn't Brandon. It was after seven in the morning when I was finally released to go home and my twenty-four hour shift was done. They didn't want me to drive, and it was actually Haley that said he'd give me a ride home after we swung by the station to grab our stuff. He was off duty as well and my place was on his way home.

Mary's Buick was in the driveway and I figured she would still be sleeping. Since it was Thursday, Mia's SUV was in her driveway as well. Even though they anesthetized the deep wound before stitching me up, I knew it was going to hurt like a mother when the numbness wore off. I winced as I got out of the car and Haley scrambled around to grab my duffel bag from the back seat. "You sure you don't need help inside, Hayes?"

"I'm fi—"

"Ash?" Mia jogged up just as I finished my slow turn in her direction. I was hoping to avoid seeing either Mia or Mary because I knew they'd both fuss. She looked at me curiously. "Did your Jeep break down again?"

My ever-helpful senior answered for me. "Big warehouse fire, Hayes here was hurt and had to go to ER after."

Worry washed over Mia's face and I hated seeing it there. "It's fine, really. I'm fine."

"She has a deep laceration where an explosion drove a six inch piece of wood into her back. She's going to need someone to check the stitches and keep her from moving around too much."

I scowled at the man and he grinned back. He knew, dammit. Mia turned to me with a look of disappointment. "Really? You get injured and have to go to the emergency room and don't even think to call me? I would have picked you up."

"I, uh, I guess I didn't want to bother you. I mean, it's not that bad." I could see it coming. After spending eight weeks getting to know each other, hanging out with her friends as a couple and even getting together with Brandon, I finally fucked up. We were about to have our first fight.

Her nearly black eyebrows went up and I was caught at how the increasing light perfectly shone on her sweaty brow. Of their own volition, my eyes wandered down the length of her, taking in the short running shorts and tank top. "Not that bad—" She stopped momentarily. "Hey! Eyes on the fire, Hayes, and not the smoke below!"

That's the point that Dan Haley lost it and cracked up. "Well, Hayes, I can see you're in good hands with your girlfriend here. I'm going to head home before my wife thinks I've run away." He turned to Mia and his face sobered. "Take care of Hayes here, she did good work tonight. Between her and the rookie, they saved a lot of people."

I was left standing in my driveway with a duffle bag at my feet and a pissed woman to my right. I sighed and rubbed my forehead tiredly. "I'm sorry." After a few more seconds Mia sighed too. We'd been dating since the night I showed up at her door and we continued to get closer as we shared more and more of our thoughts with each other. I knew I was in love with her but I continued to hold that last bit of myself back because I could never tell her everything.

"It's okay, honey. You're tired and I just worry. I'm sorry for going off on you." She picked up my duffle from the ground. "Your place or mine?"

I looked down again. "I won't be very good company."

Her hand came up to cup my cheek. It was something she did a lot and each time it touched a tender place inside me. It made me want to break my personal vow of silence to see if she could soothe the rest of me. But I never did because the fear of rejection was too great. Worse yet, I was afraid of being judged and branded a criminal, losing Mia's trust and respect. "Ash." I met those warm brown eyes and they were full of an emotion I wasn't ready to name yet. It was too fast, but more importantly, she didn't really know me. Mia knew who I was now, but not who I'd been. "I don't want to be entertained. I just like having you near me. I don't care if you just sleep all day, I want to be here for you."

My voice was a hoarse whisper and I felt myself sway. "Okay."

Once we were inside and upstairs I headed for her bathroom. "Where are you going?"

I waved my hand toward my dirty appearance and soot covered face. "I need a shower."

She crossed her arms. "Are you supposed to get those stitches wet—"

Her words irritated me and I didn't know why, and the frustration finally broke free. "I just want a goddamn shower, Mia! I'm not helpless. Look, I can just go home—"

"Please, nobody said you were helpless. But that doesn't mean you can't let me help you, for my own peace of mind."

I realized in that moment that I was being an asshole. I was pushing her away because I didn't want to be seen as weak. It was something I'd discussed with Sarah over and over in our weekly sessions. At least I was no longer having flashbacks, and I'd gotten a good handle on dealing with my grief in a productive way. The grief may have gotten significantly easier over the past four weeks since returning to work, but the guilt sat on my shoulder like a sentinel. It was a monster that would never let me go and that was why I was so afraid to let Mia all the way in. I loved her and I couldn't lose her too. I had zoned out a bit and startled when I realized she was waiting for an answer. "I'm sorry. Please, I would appreciate your help."

Mia helped me undress and put a waterproof bandage over the sutures, then showered with me. She gently scrubbed away all the soot I couldn't reach and I let her. I was too tired to even be turned on by her touch, and she knew it too. She shampooed my short hair, gently massaging the scalp before rinsing the lather away and using a fruity smelling conditioner. "I don't normally condition." I received a kiss for my comment, then she rinsed me again. Once I was clean and dry, I found a pair of boxers and a soft gray tank top in my bag. Then I crawled into Mia's blissfully cool bed and turned my head toward where she stood next to her dresser. She had put on a pair of shorts and a Detroit Redwings tee. I snorted at her. "At least that one is a winning team."

She smiled as she came over to stand by the bed. "Shut up, you! Detroit's my city, I'm loyal to our teams. Even the damned Lions."

I rolled my eyes. "You and Brandon, both!" Her sweet smile looking down on me prompted a moment of insecurity. "Will you lay with me for a few minutes? Or do you have something you need to do?"

Mia gestured at her old and fade clothes. "Do I look like I'm going anywhere? I'd love to snuggle with you. I didn't sleep well last night."

She got into the bed and arranged herself next to where I lay on my stomach. Her hand made gentle circles on my upper back, away from the stitched wound. "Why—" I fought a yawn and lost, then finished my question. "Why didn't you sleep well?"

Mia brought her fingers down to lightly rub what I knew were dark circles beneath my eyes. "Baby, you need your rest. Get some sleep, Ash. I've got you."

With her words, my eyes drifted shut. She did have me and I let her.

Chapter Thirteen

I SWAM UP from sleep slowly, my back throbbing. I glanced at Mia's bedside clock and was surprised that I managed a good six and a half hours sleep, all things considered. The things I had to do for the remainder of the day ticked through my head. My Jeep was still at the station and I had to get the prescription filled that the hospital gave me. I also promised Mary that I'd fix the latch on the gate.

"Hey, you're awake!"

I sighed and smiled at Mia. "Unfortunately. How long have you been up?"

She walked over, sat on the edge of the bed, and ran her fingers through my dark fringe of hair. "Just a couple hours. I threw your clothes in the wash because they reeked of smoke, and I called in your prescription for you. I wasn't sure which pharmacy you normally use so I took a chance on the Walgreens a few blocks away."

My cheek rubbed against Mia's soft pillowcase as I nodded. "Yeah, that's the one I use." Suddenly, the rest of her words caught up with me. "Uh, did you say you put my clothes in the laundry?"

"Yes, but I took the lighter out of your pocket first. I didn't think you smoked. Why do you have an old Zippo?"

My eyes dropped to where my hand rested on the bed. I watched her out of the corner of my eye. "It's nothing. Just something I picked up."

She cocked her head in that cute way that I love so much, but my mind was not thinking anything cute. It was thinking ugly thoughts. Her voice drove them deeper into my skull, throbbing with the pain in my back. "People don't just pick up a lighter if they don't smoke, Ash. Or if they do, they don't keep it. Does it mean something to you?"

I wanted to lash out and tell her to mind her own business. I wanted to get up and leave the house so she'd stop asking so many questions. But something Sarah said to me in our last session kept me in place. *"Running from your past gives it power. Lying to yourself and others about your past gives it power. It's time to take back your life, Ash."*

I couldn't lie to Mia, but I couldn't answer her either. I was caught. My voice was quiet, low, and pained. "Please, can we not talk about this right now?" She looked like she wasn't going to let it go. "Please, Mia."

Finally she sighed and sat on the bed next to me. "I don't understand you sometimes. Every time I feel like we're getting closer, you take a step back. You keep everyone at arm's length and I don't think this has to do with Derek anymore, does it?"

I shut my eyes. I couldn't bear to see her disappointment. "No. It's...it's something I'm working on in my appointments with Sarah. It has to do with my past and I'm not ready to talk about it yet."

Mia started running her fingers through my hair. "How bad does it hurt?"

I opened my eyes and tracked up to her face from my prone position on the bed. I wasn't sure if she was talking about my past or my back. Maybe it was both. "It hurts."

"Why don't we get you something to eat, then I'll take you to pick up your prescription?"

I started to protest. "You don't have to do th—"

Her fingers gently stilled my lips. "I know I don't, but I want to. Will you let me help you?"

It was another thing I had been working on in my sessions. It wasn't weakness, it was injury. It wasn't pity, it was compassion. "Yes, thank you. For everything." She knew I meant more than just taking care of me. I could see it in her eyes. I was thanking her for giving me more time and space to work through the problems of my past.

Getting dressed and picking up my script took nearly everything I had. I popped a pill while we were still in the parking lot and hoped for fast relief. Mia, always the voice of reason, suggested I leave my Jeep at the station. I was hesitant because parking space there was limited but she threw out a suggestion. "Do you think Brandon could help us get it home?"

I shook my head slowly, but the pain had already started to fade. The pill was kicking in faster than I expected. "No, he's on duty right now, he picked up an extra shift."

"What about Mary?"

"She can't drive a stick." My shoulders began to relax because the throbbing had dulled to a low ache. "Listen, I should be fine. If you just drop me off I can get it back home, it's not like we live far away from the fire house."

Mia gave me a worried look. "Are you sure?"

"Yeah, my pill is kicking in and I'll take it slow."

She gave me a piercing look. "Fine, but your Jeep bounces too much. I'll drive it back and you can take mine."

I looked at her in surprise. "You can drive a stick?"

She clucked her tongue at me and I smiled at how cute it was. "My dad is an engineer at Ford, the man is obsessed with cars. Of course I can drive a stick!"

I held up my hands in defeat and she started her SUV. "Fine, you can drive my Jeep. If it starts."

Mia glanced at me out of the corner of her eye. "Still having issues?"

I snorted. "When don't I?"

"And you cleaned off the battery cables like I suggested?"

I was shocked to find that Mia was a surprising fount of automotive information, though after meeting her dad three times now I shouldn't have been. Mia was like a sponge for knowledge and her dad loved to talk about cars. "Yes, I cleaned them and I've replaced the battery. I'm just going to have to face facts. The Jeep is more than fifteen years old and it's a POS. I'm going to have to get a new vehicle soon, probably any day now."

Mia gave me a curious look. "What are you looking for?"

I shrugged, then winced as it pulled the stitches in my back. "I don't know. Either a truck or an SUV. I like the clearance my Jeep has."

"Well, if you aren't going to get another Jeep, I can get you a discount on a Ford. Friends and family, and all that. Just let me know if you're interested."

As much as I didn't want to buy something new, I did want my next vehicle to last and be reliable. I had the money but it would be nice to get a discount if I found something I liked. "Okay, thanks. Let's see how the old rust bucket does first."

Seven minutes later I was sitting in the driver's seat of my Jeep, listening to it crank over but not start. After a few minutes of trying, Mia popped her head in my window. "Ash, you're going to flood it."

"I know." I shut off the key and rested my head on the steering wheel. "What were you saying about a discount?"

She reached in and rested a hand on my forearm. "Honey, we don't have to do that right now. If you need to get it out of this lot, we can just call a tow company to get it back to Mary's house."

My stubbornness kicked in. "No, I'd rather just take care of everything now. Unless you think it's too late?" I didn't feel like pulling my cell out of my pocket to check the time but I knew it couldn't have been later than three-thirty, so the dealerships would still be open.

Knowing she wasn't going to change my mind, Mia pulled out her phone. "Let me text my dad for the code. And what do you think about the place near the Ford plant in Wayne? We could probably be there in a half hour."

I gave her a tired smile. "Sounds good."

"I've got a small tool kit in the back, I'm going to take the plate off for you so you don't put any strain on the stitches."

Mia was always a nurse even when she wasn't on duty. "Thank you. Oh, and we'll have to swing by my place to pick up my checkbook before we go to the dealership."

She gave me a strange look. "You can't just use a bank card?"

"Not for that account." It would have to come out of my backup checking account, the one I'd previously only used for big projects for Mary's house. When my mom got caught up with the human traffickers, it was part of a huge case that went through the court system. I worked a part-time job my last year of high school to help pay Mary for my upkeep. I started college to be a paramedic on low income grants and Derek started with me but he had a small academic scholarship.

The case finally wrapped up a year after graduation and in the end, all the victims of the child trafficking ring got to split the money and other items seized by the cops. The victim compensations were based on the severity and length of the crime against us and I ended up getting enough to finish paying for my Associate's Degree, buy my old used Jeep, and give a little bit to Mary. Because of that compensation, I never had to pay student loans and I had quite a bit set aside. On Mary's recommendation, as soon as I got my first paycheck as a paramedic, I immediately started putting thirty percent a pay period into retirement. Another twenty-five percent went into a backup checking account and the rest remained to cover my bills or any other purchases I wanted to make each week. That was the ratio I'd continue for the past ten years. I never wanted to be poor again.

While Mia was removing my license plate I threw the few personal items I had in my Jeep into a grocery bag and locked it, then got into Mia's passenger seat. I made a call I didn't want to make after she started driving us back to my place. As luck would have it, Dave answered and not one of the guys. "Hey Dave, its Ash. I don't want anything. I'm calling to see if you want my old Jeep. It won't start so I need to get something that's reliable. Anyway, I know you fix up donated vehicles for charity, and I wanted to know if you could use the Jeep. Otherwise I'll just sell it to the junk yard." I could sense Mia keeping an eye on me while she drove and strangely enough I didn't mind that bit of overprotection. Dave was Derek's pop. "It's broke down at the station right now. If you want it you'll have to send your truck over to get it. I can drop the keys and title off at the shop tomorrow. Okay, thanks."

"Who was that?"

I leaned my head against her passenger window. "Derek's pop."

Mia put a hand on top of mine where it rested on my thigh. "I'm sorry. That must have been really hard."

I lifted my head as we pulled up to a stoplight. "It could have been harder." She gave me a strange look. "It could have been one of Derek's brothers that answered."

It was about four-thirty in the afternoon when we pulled into the Ford Dealership on Michigan Avenue. I knew rush hour traffic in Metro Detroit would hit anytime and we'd have a slow ride home. I'd never even been on a Ford website, so I had no clue what I wanted when we got there. Mia parked her Edge and we got out to walk around. Three minutes later the first salesman showed up. "How you doin' folks? You lookin' for something for the gentleman or the little lady today? My name is Brad and I know these cars inside and out so whatever questions you have, I've got the answers! For instance, I saw you drive up in a Ford Edge, did you know it debuted in two-thousand fifteen? It's one of the hottest cross-overs on the market right now." Walking up behind us like he did, he clearly didn't realize I wasn't a guy. I'd been called sir a lot because of my height, and the way I dressed and styled my hair.

Mia rounded on the man and I watched it happen almost in slow motion. One of the many things Mia was great at was putting people in their place. "First of all, I'm no one's little lady! Second, my girlfriend is the one who's here to look. I suggest that if you want to maintain your sales in the future you drop the sexist rhetoric, pay better attention to your potential customers, and not be so condescending. I probably know more about these cars than you do! For instance, it was the second generation Ford Edge that debuted in two-thousand fifteen. The first generation came out in two-thousand seven!"

Brad put up his hands and I could see the "oh shit" look in his eyes. I wondered how long he had been working there and figured probably not long. "My apologies, li—if you need anything I'll be inside." He took a card out of his pants pocket and when Mia glared at him he stuffed it back in and walked away.

"Can you believe that shit? Does he really get away with that?" She turned to look at me and I could feel the stupid smile on my face. "What?"

I reached out and took her hand. "You're beautiful."

"Oh."

We walked through the SUVs first but nothing really caught my eye. As we started through the F150s, I saw a big crew cab in bright red. I pointed at it. "That one. I want to look inside."

We checked the doors and surprisingly they were unlocked. Not all dealerships did that anymore, at least that's what Derek told me. He said there was a news report from a few years back that found homeless people sleeping in vehicles of numerous dealerships so many started keeping them locked during the day. My back twinged a lot when I stepped up and pulled myself into the driver's seat. I just sat there for a minute to let it calm down again.

"Are you okay?"

I took a few deep breaths. "Yeah, just pulled a bit. It's a long way up." And it was too. It definitely had more clearance than my old Jeep. I played with all the buttons and switches, feeling a little bit of awe. "I've never bought myself anything new before."

Mia watched me, seemingly fascinated and I wasn't sure why. "What do you mean?"

"I mean, I don't think I've ever bought anything new that cost more than fifty bucks. I've had my Jeep since I graduated and it was used. I bought my phone and stereo on eBay, and I got my weight set off Craigslist." I gave a careless wave of my hand. "I don't really count the furnace or dishwasher I bought for Mary a few years back. It's not the same."

She leaned over to rub my leg. "No, it's definitely not the same. So what do you think?"

I gripped the steering wheel with both hands and looked forward, out over the hood and into a sea of other gleaming vehicles. "I'm going to buy it. You have the code from your dad, right?"

Her gaze grew concerned. "I do. But this is an expensive

truck, Ash. Even with the discount, it's still going to run you just under forty grand. And your insurance will go up. Will you be able to afford the payments?"

We'd been dating for eight weeks, but it often felt much longer. There was something between us that just clicked. Mia got me. Even though I held back so much of my past, she really understood what made me tick and I was drawn to her, almost desperately. But I forgot that there were things besides my past that we'd never discussed. Maybe it was because we were still pretty new to each other, or maybe it was because we felt so established already. She told me a long time ago how much she made with her Master's Degree as a Clinical Nurse Leader. It was just shy of six figures, well beyond my firefighter's salary. But she never seemed to care who made what. When Mia inherited her grandma's house, she chose to move into the slow-to-revitalize neighborhood rather than sell it off and live in a more affluent place. And she knew about what I made as a firefighter. But I don't think she realized how relatively small my monthly bills were. I lived simply. Mary's house was decades beyond having a lien. I gave her half the utilities, and about five hundred a month in "rent," and did all the maintenance on the place. But truthfully, between her retirement and the fact that the house and car were paid off, she didn't even need my rent, just my help.

I rubbed my fingers along the leather grip. "I'm not going to make payments, I'll just give them the entire amount and save myself a few grand on interest."

"*What?*" Her voice rose in surprise and I turned to meet her eyes. It only took a few minutes to explain Mary's advice from so many years ago, to tell her that nearly two thirds of my income had been funneled into my retirement and secondary checking account for the past decade. Mary understood how much stability and security meant to me, even at the tender age of twenty. Besides love and a roof over my head, her financial advice was the best thing she ever gave me. Mia's incredulous face said more than her words. "Wow, Ash."

"Are, um, are you mad at me?"

Her mouth dropped open. "Are you kidding me? Of course I'm not mad at you! That's probably the smartest thing I've ever heard anyone do. And you were what, about twenty when you started doing that?" I nodded. "Amazing!" Mia smiled at me and it was the one that always made me want to melt into a puddle, and yet also squirm uncomfortably. "You continue to surprise me, you know that?"

"I don't mean to. I just…my childhood was really fucked up, you know? I don't ever want to be that kid again. I don't ever want to worry that the heat will be shut off, or there won't be any food in the house. I don't want to have to steal cupcakes from the 7-11 just so my stomach didn't growl in the morning at school. I know I can't be a firefighter forever, Mia. I guess I don't want to worry so I'm doing what I can to take care of myself down the road. If it hadn't been for Mary…" I didn't finish the statement. Anyone that knew me well, Brandon and now Mia, knew that things would have not turned out so nice for me.

"I get it and I think it's an incredibly mature mindset."

"Well, I *am* an adult, you know."

She pushed a bit of hair from my forehead, I hadn't bothered styling it before we left to get my Jeep. "But you started it not long after graduating high school. Jesus, when I think back to twenty…I was just trying to survive college, not plot out my retirement!"

We both glanced up as a woman wearing a blue Ford polo shirt and khaki pants approached from the main building. Mia grinned at me and patted my leg. "Are you ready to buy yourself a new truck?"

I grinned and opened my door. "Let's do this!"

IT WAS ALMOST two hours later when I pulled my big red beast into the driveway. Mia pulled into her own drive while I sat inside my new truck. I knew the rumble of it was a surefire way to bring Mary out of the house. Exactly as predicted, Mia was making her way across the lawn at the same time Mary popped her head out the front door. "Now who is that sitting in our driveway?" She turned and caught sight of Mia. "Evening, dear. Have you seen Ash?" Mia pointed at me sitting in the truck and I could see Mary squint in my direction. "Oh my Lord, she's finally done it!"

I slowly got out of the pickup as Mary shuffled out to see it. "Well, what do you think? The old Jeep finally died today and Mia said she could get me a discount."

The old woman looked it up and down and sniffed. "It's kind of big."

I led her around to the passenger side where there was a step for her to get in, as well as a handle. "See? You'll be fine. And when you get even older and crankier than you are now, I'll build you a little set of stairs, just like Stella Washington down the street has for her terrier to get on the porch swing."

Mary gave me a good poke in the side and I winced as it was within a hand span of my stitches. "Hey, easy there!"

"Careful, Mary, she's got stitches. Big fire last night and a few of the firefighters got injured."

Mia threw it out there, now I had to deal with the aftermath. Mary rounded on me with fear in her eyes. "You best be careful out there. I want your lily-white hide to come back here intact, you hear?"

I squeezed her bony old hand. "I'll do my best, Mary. You know I always do."

"I know, child. I know." She turned back to the truck. "You want to take me for a spin now?"

I looked from her to Mia and back. "Sure, you want to go for ice cream?"

Mary held her hand up. "Oh no, not that far! I meant just around the block. I'm watching my program and that fancy satellite system you got will only pause so long!"

Mia laughed and I had no choice but to join her. "All right, old woman. Around the block it is." As I helped her into the cab, I met Mia's gaze through the open passenger window. There was beauty in the way she looked at me and something eased deep inside my heart. Mary had been my family for a long time, but Mia too had found her way inside.

Chapter Fourteen

"HOW HAVE YOU been, Ash?"

Because we only saw each other weekly, Sarah always started my sessions by asking how the previous week had gone. She wanted to know if I'd had any flashbacks, or if I'd struggled with depression or other difficult childhood memories. "Things have been good, Doc. I got a new truck last week so no more late appointments for me."

She smiled. "Good to hear. You mentioned once that you don't like to spend money on yourself and that you've had your Jeep since college. How did it feel to get something new?"

My memory took me back to that office at the dealership.

"Why is there so much paperwork?" I stared at the stack in dismay.

Mia snorted and rolled her eyes. "It's cute how you think this is a lot! You should buy a condo. For that matter, you'd have even more if you were taking out a loan for the truck."

"Well that just seemed foolish since I have the money to buy it outright." The sales associate that had come out to the lot to greet us after Mia sent Brad running with his tale tucked between his legs moved her head back and forth as she watched our bantering. I could tell she was family just by looking at her, by the casually styled shoulder-length hair and the way she wore her polo. Well, the picture of her and her partner on the side shelf in her office gave it away too.

"You ladies are too much. How long have you been together?"

"Eight weeks."

"Ten weeks!"

I looked at Mia, confused by her answer. "Babe, we've only been dating for two months."

She got that sweet look on her face and my face turned red at her words. "I'm counting how long we've known each other because I knew we'd be together the minute we met."

"Really?"

The sales woman smiled but politely didn't comment.

Whether it was two months or two and a half months, neither was a lot of time. But we both felt like we'd known each other much longer. There was a familiarity and comfort with Mia's presence that I had felt with so few other people. I knew weeks ago that I was falling for her, dangerously fast given my history. But nothing in this world could stop the way I felt. The only thing would be Mia herself, if I ever dared to tell her the truth.

"Are you with me, Ash?"

I jerked my gaze back to Sarah. "Yeah, sorry. Just got lost in my head for a minute."

She jotted something down and looked at me with concern. "More bad memories from your past?"

The smile came over me and I couldn't stop it for anything. "No, actually. I was thinking about the day I bought the truck, Mia came with me."

"Ah, I see. And how are things progressing in your relationship? Are they well?"

As each week went by, it seemed like I talked more and more about Mia, Mary, Brandon and the kids, than I spoke about my childhood. And the abuse I suffered as a kid was the main reason I continued to see Sarah, even after she signed my work release. I thought about her question for a minute. "Yes and no..." I knew that wouldn't be an acceptable answer so I tried to put it into better words. "Some days I feel like I've known her forever. I've never felt that way about anyone I've ever met, let alone someone I loved." I stopped abruptly, realizing what I had just admitted aloud.

Sarah smiled kindly. "So you love her?" I nodded, stupidly. "Does she know?"

I looked away from those quick blue eyes. Instead I scraped my nail over the denim covered lighter that was in my pocket. "I'm afraid to tell her."

"Why are you afraid? Do you think she won't love you in return, that she won't accept you the way you are?"

I thought back to all the laughter I'd had in my adult life. I remembered joking and spending time with Derek and Brandon. I recalled those dinners and barbecues where Brandon's kids were crawling all over me. I thought about Mary giving me that smile that said how much she really cared. No, it wasn't a fear that Mia couldn't love me for who I was. It was fear that she couldn't love me for who I used to be, for what I'd done. I sighed. "I have nothing to offer in terms of a relationship. She's way out of my league."

"Ash..." I looked up and met Sarah's eyes. "From everything you've told me, Mia sounds like a smart woman. She knows where you live, she knows what you do for a living, and she knows about your struggles of late. Why would you suddenly think any of that would make a difference?"

My hands got clammy as I thought about my reason for fear. "It's...it's not about something she knows. It's about something she doesn't know."

I foolishly gave her an opening and I knew she'd probe it. "Is this about your past?" I nodded. "Have you told anyone?"

"No."

She set the pen down on the tablet. "Not even Derek?"

I let out a long drawn breath. "No, not even him. This isn't something I can tell anyone."

"You know, Ash, guilt is an anchor. While it may be tolerable in calm water, it will drown us when the water gets rough. Trust me when I tell you this, you will never be able to leave your past behind as long as this is inside you. I've been watching you closely over the past few months, that's my job. And I've seen your struggle. Whatever this thing inside you is, it eats at you."

Emotion got the best of me and my eyes welled up. I leaned forward to brace my elbows on my knees, hoping she wouldn't see the tears as they fell. "I don't know what to do. I've lived with this for seventeen years and I can never tell anyone. Not even you, I'm sorry. I don't know what to do." I dug the heels of my palms into my eye sockets, willing the wetness away. My breath hitched in my throat. I hated my sudden loss of control. It had been more than a month since I had a breakdown and I felt weak as it washed over me again. "I don't know what to do. I love her so much —" I stifled the sob as best I could. I didn't want Sarah to see me cry. It seemed like it would be a failure of sorts on my part.

But that girl inside me, the one that fucked up all those years ago, she was so sad. I should have been used to losing people at this point in my life but I didn't want to lose Mia to the void that was lurking in my past. She was the one flame in my life that I couldn't control. She was a spark in my dark room and I couldn't bear it if I lost her.

"Hey, it's going to be okay, Ash."

I drew my head up slowly and saw that Sarah had come

around the desk. She held a Kleenex box and I took three. My nose was running and my eyes felt hot and gritty. "I'm sorry."

Sarah put the box back on the shelf and turned to face me again. "Never feel sorry for expressing honest emotion. They make you human." She moved to sit in a chair nearby. "My job here is to listen to you and help you understand yourself. I can give you suggestions that will point you in the direction of good mental health, but ultimately I can't tell you what to do. But you should really take a look at this thing you're afraid of. If it's illegal, research the law. I would think that seventeen years far outstrips the statute of limitations in Michigan. If it's hurtful, you should weigh the truth against peace of mind for whomever was hurt. But take a hard look because from where I sit, this is something that has been holding you down your entire life. Don't you want to be free?"

I stared back at her, frozen. She made it sound so simple. And she was right, I wanted to be free. But was it at a cost I couldn't afford? I wasn't sure if I believed in karma or whatever, but it sure felt like I'd paid in spades my whole life. I swallowed and cleared my throat. "I want to be free." My voice was quiet in the room, barely audible over the sound of the noise cancellation machine.

"Tell me again, Ash, because you don't sound very sure."

My voice was louder the second time, more firm. "I want to be free."

She met my gaze. "Again."

"I want to be free." And there it was, like calling forth a genie from a bottle, I'd said the words aloud three times and now my heart wanted out of its chains. I could no longer go back. Sarah was right, even if she had no idea what my guilt stemmed from. Without getting it out, it would weigh me down forever. I would never truly be happy.

The rest of the session went by in a blur. It was Friday and Mia's friends, Gail and Frankie, were coming over around eight to play cards and hang out. Despite my preoccupation with all the things going through my head, I still had errands to run before I could head home and throw some paint on the fence around the backyard. My most recent injury was pretty much healed. I only had a few days off work for it and went back yesterday. My twenty-four hour shift on ended at seven this morning. I was able to get home and catch some sleep before coming in for my therapy session with Sarah. Normally I'd have three days off before

I'd have to report to my next shift at the station but I was going in a day early. A few guys had picked up extra shifts to cover for me while I was injured, so I was trying to repay the favor for a few who wanted some time off. Brandon had been doing the same.

Unfortunately, the fence ran overly long. Even though it wasn't the first time I'd painted it over the years, I had forgotten how long it took to scrape and paint both sides of the wood planks. As a result I was just closing up the big paint bucket where I had left it on some cardboard near the front porch when Mia pulled into her drive around quarter after seven. She got out of the SUV and rather than walk up to her front door, she grabbed her purse and insulated lunch bag and headed in my direction. I was a mess and I knew it. As soon as she got close enough to see, she burst out laughing. "Jesus, Ash! Did you paint the fence or did the fence paint you?"

"The jury's still out on that one." Mia tapped her bottom lip and stared at me speculatively. I questioned her mischievous look. "What?"

"Hmm, you're awfully sexy like this with your little paint rag and your bandana on. What do you say to sharing a shower with me?"

I liked it when Mia got playful and despite the difficulty of my session earlier, I couldn't help feeling my mood lighten with just the return of her smile to my day. "I'd say that your shower would probably get ruined."

She deliberately reached up to wipe a smudge of paint from my brow and as she pulled her hand back, the white seemed very bright indeed against her darker skin. Then she casually wiped her thumb onto my shirt and met my eyes with a challenging look. "Well...there's only one way to find out."

I glanced at the closed paint can, and then at the used brushes next to it. The paint would keep and I'd buy new brushes. Some things in life demanded to be a priority. And Mia had become mine. What we had between us was a fire beyond anything I'd known, and I planned to let it burn.

"SO HE'S GOT this quarter up his nose and despite the embarrassment it was sure to cause, Jenn had no choice but to take Malcom to the urgent care to see if they could get it out. To make matters worse the attending physician was some hot doctor that she had done a rotation with before going into private pediatric practice."

Mia was telling us a story about her cousin Jenn, and Jenn's son. And the way she had us cracking up, I was sad that we'd all only hung out the one time. The St. Seren crew seemed like a riot from what I'd personally witnessed the day of the barbecue and from the stories that Mia had been telling of them. Frankie chimed in while Gail and I were still laughing. "Well that doesn't sound too bad."

My girlfriend shook her head and held up her hand, the one not holding cards. "Wait, I'm not done! So, thinking she's going to prove that she's not some delinquent mom who lets her kid turn himself into a slot machine, she asks Malcom point blank if he's learned his lesson. You know what that little shit said?" We all shook our heads. "He said 'yeah, next time I'm gonna use a dime' and she said that doctor hottie just about lost his shit with laughter."

I glanced across the table at Mia and enjoyed the look she was giving me. After draining the last sip of my beer, I stood and addressed the table. "I'm going for a refill, anyone else want one?"

"I'm good."

"Me too." The married couple of our euchre night was full up so I glanced at Mia.

She stood as well. "I still have half a bottle but I'll come with you. I have to pee."

Gail coughed into her hand and murmured three letters. "TBS."

She got flipped the bird in response. "Tiny bladder this, Detective Evans!" Mia started to follow me again then abruptly stopped and went back for her cards only to stack them and stuff them into her back pocket. "I don't trust either of you!"

I snickered at Gail's outraged look but took special notice of Frankie's smile. Something told me that she'd been less than honest when playing euchre with Mia before. Mia followed me through the kitchen but when I tried to stop at the fridge, she grabbed my hand and pulled me past it. I glanced back at the table where I could see Gail and Frankie playing on their phones and tried to pull my hand free. "What are you doing, the beer's there?"

Mia gave me what I'd come to know as her naughty smile. "But I need your help with something in here." She kept pulling me until we made it halfway down the hall, then she turned and pushed me against the wall. "Have I mentioned how sexy you are tonight?"

She wasn't usually so forward but I liked it. "Shouldn't that be my line?"

"Seriously, I've got plans for you tonight so you better be ready!"

I laughed and gave her a searching kiss, one that definitely took longer than an average pee time. When I pulled back, her eyes were still closed. "I'm surprised our shower earlier didn't take care of this fire you seem to have."

Mia leveled a smirking gaze at me. "Have you ever done a shot then ordered a beer chaser?"

"Sure. Why?"

The fingers of Mia's right hand came up to scratch along the back of my head where my hair was clipped short. I shuddered at the feel of it. When she whispered in my ear, I was ready for our guests to leave. "We haven't had our beer yet."

Mia's eyes held lust greater than I'd seen in anyone else, but I didn't know how she really felt about me. And I couldn't find out unless I was ready to admit my own emotions to her. The problem was that feelings and emotions led to discussions of the future. And until I told her about my past actions, we could have no real future. I held up a finger. "Hold that thought. You pee, I'm gonna grab another drink, then we're going to win that game and start the rest of our night."

Later that evening, long after Frankie and Gail had gone home and Mia lay sleeping next to me, my mind raced with the words she had said to me. The ones we had said to each other. In the afterglow of the hottest sex I'd ever had, one of us said something funny and we both laughed until we were nearly out of breath for a different reason. In the quiet of the room, we both lay staring at the ceiling. Her head was on my shoulder and I felt my thoughts wander as I traced the skin of her arm. Light and dark, conflicted and sure, two sides of a coin. Even though hours had passed since she fell asleep, her voice was clear as a bell in my head at the memory of that moment.

"What are you thinking about?"

I turned slightly so I could see her out of the corner of my eye. "Nothing really, why?"

Mia entwined the fingers of her left hand with the fingers of my right, stopping my caress. "You just got really quiet all of the sudden."

I smiled at her, enjoying the feeling of closeness that we'd developed during our nights spent together. "I don't know I guess, just thinking about stuff. Sarah said some things in my session today that really has my mind turning. I'm sorry."

Mia pulled back from me so she could look me in the eyes, but she didn't let go of my hand. "Why do you always do that?"

"Do what?"

"You always apologize for how you're feeling. Babe, your feelings don't need apology. I understand that you're learning how to deal with some of the stuff from your past. God —" She shut her eyes and I gave her hand a squeeze so she'd continue. When she looked at me again, it was with such sadness. "When I think of how you had to grow up, it makes me so angry! I wish I could go back and just take away all the bad memories that you have from your childhood."

I sighed, understanding exactly what she meant. "I'm not going to lie, there are a few things I'd change if I could. But if I did that, how do I know that I'd be right here right now, with you? I wouldn't change any of it if it meant I didn't have you in my life." And my stomach dropped as I realized how much truth was in my words. As much guilt as I carried on my shoulders, as much as I feared for the future, I couldn't be certain that she'd still be lying on my arm if I changed any bit of my past. But it was so hard, and it hurt so much. Against my will, I could feel it start. It was nothing more than a continuation of that outpouring that I felt in Sarah's office earlier in the day. My breath stuttered and I tried hard not to let it hitch. I could feel the first tears start as I trembled beneath her.

Immediately concerned, she sat up and looked down at me. I had no choice but to put my arm over my eyes, to hide. "Baby, what's wrong? Did I say something wrong?" I shook my head back and forth but I couldn't answer as the first sob escaped. I didn't cry. I hated crying. And she'd seen me cry more times since I met her than anyone else in my life. I felt so weak. Mia pulled me toward her and just held me. She held me as the minutes went by, until I'd finally gotten it out of my system.

"I'm so —"

She covered my lips with a finger. "Don't say it. You have no reason to feel sorry. I want to be here for you, I want you to lean on me if you need it." Almost as if she could read my mind, Mia continued. "It doesn't take weakness to accept help from the people who care about you, Ash. On the contrary, it takes incredible strength to know when you are not quite strong enough."

My voice was a whisper in the darkness. "I don't feel strong enough."

Her fingers stroked through my hair, untangling the thick strands. "Can you tell me what I can do to help?"

"I don't know."

"Okay. Can you tell me what has you so upset?"

My throat felt tight with the answer. "No."

"Can you tell me anything?"

I reached up to still her hand and pull it into my own grasp. Then I looked up into her eyes, barely making them out in the room. "I can tell you that I love you. I can tell you that I'm going to be better because I want to be with you for as long as you'll have me."

Mia's grip tightened almost painfully where our fingers were interwoven. "Oh." Before I could ask what it meant, she leaned down and kissed me, passionately and explosive. It was like an incendiary agent had been thrown onto a hot coal. All the heat inside of me coalesced and flashed into the space between us. When she finally came up for air again, I pulled my hand free and traced the smile on her lips. Her last words before sleep lent reason to her response. "I have wanted to say it for weeks now, but I didn't want to push you. I didn't want to make you uncomfortable."

I smiled back at her and I knew it was a sad smile, though she couldn't see it under the cover of night. "The only thing that would make me uncomfortable is if you were to ask me to leave."

"Sweetheart, that would never happen."

Hours later, after our mutual admission of love and her subsequent fall into sleep, I lay awake thinking about her words. And I prayed to whomever would listen that what she said was true.

Chapter Fifteen

I FELT THE heat from the blaze through my PPE. For reasons known only to my captain, or perhaps they were obvious, he chose to keep me off the inside crew and with the guys that were manning the hoses. First task was connecting the hoses to the hydrants, then opening the building up and getting water inside. It was another warehouse but unlike the last one I was on, this one was close to a residential apartment building. We had concerns about the fire spreading so more trucks were called in. When you're in the heat of the fire, with the roaring and raging blaze all around you, and people yelling out orders and reports, hours can go by in exhausting minutes. It was near two in the morning before we were able to shut the water down.

Afterward, while we were gathering equipment, rolling up the hoses, and checking in with all our members, I glanced over toward the cruisers and saw a couple cops standing around. I recognized both but didn't know either very well. I was just finishing with my own duties when Brandon called out to me. He had the arm of another of our crew draped over his shoulders, helping support the man's weight. I couldn't see who it was though. "Hey, Ash. Can you head to the B side entrance? I left my axe over there and I still need to get Stevens over to the paramedic. He stepped on a nail inside."

"Sure man, I got it." B side was to the left of the front part of the warehouse, opposite the side with the apartment building. Streetlights had the area dimly illuminated but there was still a lot of smoke in the air, obscuring vision. The structure sat like a massive charred and dripping hulk. The night had quieted with the extinguished fire and I even heard a few crickets. But as I walked farther down the building, I heard a more distinctive sound. The noise was louder than the creaks of burnt wood and dripping water from flooding. It was something I knew just as well. *Ching-clp.* I peered through the gloom, trying to see where the sound came from. There was a dumpster near a chain link fence and just to one side of the dumpster was a kid. He couldn't have been more than thirteen or fourteen.

Every instinct I had said this kid was responsible. If there was one thing I knew, one pleasure I understood beyond what most people would, it was the pleasure of burning something and watching your work. And a kid that young had no call to be on the street watching a warehouse burn down in the middle of the night. It was like a kick to the gut. I had taken off my heavy coat and only wore my turn out pants and boots with a sweat-stained tank top. It was my duty to snag this kid if I thought he had anything to do with the fire. He could have burned down an entire building of sleeping people next door to the warehouse. That's not a small crime, that's serious business. I felt like a hypocrite but I bolted toward him without warning anyway. The way the fence ran around the property, I had him penned in.

As if sensing his own dilemma, the kid looked up in a panic. He wasted precious time stuffing the Zippo into his baggy jeans pocket, then ran in the wrong direction. Instead of trying to get past me toward the street, he ran for the back fence along the lot. I caught up with him as he tried to climb it and pulled his little ass down again. His clothes were soaking wet, telling me he'd been watching for a while. He struggled with me but I twisted his arm behind his back and started marching him back toward the front of the building. When we passed the spot he had been hiding, it was dry, despite the area all around it being as wet as the boy. He'd been there the entire time, unafraid of the flames and smoke.

Brandon was heading my way when I came into view. "Ash?"

I didn't answer him, instead I yelled out to the two cops that were still standing by the patrol cars. "Canter, Smith…I got something for you!"

Officer Smith laughed. "You find yourself a boyfriend at last?" He was a jackass but I knew he was also a good cop. We'd volunteered together for events in the schools and hospitals before. People weren't black and white and sometimes you had to just roll with it.

I shook my head while the kid continued to struggle. "Even better. I found this punk hiding on the other side of the building, lighter in hand. He shoved it in his pocket right before he tried to run from me."

Canter walked up and took control of the boy. "Witness or…" He trailed off, the question was obvious.

"You didn't see his face, I'm leaning more toward 'or.' He's soaked and the place he was hiding was dry as a bone. He must have watched the entire thing."

Smith walked up too. "All right, we'll take him from here. Thanks, Hayes."

I turned and walked back to where Brandon was watching me. He gave me a strange look. "What?"

Brandon pointed toward the gloomy side lot with the head of his axe. He must have got it himself as I chased the kid down. "How did you know he was hiding back there? I went over there to get my axe and you couldn't see shit in the haze on that side of the building."

"I heard him."

"Bullshit!"

The final sigh slipped from between my lips. With trepidation, I reached into my jeans and pulled out my own Zippo. Then with practiced ease, despite the shaking of my hand, I proceeded to open and close it a few times. *Ching-clp, ching-clp.* He had questions, I could see it in his eyes. "This is what I heard."

Brandon's eyes met mine. "That one's yours?" I nodded and he went on. "You okay?"

"Yeah." He knew I didn't smoke, but he didn't ask any more. He also knew I'd just lied to him. I was definitely not okay.

I BARELY HELD it together for the rest of my shift. Even though my heart continued to race and panic clawed at my conscious mind, I made sure to shower before I left the station. It had been two weeks since the purchase of my new truck and I didn't want to bring any of the burnt fire odor into the cab. My hands were shaking so badly that it took me nearly five minutes to text my therapist to see if she was available to meet that morning. I had just come off another forty-eight hour double shift that had been unusually active. I knew I was stressed and exhausted and the events with the kid had thrown me completely.

It was slightly later than normal when I pulled into my driveway, though fairly quiet as it was Saturday morning. Because it was a weekend, I wasn't surprised that Sarah didn't message me before I got home. Not knowing what else to do, I sat in my truck with my head on my steering wheel. I couldn't stop shaking and I couldn't stop the tears. I don't know how long I sat there but I jumped when someone knocked on my window. It was Mia.

"Ash?" I looked up at her through the glass and either the tears, or the look on my face, must have registered because she immediately opened the door. "Oh God, what happened? Are you okay? Are you hurt? Baby, talk to me!"

Her hands were everywhere and my heart wrenched again at the pain in her voice. "I...I'm not hurt. I'm sorry for scaring you. I'm okay." I ran a shaking hand through my hair. "I'm all right—"

Mia had stepped up on the runner below my driver's door and grabbed my shaking hand with hers. "You're not all right. Tell me what happened."

I wiped my wet eyes with the hand she wasn't holding. "Mia..."

The look she gave me was tender, heartbreaking almost. She tugged my hand. "Grab your bag and come with me."

I did as she said but I didn't even have the energy to lock my truck when I got out. She took my fob from my hand and guided me away as the locks engaged. She never let go of my hand, all the way over to her house and up her steps. Still in a fog, I asked the only question I could think of. "How did you know I was home?" She was in sweatpants and a t-shirt, and a pair of flip-flops. Mia wasn't normally an early riser unless she had to work or she wanted to go for a run.

We entered, and Mia locked the door behind us then led me straight upstairs to her bedroom. She sat me down on the bed and helped me remove my shoes. "Brandon called me, he was worried about you. He didn't tell me what happened, just that you didn't seem right when you left."

When she started unbuttoning my shirt, I stilled her hands. Her light brown eyes held nothing but concern for me and I knew that I couldn't face that on top of my own guilt. "Mia...I should probably just go. I'm not good company right now."

"Dammit, Ash! I don't care if you're good company! I care about you and you're hurting. Let me help you!" Her eyes grew liquid in front of me. "Why won't you let me help me?"

I stood abruptly, causing her to step back. "Because I don't deserve your help! I don't deserve your love or your caring! I'm no good for you, and I'm not worth it. I'm just... just shit, Mia, why can't you see that?" I paced as my emptiness filled with energy that I didn't have to spare. "You want to help, you say you care but no one can really care. None of you know who I am or what I've done—" I stopped as it felt like cold water washed over me. Like a puppet with my strings cut, I slid down the wall at my back. Then I wrapped my arms around my knees as the sobs tore from my heart, up through my chest, and out from between my lips. My body shook and it hurt knowing that the truth was coming and I couldn't stop it. I didn't know how to keep it silent any longer.

Mia settled on the floor next to me. "Ash." Hiccupping sobs continued but I managed to pull my head up off my knees to look her in the eye. She was afraid, I could see it plain, but she also had her stubborn look. "I love you. It doesn't matter what you've done, I will continue to love you. Tell me."

The tears kept falling but I slowly and resolutely reached down and pulled the lighter from my pocket. With a few practiced motions of my fingers and thumb, I opened and closed the lid as my wrist rested on top of my knee. *Ching-clp, ching-clp.* The motion ended when I ran my thumb casually over the wheel and flame sprung to life. "We had a warehouse fire tonight. Afterward, I was heading around to the side door to retrieve Brandon's axe for him and I heard something in the darkness." I shut the lighter again, extinguishing the flame. Then I opened and closed it a few more times. *Ching-clp, ching-clp, ching-clp.*

Her hand stilled my motions. "Ash..."

I continued with my story as I stared at her hand on my wrist. "There was a boy, probably not more than fourteen, hiding by the dumpster. I could hear him, opening and closing a Zippo, just like mine. He was standing there in the darkness, soaking wet and staring at the burnt-out building. And I knew, Mia. I knew he was the one that set the fire."

"What did you do?"

"I took off after him and caught him as he was trying to climb the back fence. Then I turned him over to the officers that were on site as a suspected arsonist. I probably ruined that boy's life tonight." I shook my head slowly but it didn't clear away any of the guilt or pain. "I am such a hypocrite."

Mia moved her hand from my wrist down to my leg and gave it a squeeze. I recognized her encouragement. "What makes you think you are a hypocrite? You did the right thing, arson is dangerous and someone could have been killed."

Her words burned me worse than any fire. I knew then that I had kept the story inside for too long and it was time to let it out, come hell or fury. Come fire and flame, it was time to face retribution. "I stole this lighter from one of my mom's boyfriends when I was eleven. Dave wasn't as bad as some of them. He never tried to touch me and he wasn't into drugs like the rest. But I was so fascinated by it, I had to have it. They broke up not long after.

I carried the lighter with me every day since. It kept me company when I was lonely or scared." I stopped talking, trying to understand the best way to say the important parts, the hard part.

Mia's arm came around me and drew me closer to her. Her voice was quiet and I shivered at her warmth. "Go ahead, I'm listening."

"I used to go into a warehouse nearby and burn papers and stuff in the empty barrels inside. I had to be careful of the dealers, druggies, and homeless people. Sometimes my mom would be drunk and after me, or worse, one of her boyfriends would try to get in my room and I'd sneak out the window. I wasn't safe at home. Sometimes I'd go hang out at Derek's for hours but I always got the impression that his family merely tolerated me. They knew I didn't have a good home life but I think they saw me as a bad seed. They were right."

"Hey," Mia turned my face toward hers. "No they weren't! You're one of the kindest and most selfless people I know! The opinion of one small-minded family doesn't matter."

I shook my head and her hand fell away. "I know what I am, Mia. No matter who I am now, some stains just can't be washed away. I—" Fear froze my words as the enormity of what I was about to do rolled over me like a flash of flame. I could feel the shaking begin and I locked my arms tighter around my up-drawn legs. I'd told Mia a lot about my past. She knew some of the stuff I'd been through, and some of the worst things my mother had done. But this was different. This was the worst thing that I myself had done.

I cleared my throat, more frightened and yet more determined than ever for my misdeeds to come out. "When I was thirteen, one of my mom's boyfriends tried to get into my room. She passed out and he wanted some action from me instead. I knew he would do it too because he was always making comments when she wasn't around. He'd cop a feel, or whatever. I was so scared." Even in the retelling I could feel the fear of that moment in my life.

"I always wedged a butter knife into the doorjamb, to keep the assholes out of my room. When I saw the knife bending inward I had to get out of there. I snuck out the window and down the fire escape, like I'd done in the past. I went to my favorite warehouse a few blocks away to burn some newspapers and stuff in a big barrel, just like usual. There didn't seem to be anyone inside the big building so I took a chance on a bigger fire since it was chilly outside. Pallets and stuff like that were always lying around. After I'd been there a while I heard voices upstairs in the offices above the warehouse floor. I could tell they were shooting up by what they were saying. Then I got scared because one of them saw the light from my fire. I heard two voices at first then only one." I stopped, because of everyone on the entire planet, only I knew what happened that night.

Mia's hand gave me a squeeze again when I'd been silent too long. But that was the root of all my problems. I had been silent too long. "What happened?"

I gritted my teeth and clenched my fist around the lighter in my palm. "Fuck. I panicked. I tried to put out the fire by throwing a big cover of some sort over the top of the barrel, but it only made it bigger and the fire started to spread. I didn't know what to do after that and...and I ran. I fucking ran away like a coward and left those guys to die! I was just a stupid fucking kid but I killed two people." I shut my eyes and the flames of that fire burned behind my lids, replaying like a home movie.

Mia stiffened next to me, then quickly relaxed again. I didn't want to look into her eyes, I was afraid of what I'd see. Her voice was quiet in the room. "How do you know you left them there to die? Maybe they got out."

Back and forth, my head moved of its own volition. The truth had ways of moving us all. "I saw the headline the next day. Two men died in the fire. They died because of me!" I slammed my fist into my chest, the hand that was holding the lighter. But the physical pain didn't even register over what I was feeling emotionally.

Her free hand grabbed my fist to still it and Mia rocked me as the sobbing started again. It was pity. It had to be because I was nothing more than a monster. I had taken two lives when Mia's entire life was dedicated to saving them. "Shh. It's going to be okay, Ash. It's going to be okay."

Shuddering breaths moved in and out of my lungs. "It's not. It's never going to be okay. I can't take back what I did. My mom used to say I was worthless, and no matter what I do she'll always be right." As the emotion continued to rise, so too did the panic. I'd just told someone my worst secret, my shame, and I had to get away. Mia wouldn't want me near her anyway. I pulled away from her and quickly stood. "I should go. I'm so s...sorry for putting this on you and I think it's best if we just end things he...here." I glanced her way then quickly looked down again, searching for my stuff. "You can do what you want, turn me in or whatever. I deserve it."

Strong hands grabbed both my shoulders, preventing me from moving. I looked up only to see a mix of love, anger, and fierce determination in Mia's eyes. "You are not dropping all that on me then walking away! Did you think I lied to you when I said I wouldn't love you any less? God damn it, Ash! I wish you would trust me. Please?"

I stopped trying to pull away. I was so tired. "I'm sorry."

She led me over to the bed and turned down her covers then pushed me to get in. "It's all right, you have to be exhausted right now. You should try to get some rest."

"No, I should go home. I shouldn't bother you anymore." Because that's what I was, a bother. Her hands tightened their grip when I tried to sit up again. No, I was a murderer.

"Hey, shh." She tilted my chin up so I could see her face. "You're not a bother to me and I don't want you to go anywhere. I love you and I want you here." I didn't answer because I didn't understand her words. She repeated them again and they finally made sense. "I *want* you *here*. We'll figure this out. Okay?" I nodded and let her lay me back down. The last thing I remembered before it all went dark was the feel of her fingers running through my hair. It was comforting and I was finally able to still my thoughts.

Chapter Sixteen

BEAMS OF AFTERNOON sunlight came through Mia's blinds when I woke. My body still felt tired and it took me a minute to remember how I had gotten into Mia's bed. Memories of the morning flooded back and filled me with dread. When I realized that I had admitted everything to her, my stomach roiled and I bolted for the bathroom. All that came up was bile and some chunks of apple from the night before. I knelt there for a few minutes with my hands on the back of the toilet to keep me steady. My entire body shook with exhaustion, fear, and sickness. Mia's voice drifted into the bedroom, filling me with dismay.

"Ash?" I was physically unable to answer. My throat was raw from vomit and tight with fear of rejection. She was going to ask me to leave. She rounded the corner but I didn't see any judgment in her eyes, only concern. "Hey, are you okay? Here..." Mia quickly ran some cool water on a cloth and gave it to me to clean my face.

Once I was done I threw it into the sink then turned to lean against the cabinet. She filled a glass from the counter with water and I drank it down gratefully, letting it dangle from my fingertips when I was done. I continued to stare at the tiles on the floor but I needed answers. "Why are you being so nice? Why haven't you asked me to leave yet, or worse, turned me in? I don't get it."

Mia sighed and it sounded loud in the small space. "Do you think you're going to get sick again?" I looked up at her and shook my head. "Good." Mia held out her hand. "Let's get you off the bathroom floor and go someplace where we can talk.

I made a face because my muscles were still trembling. "I don't think I can stand yet."

The hand never wavered from in front of me. "I'll help you." She wasn't going to take no for an answer so I let her pull me up and steady me while we walked back into the bedroom.

Her room had become familiar to me over the last few months as I sank gratefully onto the pillow-top mattress. We sat there in silence for the longest minute of my life. "Well aren't you going to say something?" My words came out harsh and I regretted them immediately. I had no reason to be angry with her, I was angry with myself.

"I'm not sure I should be the one talking right now."

I peeked through my lashes, trying to get a read on her body language and the expression on her face. "Are you mad at me?"

Mia picked at a thread on her dove gray comforter. "No, I'm sad—"

"I don't need your pity!" Anger returned to the forefront. Mia's head jerked up and her eyes narrowed. The last thing I wanted to do was piss off my girlfriend and I resigned to keep my mouth shut. "I'm sorry. I'm an ass and I don't know why I'm so angry right now."

"Sadness isn't the same as pity, Ash. After thinking about everything you told me, and knowing your life since then, I can see how you ended up in this place. I mean, Jesus, Ash! You had the shittiest of childhoods and rather than get any kind of help dealing with that, the state simply signed off on your emancipation paperwork and turned you loose. I've never seen such a case of 'good luck and fuck you, kid' in my life. I'm sad that you had to go through that and I'm furious that you fell through the cracks."

The deep breath slowly filled my lungs and I released it again. Bad childhood or not, I was still accountable. "That doesn't excuse what I did though. I burned that building down, and two people died."

Mia cocked her head. "Didn't you say it was an accident? Or were you trying to burn down the warehouse?"

I looked at her in dismay. "No, of course I wasn't trying to burn down the building! I just wanted to have a fire in the barrels. It was chilly and I liked to see the flames. I still like to see them." The last bit was an admission as much to her as to myself. I rested my elbow on the knee that was bent and ran my hand through my hair.

"Ash, I'm not denying that you don't have an addiction of sorts, maybe one that has become a coping mechanism. But I don't know that I would call you an arsonist either. That kid last night, the one you caught, do you think he meant to set that warehouse on fire?"

The boy's face was still vivid in my mind's eye. He looked at the burnt-out building like he was in a trance. That kid stood there for the entire burn. Guilty people run away. Remorseful people don't stand and look at their work in awe. And if anyone knew that truth it was me. "No, he meant to set the fire. I'm almost certain."

"So there is a difference between someone who is an arsonist and someone who has a foolish obsession with fire?"

"Yeah, I guess."

She smiled and took my hand. "I did a lot of reading online while you slept. I couldn't find anything but the main story in the Detroit Free Press archives, but I researched a few other things. An arsonist is a person who commits a criminal act, who deliberately sets fire to property. What you did was not done with criminal intent, it was an accident. That puts your crime at manslaughter, and you were a troubled minor at the time. A juvenile."

"So I should have gone to juvie then, and served my time there. Is that what you're saying?" Mia was smart and even if I was afraid of what was to come, I knew I'd listen to her because I was tired of hiding and hurting.

She took slow breaths and I braced myself for her words. "If you had gone to juvie, would you have become a firefighter?"

"Probably not. I know juvenile records are sealed, but they're still visible to the courts, law enforcement, and government agencies. I don't think I could have been hired as a paramedic even, not with that charge on my record."

Mia continued. "How long have you been a paramedic and firefighter?"

Even though I was confused I still managed an answer. "Paramedic with the fire department for two years, and about eight and a half as a firefighter." That was an easy question but I sensed something in her eyes, more difficult things to come.

"And in the past ten years, how many lives have you saved? How many people did you save as a first responder, how many have you carried out of burning buildings? As a firefighter you do more than just put out fires. You save people, property, pets, you keep fires from spreading, and you even run down arsonists." I looked down to swallow the lump in my throat, but Mia wasn't going to let me get away with that. "Ash, look at me please?" I met her eyes again. "How much good would this city have lost if you had never become the driven and caring rescuer that you are today? Whether you admit it or not, firefighters are heroes. You are a hero."

Frustration caused me to pound my fist on my thigh. "But two men died!"

I'd never seen her look so serious. "Yes, they did. And you

will have to live with that for the rest of your life. But there is a part of me that respects the fact that you didn't give up and didn't give in to that darkness you were raised with. You learned from your mistake and you strove every single day to be a better person. That's good on you in my book."

My breath caught in my throat and hope slowly rose within me. "D...does that mean that you forgive me?"

She shook her head and my heart plummeted. "Ash, I can't forgive you because it's not my place. You haven't done me any harm. Only you can forgive yourself, when you're ready."

"Oh."

Mia shifted nervously on the bed. "I have something to tell you and I'm not sure if you're going to be happy with me. I spoke with Gail today —"

"*What?*" My entire body tensed with panic and I was seconds from bolting when I felt her hand close gently around my wrist.

"No, wait...please?" I paused, taking pleasure in the feel of her soft fingertips against my skin. She had listened to my words when I knew that the sin of my past was the last thing she wanted to hear. I could do no less than to listen to her, even if the mere thought of telling her cop best friend terrified me. I forced myself to relax and she relaxed as well. "I didn't give her any names or reasons, I just asked her to do me a favor and look into the ware-house fire from seventeen years ago. I told her two people had been killed and that it was suspected arson. She said she'd do some digging and let me know what she found out. I promise, I didn't tell her it was you that I was asking for."

I let out a long sigh. "She's not an idiot, Mia, she'll figure it out."

"Maybe, maybe not. I've had her look up a few other things over the years, things about friends and people who have come through the hospital. So she may not put it together."

"So what do we do now?"

She gave me an understanding look. "We wait, and you keep living your life. I want you to have all the facts before you decide which way you should go. But I'm here with you for whatever you choose. Okay?"

I swallowed hard and fought the tears away. "Okay." I looked around after that, searching for something to wear. "I should probably go next door and get some clothes from my place."

"I already did. I put some of your things into a duffle bag and brought them back over here earlier."

She continued to surprise me with her thoughtfulness and foresight. "When did you do all that?"

Mia shrugged. "When I went next door to invite Mary to dinner."

With a stupid look on my face, I stood with my mouth open for a few seconds before words could come out. "Dinner?" She nodded. "Here?" Mia nodded again. "What are we having?"

I saw Mia's look turn teasing and I knew it would be good. "Buttermilk fried chicken, mashed potatoes, and corn on the cob. Mary gave me some green tomatoes from your garden for frying, and she's going to make homemade biscuits."

"Holy shit, that's a lot of food!"

"It is. That's why I also invited Brandon and his kids over as well." I grew leery at the thought of being around so many people while I felt so raw emotionally and she could see it on my face. Mia immediately pulled me into an embrace. "Babe, you need your friends. I think I know you well enough by now that I can say your first instinct is to wallow and hide from the things that upset you. But it's time to start facing them and moving forward. Leave the past behind, Ash."

I laughed, brokenly. "You make it sound so easy." I glanced to my right and her face was very close to mine. I watched, fascinated, as her full lips moved to form words to answer my own.

"Isn't it though? The way I look at it, your past is a mountain. Sure, it's hard as hell to get over, but you take it one step at a time. And the real secret is that you don't keep facing back. You face forward and move your damn feet."

"That sounded just like something your grandma would have said."

"It is." She smirked.

That time my laugh wasn't broken. It was quiet and full of burgeoning surety. Mia had that effect on me. I decided to change the subject because I was tired of looking back. "Can you even make fried chicken?" My question was valid, I'd practically grown up on Mary's home cooking and I had high standards when it came to chicken.

Mia pulled back and made a face. "For real? You did *not* just ask me that, Ashley Hayes!"

I grimaced at the use of my full name. "Ugh, please don't call me that! And my question is legit, I mean, Mary's cooking sets a pretty high bar."

She held a hand up. "Girl, please. Grandma Letty taught me her secret recipe when I was ten years old."

I raised a skeptical dark brow. "And you remembered?"

"Damn straight! I remembered everything around Grandma Letty, she had a drawer of wooden spoons that guaranteed it!"

Her words brought a smile to my face again and I wanted to kiss her but I was very aware of my breath from getting sick. "I'll be right back." Two minutes later I returned and she gave me a curious look. Rather than answer, I pushed her back on the bed and gave her a minty kiss. I wasn't always good with words, and emotions were just too hard sometimes. That was why I tried to put as much as possible into my kiss. After everything I'd gone through over the past twenty-four hours, I needed to feel some sort of connection. I wanted to be reminded that I was human, that I could love and be loved. And Mia was there for me, just as she promised. Perhaps she needed to know that she was loved in return. She definitely was. Grandma Letty's chicken would keep just fine.

EVEN THOUGH I stayed busy with dinner and friends Saturday night, and with a variety of projects for Mary on Sunday, the weekend went by at a slow burn. Mary didn't ask why Mia came to get my own clothes after work Saturday morning but I knew from experience that she could tell something was bothering me. I suppose that wasn't saying much though since I'd spent my entire life with something bothering me.

Monday morning I got a text from Brandon, pulling me out of restless sleep. Mia's even breathing let me know that the vibration of my phone on the nightstand didn't wake her and I was glad. We both had to work again the next morning and I knew she cherished her days off as much as I did. When I texted him back asking what was up, he responded with an unusual request. A sigh escaped my lips even as I closed my eyes to think about it. Finally my fingers flew across the screen again as I told him I'd be there.

"Morning."

Mia's voice was sleepy and rough, and when I turned my head to look at her there was affection and worry shining in her eyes. I told her Sunday about trying to contact my shrink when I got off work and not hearing back. Maybe she thought Sarah was texting me since it was now Monday morning, if a bit early.

Warm affection washed over me as I gazed into Mia's light brown eyes. Even with sleep wrinkles creased into her skin and a white film next to the corner of her mouth, she was beautiful. "Good morning, gorgeous."

She rolled her eyes like I knew she would. "Oh, please. It's too early for so much sweet." She protested my words but I knew they made her happy.

I love her. The thought hit me low in the stomach, where it always did and my heart fluttered in my chest. Maybe it was because my past had opened me up, or perhaps it was my therapy sessions, but either way, Mia had walked into my heart like she owned the place. I would do anything for her, I would be anyone. Even if the person I needed to become was just a better me. In that moment I felt good about my response to Brandon's question. I smiled back at the woman who shared her strength with me each day. "It's never too early to love you."

Mia didn't respond but her smile was laced with tender affection. It looked the way I felt inside, all warm and happy, content. She nodded toward the phone in my hand. "What's up? Did Sarah text you back?"

I shook my head, listening to the *shoosh* of the pillowcase against my shorn hair. "No, her office doesn't open until nine. That was Brandon. Apparently Matt neglected to tell him until this morning that it is career day and his teacher had asked the class if anyone's parents or family were in the emergency services. She does a special program on those careers, with a short film and slideshow. He wanted to know if I could come in with him to speak."

"Well are you?"

"I don't have a reason not to so I told him yes." My phone buzzed again and I looked at Brandon's response. "Damn it."

Mia's hand tightened on my bicep. "What's wrong?"

I sighed and shut my eyes. "Nothing really. He's going to swing by and get his turnout gear to wear for the class, but he asked me to wear my class A uniform." Mia stared at me blankly so I elaborated. "My dress blues."

The blank look was quickly replaced with one I hadn't seen before and she bit her bottom lip. Before I could ask Mia what she was thinking, she broke the silence with a grin. "Now that I would pay to see. I worked in the ER back in the day, you think I could tag along?"

I thought about where I was going and made a face. "Why

would you want to go to some elementary school full of scream-ing kids?" Then it dawned on me and I pointed a finger at her in accusation. "You just want to see me in uniform!"

"I think it's a really interesting project for the teacher. I wish more kids would get interested in things like emergency response. It's a dangerous and hard job without a lot of the bene-fits you get from other professions." I stared at her straight face. Her answer made sense but I could still see the smile peeking from around the edges of her mouth. The longer I stared the more the smile grew until Mia finally broke. With a grin and that famil-iar eye roll, she huffed. "Fine, and I really want to see you in uni-form."

I texted Brandon again. I didn't have to wait long for his response. After reading it I smiled up at Mia, who had propped herself up on an elbow and was tracing the bare skin of my shoul-der with the index finger of her free hand. "He says they don't get much of a turnout for the special portion and thought the teacher would appreciate more people."

"He texts fast for a man."

I snorted and tried not to get distracted by her wandering touch. "You have no idea. Brandon's a total phone slut. He texts faster than anyone I know, including you."

Her dark brows went up. "Excuse me, are you calling me a phone slut because I text fast?"

I knew she was kidding but just in case, I started sliding out under the covers as I answered. "Uh, nope. Not at all. I need to…" I pointed at the bathroom then quickly left the warmth of her bed.

"Mmm hmm." I knew she'd follow soon enough.

Forty-five minutes later Mary met me with a whistle as I came down the stairs at our house. "I thought I heard you come and go skulk around upstairs. Let me guess, career day?"

I couldn't even answer for a second because she caught me completely by surprise. "How the hel—" I paused at the look on her face and quickly amended my choice of words. "Hello, how do you know that? Matt only just told Brandon this morning."

Mary cackled. "Tanesha's granddaughter goes to the same school and brought home papers for it two weeks ago." I knew Tanesha was one of Mary's good friends. The poor woman had taken over raising her grandchildren when her own daughter couldn't seem to stay clean.

Her words made me laugh. "Figures. Leave it to Matt to wait till the last minute to say anything."

Mary paused as I came to stand beside her and she looked hard at me in my dress blues. I waited as her old eyes wandered to take in the ribbons and medals on my chest, then moved to where I had my white gloves tucked into my belt. My hat held loosely beneath my left arm. "You look real good, Ash. I know I forget to say it sometimes, but I'm real proud of the woman you've become."

Breath caught in my chest and I could feel the sting as tears filled my eyes. But more than anything I didn't want to cry at that moment. While Mary may not have known my entire past, she certainly knew where I'd come from and who I was now. Her words were a balm to my still burned psyche. I pulled her into a hug, not caring a bit if my hat rumpled. "Thank you." My words were a whisper in her ear and she patted my back as if she knew how close to breaking I was.

A knock on the door pulled us apart and I discretely wiped the one tear that did manage to fall. "That's Mia, we have to go. But I'll come back after we're finished at the school."

Mary looked from me to the door, then back at me. She smiled and gave me a wink. "Oh, I know what a handsome woman looks like in uniform, Miss Ash. I don't think you'll be back as soon as you think. I think Mia is gonna get one good look at you and fill your afternoon."

I rolled my eyes at her, a habit I was sure I picked up from Mia. "You know that you're not always right, old woman!"

Her dark brown eyes crinkled at the corners and I recognized imminent mischief. "Oh please, child! I'm not so old that I don't remember what it was like when Marge and I were still in the Army. Mmm hmm, you may even get more than your afternoon filled —"

The door opened just as my jaw dropped. "Ash?"

"Mary!" My voice was both, shocked and indignant at Mary's words.

Mia looked back and forth between us and Mary started laughing again. "Mornin', Mia!" Then she clucked her tongue at us and walked back toward the kitchen.

My girlfriend listened to the old woman's laughter fade down the hall, then noticed my red face. "What was that all about?" Before I could answer, Mia's eyes widened and she held up a hand to stop me. "Hold up!" Then with deliberate slowness, she made a point of checking me out from top to bottom. "Damn, girl." Before I could respond she slipped her cell phone out of her back pocket and snapped a pic of me.

I tried to ignore the heat that continued to flush my cheeks. "I told Mary that we could visit with her after we finished at the school."

"Maybe later." She pointed back and forth between us. "You and me have plans after we're done playing dress up."

I rolled my eyes but grinned anyway. Sometimes I liked it when Mary was right.

Chapter Seventeen

CAREER DAY WENT as well as expected. Two kids asked if I was a boy or a girl, one asked if I was a mommy or daddy, and another said I couldn't be a firefighter because only guys were firefighters. On the flipside, I had three girls and two boys come up and tell me they wanted to be firefighters when they grew up. It was still too early for lunch when we left, so after saying goodbye to Brandon and the class, Mia and I went back to her place.

I had one missed call from my shrink's office when we left the school and as much as I wanted to get out of my uniform, I thought it best to call Sarah back. We spoke for nearly an hour and I felt a lot better about my state of mind once we hung up. She had an opening Wednesday afternoon, which gave me time to get off shift and catch some sleep before going to my appointment. After I hung up I went to search for Mia. Knowing who I was talking to on the phone, Mia wandered out to one of the chairs on her back porch to read. She really was too good for me. When I stepped outside, Mia looked up with a smile. I wasn't really sure what to say and everything suddenly felt awkward. I felt stiff standing there in my dress blues while she had already changed to scrub pants and a light hoodie. I pointed toward Mary's house with my thumb. "I, uh...I should probably go change and hang up my uniform."

Mia slowly shook her head back and forth and stood from the chair, carefully folding the corner of the page over to mark her place. I watched her hands closely and she mistook my gaze for something else. "I'm a monster, I know. A barbarian."

I looked at her in confusion, brows furrowed. "What?"

Her eyes crinkled at the corners when she smiled mischievously. "Never mind. What if I don't want you to change just yet?"

"I, um, guess I could leave it on for a little while longer. I was just hoping to keep it clean so I wouldn't have to take it back to the dry cleaner—"

"Ash." She interrupted my strange rambling and moved over to her porch swing. She patted the cushion next to her. Dutifully I took a seat, the swing swaying with my momentum. "Will you tell me about the medals and ribbons?"

"What? They're no big deal really."

"Please?"

When I looked into those light brown eyes I was lost. "Sure. What do you want to know?"

Mia's fingers lightly traced the medal hanging from a blue ribbon. "What is this from?"

I swallowed, unaccountably nervous to talk about the things I'd done with the fire department. "That's a medal of valor. It was my very first award. You know the scar I have on the back of my arm?" She nodded. "That was from jagged metal of a wreck back when I was still an EMT. We got called to an accident with the fire department because one of the cars was on fire. One of the cars had flipped over and the driver's door was stuck. The fire was on the other vehicle but it was so close that I worried the flipped one would catch. First I used the rig extinguisher to put out the engine fire while my partner worked on getting the driver out." I paused remembering back nearly ten years.

"Hayes! I've got this one, go check the flipped car." Bennitz pointed to the black SUV that had clearly rolled several times.

"Roger that. I'm going to leave the extinguisher here in case it flames up again." I set the canister down and grabbed my bag to jog over to the SUV. There was an unconscious man inside. The driver's window was smashed and he sported a contusion on the side of his head. I wasn't sure of the state of his neck or spine with him upside down, so I grabbed the neck brace. I'd have to get him stabile before we could extract him. I was just securing the brace around his neck when I heard a sound. It was faint but out of place. My arm jerked against a piece of jagged metal in the window frame and I felt my sleeve catch. I quickly ripped it free to focus on the sound.

"Daddy?" The voice was tiny and frightened. Whimpering started next while I scrambled around to the other side of the vehicle. That put me down in the median between north and south bound lanes of I-275. Water splashed up past my knees with all the spring runoff. It was dark and the windows were tinted so I never even realized there was another passenger inside.

I called out to Bennitz when I made it to the back passenger door. "I've got a child back here. Driver's neck is secure and waiting for extraction." Then I opened the door. The little girl couldn't have been more than four and I said a prayer when I saw her securely strapped into her booster seat. She was clearly frightened but didn't appear to have any other injuries as she hung upside down. "Hey there, sweetie, my name is Ash. I'm here to get you out."

"Where's my daddy?"

I pointed to the front where his body was slumped. Luckily there was no blood visible from our angle. "He bumped his head when you crashed so he's sleeping. But we need to get out of the car now because it's broken, okay? Can you tell me your name?"

"I'm not s'posed to talk to strangers."

"Are you allowed to talk to police officers?" She nodded. "And are you allowed to talk to firefighters?"

Her voice was so small. "Yeah."

"Well, I'm an emergency medical technician with the fire department and I'm here to help you and your daddy."

As if I had said the magic words, her name slipped out. "My name is Callie Stephens and I live on four thirty-seven, Oak Park Terrace."

I smiled at what was clearly a memorized spiel. "Okay, Callie, I'm going to get you out of those straps. It might be a little scary because you're upside down but I'll catch you. Can you be brave for me?"

She waited a beat then her bottom lip started to quiver. "I'm scared."

"I know, but this will only take a second. Ready?" I braced her upper body with my left arm as best I could and unlatched her seatbelt. I breathed a sigh of relief that it separated easily. As soon as she started to fall, she gave a little scream and I quickly caught her in my arms. "It's okay, Callie, I've got you. Let's get you away from this car now." I quickly slogged back though the water and up the hill to where our rig sat. Another truck had arrived, as well as two more ambulances. Bennitz had gotten the woman out of the car that had been on fire and the firefighters of my crew had made sure there was no more danger from that vehicle. I left Callie on a gurney in the care of another EMT. "I'll be back in a few minutes, we're going to go get your daddy. Stay strong, all right?" She nodded and I met my partner to fulfill my promise.

Before we could start the extraction, Bennitz grabbed my arm. "Holy shit, Hayes! What did you do?"

I glanced down at a bloody tear in my sleeve, not even realizing that I'd been injured. "I must have caught it on the door." He quickly wrapped it in a bandage then we went to work on the driver.

Mia's voice brought me back to the present. "Was everyone okay?"

The image of the burned and wrecked vehicles was still fresh in my head as I continued. "Shockingly yes. The little girl had no injuries and the man had a broken arm and a few sprains. The ones I didn't take care of had a variety of other injuries but none of them life threatening. For the longest time afterward, all I could think about was, what would have happened if that SUV had rolled over into the water? It was deep enough in the middle that the little girl would have drowned."

"But she didn't." Mia's smile and comforting hand over mine pushed away the last of the memories from that scene.

I smiled back. "She didn't."

Mia reached down to finger another, one with a red and silver striped ribbon. "What about this one?"

With the description of each medal she pointed out, with each story told, that ball of fear in my stomach unknotted a little more. The honors I'd been awarded told a story about my life. Some of them involved my entire crew, and one involved just me and Derek. But each one was a reminder of the things I'd accomplished during moments of fear and uncertainty. Each medal and bar was tangible evidence that I had done more good in my life than bad. By the time I had explained the last addition to my uniform, it was lunchtime but neither of us moved. I had my arm around Mia's shoulders and we cuddled together in the warming day.

I glanced down at her face and took in the long dark lashes that just brushed the tops of her cheeks. She did this. She pulled the memories out of me to remind me that I was more than my past. My girlfriend was subtle and I loved her even more in that moment. With a sigh of contentment I squeezed her closer. "Thank you."

Mia's eyes fluttered open and tracked up to my face. "You're welcome."

The rest of our day off was uneventful. We had dinner with Mary and I chose to go home to my own bed that night. It wasn't because I wanted to be alone, but rather I knew that Mary slept better when I was in the house. And with Mia having to be at the hospital and me at the station early the next morning, it made sense. But more than anything, I hoped for a day when I didn't have an axe hanging over my neck. I wished for a time that I could give my future to someone, to Mia, and not have to worry about the consequences of my past. I needed to get over my mountain.

MIA DIDN'T HEAR anything from Gail before Tuesday and I felt morbidly grateful for an unusually heavy shift at the station. Two three-alarm fires was a lot even for Detroit. One had been set deliberately in an abandoned house on the southeast side. After that my crew went out for a car fire on the highway. The fearlessness of rubberneckers on the road always amazed me. I mean, if a car is on fire, wouldn't normal instinct tell someone to get by it as fast as possible? But no, they all go slow so they can stare at the wreckage. I even saw people driving with their cell phones out.

The other big fire happened Tuesday night, just after midnight. Someone fell asleep with a lit cigarette and caught their apartment on fire. Lucky for us the place was up to code and the alarms got everyone out of the building. But the blaze itself burned hot and it was a battle to get it under control. We were the last crew to arrive and immediately scrambled to assist. I was back on the inside team and I could see people in pajamas and other states of undress standing away from the action. Some openly sobbed and others just had a look of weary horror. I grabbed my axe but held back from heading into my assigned door when I heard one little girl crying out a name.

"Lacy! Where's Lacy?"

I jogged over to where her mother held her tight. "Who's Lacy?" If there was someone missing who could still be inside, we needed to know.

The mother was the one who answered. "Lacy is our cat. It was so smoky that we couldn't find her. I knew we had to get out." She took a shaky breath and glanced down at her crying daughter. "Her grandma gave Lacy to her a few years ago, right before she died."

I sighed, knowing I was going to look for that damned cat. "Which apartment were you in? And where does Lacy like to hide? They're starting to get the flames under control and if your apartment's not engulfed I'll see if I can find her."

A look of relief came over her face. "It's three-oh-one and she likes to hide under the couch. And thank you so —"

"Hayes!"

"I gotta go!"

I took off back to my crew, pulling my mask on as I went. I was partnered with Camden and we were tasked with making our way through the floors to search for anyone left in the building. The fire was still contained to the sixth floor but I knew the smoke and fumes built up inside would be toxic so the quicker we found people, the better. We made it through the first two floors with all clear given and as luck would have it, the first apartment Camden and I searched on the third floor was 301. The apartment was already full of smoke and I immediately went into the living room.

"Hey, where are you going?" When I didn't answer he whined. "Come on, Hayes! I'm tired as shit and this is our last floor to check."

His voice was muffled through the mask. "I spoke with the tenants of this one outside. There is no one here but I want to find their cat."

I couldn't see his face well in the gloom and dim light from our helmets but I didn't need to. "Are you fucking kidding me right now, man?"

I got down on my hands and knees, ignoring him. I spied a set of glowing eyes and called out. "You can start the next one if you want, I'll be there in a minute."

They had already called out that the fire was under control while we were on the second floor, we were just there to finish the search. Even with no active fire, there was enough smoke to kill someone if they didn't evacuate with the rest. Just as promised, I caught up with Camden a few minutes later and we finished the floor without any issues. It was a good day when everyone got out safe.

Once we were outside again, I found the nearest paramedic that wasn't busy treating anyone. It just happened to be Jackson. "Hayes, how's it hangin'?" He watched as I held the front of my coat carefully. "You all right?"

"Got a favor to ask." Even as I spoke I was busy pulling a fat and lethargic cat from the inside of my turnouts. In a way I was glad she was only half conscious because I wasn't a fan of being clawed up. "I think she got some smoke, her name is Lacy. Is there anything we can do?"

He glanced around to make sure no one was watching, then

waved toward the back of the ambulance. "Yeah, wouldn't be the first time. But not a word of this gets out, hear?"

I grinned back at him as he went to work shoving the human mask over the cat's face. He cranked up the oxygen volume and looked back innocently. "Not a word of what? I was never here." The cat responded well to the oxygen and I was pretty sure she would be fine. Like Jackson, it wasn't the first pet I'd rescued. I just had a soft spot for crying girls and helpless animals.

By 3 a.m., my engine was back at the station and I found myself freshly showered. As I walked to my bunk I got razzed by the guys while the rookie looked on and scowled. The comments were crude but accurate.

"Ooh, someone got a little pussy tonight."

"I heard Hayes even gave sweet little Lacy mouth-to-mouth—"

Gomez interrupted Gil Stanton before he could tease me further. Unfortunately for her, she had no idea what they were really talking about. "What the fuck, dude? That's not appropriate!"

I called out to her. "Chill, Rookie."

She turned her angry look my way. "The name is Maria Gomez, or just Gomez. Not Rookie!"

I held up my hands in surrender and smiled. "Hey, sorry. You've done good work since you came on, I think you've earned your way past rookie by now anyway. But lay off them, they're not talking about what you think."

Gomez's look turned from anger to confusion. "What *are* they talking about?"

Stanton snickered and I ran a hand through my hair. "Lacy was someone's cat. I found her and brought her out, got her some oxygen. But—" I pointed at Stanton. "I didn't fucking give her mouth-to-mouth, you sick bastard!"

Laughter ensued, mostly giddy. It had been a long twenty hours since we started the shift and every one of us needed sleep. Lucky for me another one of my brothers stuck up for me. "No, man, it's true. She wouldn't cheat on her girl like that. Her girl is fine!"

I blushed at Blake's words. "What the fuck do you know about it?"

He laughed. "That woman that brought you lunch a few weeks ago? That's your girl, right?"

We had never talked about it, no one had ever talked about it. But something had clearly changed. Maybe it was Derek's death that brought us all together, or just the knowledge that we only had each other when things got dangerous, but I had finally found acceptance of a sort. As I looked around the room, I saw tired smiling faces and another part of that knot eased inside me. They knew and they didn't seem to care. I turned back to Blake. "Yeah, that's my girlfriend. Her name is Mia."

More voices chimed in. Sometimes the guys in the firehouse were worse than gossiping old ladies. They talked about what was going on with everyone, who was dating, and who was single. I had just become another subject for station gossip. Gomez surprised me when she asked first. "How long you two been together?"

I glanced around. Some of the guys were still listening, but others had crashed back into their bunks. "About three months."

She smiled. "Is it serious?"

I couldn't help the grin that curved my lips into a happy smile. "Yeah."

Gomez clapped me on the shoulder. "Good for you, Hayes." Then she was gone, sliding between her own covers in search of a few more hours of sleep. I went over to my own bunk after that, ready for the shift to be done.

Chapter Eighteen

TWELVE HOURS LATER I sat on the leather couch in Sarah's office, leg nervously jiggling up and down. Despite everything I'd gone through over the past three days, I was strangely good, mentally. And because of that I felt stupid that the only reason my appointment had been moved up was because of my panic attack. I missed the familiar lump that had always before been in my front jeans pocket. I was as much focused on the fact that my lighter sat at home on my dresser as I was on Sarah's words.

"You seem nervous, Ash. You mentioned Monday that you were feeling a lot better, has something changed?"

I ran a hand through my hair and stilled my bouncing leg. "No, I'm still good. Mostly I just feel like an idiot because I panicked and we moved my appointment up for nothing."

Damn those blue eyes of hers. She stared at me in silence for nearly a minute. "I listened to your message three times and while it sounded like a lot of things, *nothing* was definitely not one of them. Can you tell me what happened leading up to your phone call?"

I wasn't sure what to tell her, or how to say what needed to be said, without giving away the secret I kept. It was one thing to tell my girlfriend about the warehouse fire from my past, it was another to tell a medical professional who would be required to report criminal activity. After a deep breath I made an attempt. "There was a fire and afterward I caught a kid nearby, with lighter in hand. I turned him over to the police as a suspected arsonist but something about the entire event triggered a memory from my past. I..." I felt the dark memory rise again but quickly pushed it back down. It was a time for healing, not reliving the sins of long ago. "Mia found me when I got home, I was a wreck. She took me to her house and eventually she got me to tell her what happened. It just...brought up so much and I couldn't do it anymore."

Sarah tilted her head and gazed back at me. "Couldn't do what?"

I took a long, deep breath. "I couldn't keep it inside any longer. I told her about the worst memory of my past. I was so afraid

I would lose her but she...she didn't run or ask me to leave."

"Hmm..." Sarah made a few notes and glanced back up at me. "What did she say?"

"She, um, said that we would face it together. She actually called a friend while I was sleeping and her friend is looking into some things. We haven't heard back yet but I guess that part is still making me nervous."

There was a smile on her face when I looked up from where my fingers rubbed against my empty pocket. "How do you feel today, now that you've told her your secret? Just give me the first word that comes to mind."

"Free." I didn't even take a second to think about it, the word fell from my lips with no resistance. "It's crazy but I feel lighter than I've ever felt before."

She nodded and made another note. "If you think you're good on the reason we rescheduled your appointment, I'd like to move on to something else."

My curiosity was piqued. "Sure, I feel pretty good right now. Like I said, Mia and I did a lot of talking over the weekend and she made me see a lot of stuff I hadn't considered before. What is it you'd like to try?"

"One thing I've noticed about you is how you seem to get caught up in those bad memories from your past. You cling to them and you've said it yourself that you relive them at times. What I'd like to do is have you think about your happy memories. I know some people find it helpful to be able to call up those good times when things seem darkest. So...tell me about your first happy memory of Mary."

I thought for sure she'd start with Derek. Her question took me by surprise and I had to think for a minute in order to come up with what she wanted. Nearly as soon as I thought of it, I fell backward in my memories.

The cops took me to the hospital the night my mom was arrested and I was treated for my injuries. The nurse on duty saw that I was all alone and had no one to help me out. She told me that she knew someone who could take me in for a bit and I was too numb to do much more than nod my head. Nothing felt real. I was hurting both physically and emotionally at my mom's abuse and betrayal. Thirty minutes later a feisty old black woman walked into the treatment room.

"You the girl that Tammy called me about?"

I was still dazed and the name didn't ring a bell. "Tammy?"

The woman rolled her eyes. "I swear to the Lord...Tammy is the nurse on duty. She said you needed a place to stay?"

"Oh." My face flushed with embarrassment that I hadn't even caught the nurse's name when she offered to call someone for me. "Yes, I'm sorry." I got down off the table and held out my hand. "I'm Ash. Um...Ash Hayes."

She took my hand in both of hers and I watched her size me up. My face was a mess of bruises and swollen from tears. "You don't have to apologize, I understand. My name is Mary White. I was a nurse here for thirty some years before I retired. They sometimes call me to help with strays. Have you been released yet? We can go whenever you're ready."

Strays. That was all I'd become to the world. Nothing but a stray bitch. My mom was in jail and probably not getting out for a long time. I had no home and no job. Guilt was crushing and I couldn't put the burden of myself on a nice old lady. "It's okay, you don't have to take me. I don't want to be a bother—"

"None of that, now! No child on God's green earth is a bother. Now you're coming with me and you're gonna let me put some meat on your bones, you hear? Everybody needs somebody else in their life that's got their back, and now you have me, Ash Hayes."

"Okay. How much will it cost?" Nobody does stuff for free. I'd known that for a long time.

She smiled, smooth dark skin crinkling around her eyes, and a gap between her teeth to give her character. "It's expensive for some, but cheap for others. I don't charge money for my help but it will cost you. Respect and communication, contribution, and schooling." My face must have been awash with confusion. "You stay in school and keep your grades up, help around the house, don't sass me, and respect my rules. That's what I'm asking for now. We've got a bus stop not far from my place that will get you to school or a job after school, if you have one. How does that sound?"

"I..." I didn't know what to say in the face of such kindness. It was not something I'd ever experienced in my barely seventeen years of life. Nothing prepared me for unconditional compassion between two strangers. Mary White was offering me more than I'd ever gotten from my own mom. It was embarrassing that my lip quivered before I could answer. I was a tough Detroit girl and we don't cry. It was humiliating as fat tears ran down my cheek. I sobbed even harder when she wrapped me in a hug and held me tight.

"It's okay, child, I got you. Just let it out."

My words ended with the memory and a part of me wasn't even aware that I'd been speaking out loud. "You love her very much. She's more than just your landlady, or even your friend."

The memory slowly faded leaving ghost images behind my eyes. "Yes. She's family more than any other blood relative I've ever met. She's my mother, or rather, my grandmother. She's always been there for me since that day in the hospital. I don't know what I'd do without her in my life."

"What about Derek? You've mentioned on multiple occasions how he was a brother to you, family. Was it different for him than it was for Mary?"

With closed eyes, I thought about her question. I knew what she meant, my relationship had always been different between the two most important people in my life. They were both family, and I had known Derek a lot longer, but I always felt safe with Mary. Always. "With Derek...we were best friends. We'd known each other for decades and just got each other, you know? We loved each other, and he was definitely my brother. But the difference was that I had no one else to love. He was the only one I'd let into my heart, and the only person I had that really felt like family for a long time. But he had his own family. His mom, dad, and brothers were blood and they would always take precedence over our friendship." I paused to clear my throat.

"His love was real, but fractured. His support was strong, but conditional. Sometimes he wasn't there when I needed him most, couldn't be there. We were kids and because of that we didn't really have control over our own lives. But Mary, she was an adult. She had no one telling her she couldn't love me, that she couldn't help me, or put my needs above hers. She chose to be there for me and didn't let anyone stop her." My throat was sore when I stopped talking, not used to saying so much at one time. Sarah must have sensed my need because when I opened my eyes again she held out a water bottle. "Thank you." I twisted the cap as she made her way back to her desk.

"So would you say your relationship with Mary feels more familial than the one you had with Derek?"

Strangely enough, her words didn't provoke pain or memory. And they didn't make me feel guilty for loving Derek and Mary in different ways. "No. I think Mary became my parent, she was my grandmamma. Derek will always be my brother. I miss him." I snorted because that much was obvious. "His absence is like a hole in my life. I think the pain became unbearable when I realized how much I had lost with his death. I never had much to begin with, but I finally felt complete these past few years. I had Mary, Derek, Brandon and his kids, and a whole mess of other people that all felt like family. I forgot how much it hurt to lose someone. I guess snow feels that much colder when you've been standing in the warm sun."

My watch beeped and I was surprised to see my hour was up. By the look on Sarah's face, she hadn't expected it to fly by that fast either. She made one final note in her book then moved her eyes up to meet mine. There was a smile on her face and for the first time I smiled back and meant it. "Well Ash, I feel like you've made tremendous progress in just the past few weeks. You've shown a lot of insight today that I had not previously seen from you. Now you mentioned that you and Mia were waiting for information from one of her friends. This is something that could potentially be troubling, correct?"

I swallowed the lump in my throat. "Yes."

"If you have any issues, or panic attacks like you had over the weekend, I want you to call me." She took out a business card and wrote a phone number on the back. "This is my personal cell, I trust you not to abuse it or give it out to anyone else. But I will also trust you to call if you're feeling overwhelmed again, okay?"

My eyes burned but I refused to cry. "Thank you, Sarah."

She tilted her head. "You want to keep your next scheduled appointment two weeks from now?" I nodded. "Okay, we'll see you then. And for what it's worth, I hope you get good news."

My words were almost a whisper as I stood to head for the door. "Me too."

I HAD GOTTEN a text message from Mia while I was in my appointment. All it said was that Gail called and she'd be over after Mia got home from work. Since Mia didn't usually get home until twenty after seven, I had nearly four hours to kill. First I went to the station and spent some time in the gym. I had a locker and some clothes and shoes there, I just rarely ever used the facility unless I was on a twenty-four or forty-eight hour rotation. At least that had been the case since Derek died. Before that, the three of us worked out there all the time.

Brandon was on duty and opted to do some weight sets with me. I knew he felt the loss of our third musketeer in his own way as much as I did. It was a lucky thing that no alarms interrupted our workout. The room was quiet with just the two of us and we spotted each other on the bench press. "You okay, Ash?"

Brandon was a perceptive guy and he knew something had been bothering me but didn't push it when he brought the kids over for dinner over the weekend. And he didn't push it on Monday at the school during career day either. Of course he didn't ask if I was okay until I was pressing two-hundred pounds for my last set of reps. I grunted and briefly met his eyes. "I'm good." I focused on my reps until I hit ten then sat up and wiped the bench down for him to go. He popped a few more plates on the bar and took my place.

I counted out reps for him and he spoke over me. "I worry about you, Ash. You'd tell me if things were bad for you again, right?"

While my focus was on his bar, his words echoed in my head. I threw the towel at him when he finished and glanced around. We were the only ones in the room but I didn't want to chance anyone overhearing. "I...I've been working through something lately. Both with my therapist and with Mia. I'm going to get some information tonight and I guess I'm just nervous."

His dark eyebrows went up in surprise. "Information? Like what, an STD?"

"*What?*" His response completely took me by surprise. "Holy shit, man, no!" I scrubbed my face with both hands while he laughed and wiped down the bench. "No." I shook my head in disgust. "Ugh, no. It's just something about my past. I can't say more about it, okay?" Brandon looked hurt and I rushed to reassure him. "It's, um, it's not something I've told anyone about except for Mia."

"Not even Derek?"

I swallowed thickly. "No. Not even Derek. I may tell you someday, but I need to get more information first, okay?"

He put his hand on my shoulder. "I get it. And whatever it is, I'm here for you."

"I know, and thanks. No more going it alone for me, I promise." Even as I said the words, I wasn't sure if I could make them true.

"Good." *Snap!* His sweaty towel snapped me on my right ass cheek.

I spun around and held out my hand to block another shot. He only gave me a boyish grin, completely unrepentant. "Gotcha!"

The laughter bubbled up even as I flipped him the bird on my way out the door. "Asshole!" I walked away, feeling better about the impending news than I had all week.

After a shower at the station, I texted Mary to see if she needed anything and she sent me a picture of our grocery list. She had grown quite good at using all the apps on her phone, mostly due to Mia's instruction. Taking my time, I washed and gassed up my truck then did some shopping. But no matter how much I tried to cram into my afternoon as a distraction, I still found myself upstairs in my weight room, lighter in hand. In a fit of guilt-fueled restless energy, I removed the cigarette papers and lighter fluid from my drawer by the recliner and threw them in the big trash bin outside. Five minutes later I sat in the quiet, lulling myself with the comforting sound of my childhood. *Ching-clp, ching-clp, ching-clp.* I wanted to throw it away too but I couldn't. I went as far as pulling it out of my pocket but my hand started to shake. I knew what that meant. Mia was right, I have an addiction.

I wasn't sure how much time passed while I sat there but the vibrating phone in my pocket surprised me. I pulled it out and seeing Mia's name on the screen answered. "Hey." I stuffed my lighter back into the right front pocket as I spoke.

Her voice was so clear on the other end, as if she were in the room with me and not right next door. "Are you all right? I thought you'd be waiting for me here when I got home."

I sighed quietly, unsure about what she wanted to hear. "I just needed to think for a bit so I came home."

"Gail should be here any time, are you coming over?"

I closed my eyes as nervousness rose within me. "Yeah. Be there in five." She hung up and I stared at the dark screen of my phone for too long. Then without spending more worry, I grabbed my keys and slipped the phone into my back pocket. Mary was at a friend's for dinner so it was quiet as I made my way through the house. I no longer knew if I was waiting for the truth, or if the truth was waiting for me. Either way, I had to know.

I walked next door like a prisoner leaving the table after their last meal. My feet felt like lead as I wandered the familiar path across our front yard and into Mia's. Gail's Range Rover was already in the drive when I walked up the steps of the porch. I could hear quiet voices as I came through the door and followed the sound around the corner to the kitchen. Gail and Mia sat on opposite sides of the table, a folder laying ominously on the table next to the detective.

"Hey, babe, why don't you have a seat next to me?" Mia pulled out a chair to her right and I tried to swallow but my throat was tight with fear. Good or bad, just being here with Mia meant Gail would know my secret. I was aware of that fact before I walked off my porch.

Mia took my hand and squeezed but my eyes were locked on the detective's calm gaze. There was no point in beating around the bush. "What did you find out?"

Gail took a deep breath and placed her hand on top of the file. "Before I give you the details of the report, would you like to tell me what happened that night?"

My right hand shook as I discretely rubbed the lighter through the fabric of my dark jeans. The story had only been told once with Mia. My past misdeed left burns when it came out and I still felt raw. But Detective Gail Evans simultaneously held my past and my future under her hand and deserved the truth from me. I told her everything. She was a cop so I gave her facts and details. My mother, my lighter, the string of abusive boyfriends and users all came out. I told her about lighting fires in the barrel inside the warehouse, and about trying to put out that one fire just like I'd been taught in school. I told her about the newspaper the next day and my regret for what had happened. Mia only got up once while I spoke, and that was to grab all of us a beer. When I was finished, I didn't feel the overwhelming sense of grief that I had with Mia. Instead I felt numb and broken.

My first swig of beer went down cold and I couldn't maintain eye contact any longer. In the silence, Gail slid the file in front her and opened the cover. "I read through the entire report. I'm just going to paraphrase the main parts for you, okay?"

Gail stopped talking and I looked up at her. She was waiting for an answer. "Okay."

"Roughly seventeen years ago there was a warehouse fire with arson as the initial suspected cause. Two men, age twenty-two and thirty-one were found dead in an upstairs office. After the fire investigation was complete, the conclusion of the investigator assigned to the case determined the fire started in a barrel near the back entrance of the warehouse. The cause of the fire was ruled accidental since the warehouse was, on occasion, used by vagrants and squatters."

My breath left me in a rush but she wasn't done. Gail shuffled a few papers aside and continued. "Autopsy reports for George David Hill and Deshawn Travis Willes found no evidence of smoke inhalation. Hill had a cocktail of methadone, THC, and alprazolam in his system, which was the cause or contributing factor in his death. Willes suffered a heart attack directly caused by a combination of methadone, cocaine, and hydromorphone. The coroner's conclusion ruled that both deaths were a result of drug overdose and unrelated to the warehouse fire."

Silence crashed over me and my vision went dark. I shoved back from the table to stand and immediately crumpled to my knees. "Oh God..." Seventeen years of darkness only to find that I wasn't the cause. "Fuck." The chair scraped next to me and I brought my hands up to my head in an attempt to hold it together. I didn't kill those men. Hands scraped along my scalp and tightened into the longer hair up top. My hands, the ones that had started so many fires and put out even more. The tears came in a rush as the words fell from my lips like a prayer of penance. "Oh God, oh God—" My rambling words were interrupted by a sob as it tore free from my lips.

Sound to my left went unheard. "Ash..." A hand touched my shoulder and tried to still the rocking as I processed my simultaneous grief and happiness. I no longer knew what to feel or how to feel it. "Baby, look at me. Come on, Ash look at me."

My breath shuddered and gasped inside me but I couldn't look at her. I was afraid it was nothing more than a dream. "No, I can't—it's not real."

"It is real. Honey, it wasn't you. The fire was an accident and you didn't kill anyone. It wasn't you."

Finally, after nearly two decades of tears had extinguished the fire of my guilt, I opened my eyes. "Mia?"

She smiled, her own eyes wet. "I'm here." She was on her knees next to me, arm wrapped around my shoulders. She never let me go.

I swallowed and ungracefully sniffed the running snot that had come free as I cried for my own lessened pain. I was a mess. "I—it wasn't me."

She stood and quickly grabbed a few tissues from a box near

the microwave. After I blew my nose, she held out a hand to help me stand. Once I was on my feet again she drew us together and hugged me tighter than she ever had before. Her words were a whispered balm to my ears. "It wasn't you."

Part Three: Ash

Chapter Nineteen

THE RED NUMBERS of Mia's alarm clock changed to 12:03 as we lay in her bed, sweat cooling in the spring air. The windows were opened after a long winter of too much snow. Parts of Detroit had been flooded with the runoff, making it harder than normal for our engines to get to the fires. But I didn't care about any of that. I was off duty for another day and a half and it was the first night we'd spent together all week. I knew she was still awake because I felt her shiver as a light breeze came through the screen. I sat up, interrupting her fingers where they traced the tattoo on my bicep in the dark. "Where are you going?" Her voice was soft and quiet, unlike just a short time earlier.

"Just grabbing the blanket." I felt around the end of the bed until I found her comforter and pulled it up to cover us.

Once I was back on my pillow, she moved over to snuggle again. "I missed you this week."

I squeezed her a little tighter, thankful for each day we spent together. While nine months in a relationship wouldn't exactly be considered long-term by most people's standards, the length of all my previous ones could be counted in weeks. On one hand. After everything I'd been through, after all my losses, I found someone to hang on to. Someone that would hang on to me. "I missed you too. It was rough pulling a double, especially knowing it was on your days off. Then with you going out of town for your continuing education classes..." My voice trailed off and I sighed.

Suddenly Mia's fingers stilled where they had begun tracing my arm again, and her muscles tensed against me. I wondered for a second, curious why she would react like that when I brought up her work. I worried too, always full of self-doubt about my worth in her life, knowing she absolutely deserved better than me. "Ash—"

"What's wrong?" My voice was too fast, not even giving her a chance to finish her question. Low self-esteem stemming from an abusive childhood was just one of many issues I continued to work on with Sarah. Things were so much better for me now, but I could never forget where I came from. She had also been helping me work through my feelings about the warehouse fire. Even though I didn't kill anyone and the fire was ruled an accident, I spent a lot of years carrying that guilt on my shoulders. It was hard to set it all free. I wasn't sure if I would ever have the guts to say what I needed to say to Mia. She was quiet too long and I suddenly realized that I interrupted her train of thought. "I'm sorry, what were you going to say?"

I tensed too, curious about the words that would come out. I loved her, but was it enough for Mia? "Will you move in with me?"

My breath left in a rush. I didn't even realize I had been holding it in. "What?" I pulled back slightly and looked at her with wide eyes. She smiled in the near-darkness. With the window open, the room was just barely lit by the streetlight outside.

"Baby, I want you to live here...with me. What do you say?"

"I—" Her face fell and I rushed to answer. "Yes! Uh, no. Damn it." This time I did sit up, covers pooling around my waist as I turned to look down at her. "Are you serious?"

Dark eyes stared back, so vulnerable. "I wouldn't have asked if I wasn't."

No, I knew she was serious. "I want to say yes right now, and kiss you like crazy..."

The smile that started across her lips faltered and dropped away. "I sense a *but* coming."

"It has nothing to do with you. But I can't just leave Mary by herself in that house."

A look of understanding washed over her face and her eyes went wide. "Oh, damn. I forgot about that." Her bottom lip came out in a pout and I leaned down to kiss it away.

"Let me see what I can do, okay? Maybe one of my unit needs a place to stay or something. Just the other day the rookie mentioned that she hated her apartment."

Mia made a face. "Is she really still a rookie?"

I laughed. "No. It just pisses her off when I call her that. But anyway, let me do some checking around, all right? Because I would love to wake up with you every morning that I'm not at the station."

"Yeah?"

It was the first shy look I'd ever seen from Mia and I loved it. And I loved her more than I'd ever thought possible. The truth did more than cast off my guilt, it also set me free. Mia was the first person I didn't guard myself with, for her I was nothing but an open book. I kissed her again just so there would be no mistaking how I felt. "Yeah."

She wrapped her arms around my neck as I held myself above her face. Mia's voice changed and I recognized the tone. "What do you have planned for tomorrow?"

I thought for a second, recalling the note that Mary had left for me before going off to play euchre at the community center. "Well, I wanted to wash my truck, do some laundry, and Mary wants me to look at the trellis against the back por—"

My words were cut off with a kiss. It took a few minutes for us to come up for air, both laughing. "So, you're free to sleep in then?"

"Wasn't that what I was saying?" She kissed me again.

"I GOT A call from Tammy today." Mary was busy dropping eight-inch tall tomato plants into the holes I had dug in a neat little row. It had been a month since Mia asked me to move in. There never seemed to be a good time to bring it up to Mary. First there were a ton of spring projects outside, then it was time to plant the garden.

Her words stopped my trowel. "Who's Tammy?"

"Really, Child? After all these years you still can't remember Tammy's name? She's the nurse who called me the night you got taken to the hospital.

I remembered then. "What did she have to say? Does she call you a lot?"

My trowel continued along in the soft soil as I waited for her to start talking again. "Oh, she's called off and on over the years. Always about a stray. I know a lot of people so I can usually come up with something or someone that can help. But today she called me about a young woman in a situation similar to what you were in all those years ago. She's staying someplace temporary, but I was thinking about letting her move in here."

"Are you ready for that? It sounds like a pretty big challenge and you're not getting any younger, Mary. I mean, I know I was a handful at times."

She clucked her tongue. "Oh, Child, you were always worth it though. I have loved having you here with me. But you don't need my help like that anymore. And...I'd like to do more if I can, to be there for others that don't have anyone they can count on. But I don't want you to feel like I'm shoving you out. I just have this need to help, you know that." She was right, I did know. I'd often compared her with Mia in my head. Both were healers, nurturers of body and soul. I always suspected that was why they got along like two peas in a pod.

I glanced at where she sat. "I get it and I think it's wonderful the way you help people."

"Well...I'm kinda glad you said that because I may have told Tammy that I could probably take in Samantha next week. She's just finishing up her junior year of high school and it would be nice if she can have the summer to settle in before her last year this coming fall."

I stopped digging completely. I wanted to meet this girl, if only to make sure she wasn't going to take advantage of Mary's good nature. "Really, that soon? Do you need me to clean out my weight room? I bet Mia would let me move my equipment over to her place."

Mary started laughing and threw a clod of dirt at me. "When is she going to let *you* move over to her place?"

"What?"

The woman who practically raised me sat back on her little stool and gave me her "lecture" look. I knew it by the way she drew back her shoulders and narrowed those dark brown eyes. "Now, Ash, you've been living here going on fourteen years and I have loved nearly all of it." I snickered when I remembered the dish soap in the washer incident. Mary gave me a dirty look and continued with her speech. "But I see the way Mia looks at you and I think it's time you started planning for your future. Every baby bird needs to leave the nest sometime."

I couldn't help the laughter that came out after her little speech. "Really, old woman? You're giving me the baby bird speech and kicking me out of the nest?"

Suddenly she looked a little less sure. "I am not kicking you out of the nest, Ashley Marie Hayes! I would never do that to you."

"Did I just hear your full name? Does this mean you're grounded and can't go out with me tonight?"

The sounds of Mia's voice made me jump up and smile. "Mia! I thought you were going to have lunch with your mom?"

"Hi Grandma Mary!" She turned back to me after giving Mary a quick hug and a quick kiss on the cheek, careful not to get dirt on her clothes. "I was, but it turns out my dad surprised her with tickets to see *Wicked* this afternoon, for their anniversary."

After greeting Mary she made her way around the garden bed and gave me a quick kiss as well. I had been the one that tilled the entire garden that morning so I was pretty sweaty and gross. I didn't blame Mia for keeping her distance. "Aww, that was sweet of him."

"How many years have your parents been together, Mia?" Mary was back dropping plants into holes but she was still in the conversation.

Mia's entire face lit up when she smiled and I had to purposely turn away from her so I didn't stare like some sort of idiot. "Thirty-five years tomorrow, and still in love as the day they met."

Mary chuckled. "Sounds like they made a good match then."

I knelt again since I only had a few holes left to dig and Mary was nearly caught up with me. But I didn't miss the love in Mia's voice, or the way her eyes softened when she thought about her parent's marriage. I wanted that too. Lately I'd been having dreams that Mia and I had grown old together, that we had two children and a cat. I'm not sure where any of it came from because I didn't want a cat and the thought of kids never occurred to me before. I doubted I'd be a good parent anyway since I didn't exactly have a good family model while I was growing up. Mia's voice startled me from my deep thoughts. "Do you two need any help? I can go change into some old clothes."

I wasn't surprised that the old woman waved her off. "Pssh! We're just about done here. As a matter of fact, Ash there is just playing in the dirt now, so if you can get her out of my hair that would be a fine thing."

"Mary!"

"You never told me what she used your full name for."

I started to answer but Mary beat me to it. "Ash was just bein' stubborn like always. I swear, that child is dumber than a chicken with her head in a sock sometimes."

My trowel made a clatter as I tossed it into the big five gallon bucket we used for tools. "Oh my God, woman! What does that even mean?"

She pointed her dirty finger at me. "Don't you take the Lord's name at me! Now answer Mia's question." She had five plants left and shuffled her rolling stool down a little farther.

Mia looked confused so I gave her a tender smile. "Funny thing, Mary just told me she was thinking about taking in another stray. Some girl needs a place to stay and she asked when I was going to move in with you."

My girlfriend burst out laughing. "For real?"

"Apparently. Yeah."

"What's so funny?" Mary wiped her hands on the apron tied around waist and stood up with a groan. "My old bones ain't like they used to be."

I quickly gathered up the rest of the tools before she could get her hands on them. "I think it's time you call it a day then, right Mia?"

"Absolutely! And we're laughing because I asked Ash to move in with me last month. But she didn't want to leave you all alone in the house."

The look on Mary's face right that moment was one I'd seen a little more than a dozen times before. I saw it the day of my mom's sentencing. And I saw it once a year since I came to live with her, always on her anniversary with Margie. It was the purest love that Mary could give. For once, the old woman was at a loss for words so I gave her some. "You're my family, more than any other I've had. You scolded me, loved me, and taught me right from wrong. You raised me more than that woman ever did, Mary. You're my family and I'd never leave you alone." Then I walked over and gave her a hug that was just shy of hurting.

When she pulled back she placed a dirty hand against my cheek as tears pooled in her eyes. "Oh my Ash, what did I ever do to deserve you in my life?"

"I ask myself that every single day." I glanced at Mia to know that she was included in the statement.

Suddenly Mary slapped her thigh. "You know what this means?" Mia took my hand and we both shook our heads in confusion, trying to keep up with Mary's rapidly changing thoughts. "This means we need to have a barbecue to celebrate your move!" She quickly untied her apron and threw it in the bucket. "I'm going to clean up and go to the store. I'll let you girls gather up the garden tools and fire up the grill." Then like a whirlwind, she was gone with a slam of the back porch screen door. Ten seconds later her head reappeared. "Don't forget to invite Brandon and the kids!"

I looked at Mia, still feeling a bit of shock at the rapid shift of events. "I..." I couldn't even finish a sentence.

"Did that just happen?"

Mia's eyebrows quirked up in confusion and I couldn't stop from stealing another kiss. "I guess you've got yourself a room-

mate if you still want me." I looked down, shyly, but the serious-
ness of her voice pulled my gaze back up.

"You still don't get it, do you?"

"Get what?"

Mia smiled softly. It was the sweetest little upturn of lips and
she took my hand in hers. "I'm never gonna stop wanting you."

My breath caught as my stomach did a little flip. "Oh." It was
a stupid word in the face of her brave ones. But before I could say
another stupid thing, I pulled her into the same tight hug I'd
given Mary. I wasn't good with words, but I'd try my best every
single day to show her I felt the same way.

Chapter Twenty

"SO HOW HAVE you been? Things still going well with Mia?"

I smiled at Sarah, unable to contain my happiness. Mia and I had been living together for months. "Yeah, it's been great! I mean, I stayed there all the time before the move so we were kind of used to each other by then." It wasn't all roses though. I learned early on that we couldn't share a toothpaste tube because she killed hers dead on a regular basis. I also learned that for someone so messy with a toothpaste tube, she was a neat freak with everything else. It made no sense. But after two months, I still felt so amazed each morning I woke up next to her in our bed.

Sarah flipped a page on her ever-present notebook and clicked her pen. "Okay, the last time we spoke, we covered your addiction to fire and I gave you some brochures on emotional and psychological dependency. Did you get a chance to look at them?"

The papers she sent home with me the month before were eye opening. In her continued effort to provide support for me while I dealt with everything, Mia had also been reading the materials that Sarah sent home. I absently rubbed the lump in my right front pocket. It had been gone for a long time, so it seemed strange to feel it back again. Different. The familiar motion was soothing and simultaneously nerve-wracking. "Both of us read them. I never considered all the ways that addiction could affect a person, both mentally and physically."

"In which way are you referring?"

"I mean, I knew that drugs would cause your brain to release chemicals and stuff. But I had no idea that any kind of addiction would have the same effect. Like, uh, dopamine and stuff. I never realized that every single time I started a fire, I was fueling the addiction. That each time I opened and closed my lighter, it just sent little signals to my pleasure receptors and stuff like that. That just seems crazy, doc."

Her blue eyes always drew my attention. There was a window between us, on the left side of the room, and the light made them seem brighter. She folded her hands in front of her, not bothering to make any notes. "Speaking of your lighter, you mentioned at our last appointment that you still kept it. You also said that while it was a reminder of your childhood, it was also a reminder of your obsession with fire. Have you decided what to do with it yet?"

My memory folded back to three weeks ago. It was Monday night and Mia was getting underclothes out of her dresser to lay out for work the next day. She had the top three drawers and I had the bottom three.

"Ash?" I was in the bathroom brushing my teeth when she called me.

I quickly spit and rinsed before coming back into the bedroom. "Yeah?"

Mia pointed at the small silver rectangle that sat in a dish on top of the dresser. "When are you going to get rid of that?"

I froze and a tremor ran through my right hand. "Ge—get rid of it? Like, throw it away?"

"Yes."

No, I wasn't ready to part with my lighter. I wasn't ready. "I can't do that!"

Her head tilted. "Why not? You don't use it, right?"

"No, I don't even carry it anymore either. You know that." The burnished silver of the lighter seemed to glow in the bright room. Both nightstand lamps were on, as well as the overhead light and my eyes remained fixed on it. The lighter had been a part of me for two decades.

"Ash..." My gaze was pulled back to Mia by the tone of her voice. "Why can't you get rid of it?"

I swallowed and clenched my hands to keep them from shaking. "I—I don't know."

She caressed my cheek. "Yes you do."

A sigh escaped but I wasn't sure if it was mine or hers. "I'm afraid."

"You remember what Sarah told you. You can never fully move on as long as you're holding onto that piece of your damaged past, that symbol of your addiction."

"I know. I just don't know how to let it go."

Mia leaned toward me and delivered the sweetest kiss on my lips. They trembled beneath hers. "I'll be with you every step of the way. We can do it together."

"Together." She waited and I watched the emotion swirl in those light brown eyes I'd grown to love so much. Then before I could overthink it, I snatched the lighter from the dish and held out my hand to her.

She hesitated. "Babe, you're only wearing boxers and a t-shirt."

"Don't care. You coming?"

Mia smiled and took my hand, following behind me as I led us down the stairs to the kitchen. When I started to lead her toward the back door she pulled me to a stop. "Where are you going? The trash is over there." She nodded to the other side of the kitchen.

"Not yet, there is something I have to do first." Then I released her hand and took two quick steps and pulled open the drawer next to the back door. Inside was a collection of house-hold tools, including a hammer. My hand paused for just a second before closing firmly around the wooden handle. She was with me when I unlocked the door and led us out to the concrete back porch. She placed a hand on my left shoulder when I sat on the top step in the cold night air and flicked the lighter open and closed one last time *Ching-clp.* The fluid had evaporated months before, it had no fire left to give. I placed it next to me and with three good swings, I reduced it to bent metal and broken pieces. Then I calmly set the hammer down next to the mess. Mia held me while I cried.

I swam up from my memory feeling lighter than any of the other times in Sarah's office. "I smashed it, a week after our last appointment."

I think I surprised her for once as a pale brow went up and her eyes widened at my words. "Oh! And how did it feel? Have you had any lingering sadness or anxiety?" She knew that I had used the lighter as a crutch for many years. I wasn't just addicted to the fire. I had, in some way, been addicted to the lighter as well. Every part of the process drew me, from flame to ash.

I smiled to reassure her. "Actually, no. It was like another weight being lifted off my shoulders. I felt, *hmm,* free."

Her smile for me was so big, and I wondered if our time together was finally coming to an end. Six months ago Sarah had discussed the possibility of a time when I no longer needed her services, or at least a time when I didn't need them as frequently. There was the slightest quirk to Sarah's lips. "That was the last piece of your past, Ash. The last thing that held your mind trapped in the heart of that girl that you were. Tell me in your own words why you're here today."

My entire body stilled as I took a deep breath. I remembered her words from our very first appointment together. "I'm here to tell you that I've been reborn."

Sarah clicked her pen off and dropped it back into the holder on her desk. Then she slowly closed the notebook that had become so familiar over the past year. "You continue to amaze me, Firefighter Hayes. What do you say we schedule your appointments 'as needed' going forward?"

There was no anxiety at the thought of no longer having my monthly appointments. I felt healthier and happier than I'd ever been, and I had so many people to thank for it. Doctor Sarah Caplin was only one of them. "That sounds good." I stood then, conscious of that hard square in my pocket. Our one year anniversary was coming up in four days and I held happiness in my hands.

Sarah stood as well and walked me to the door. "Do you have any plans for the weekend?"

I grinned. "It's our one year anniversary."

"Oh? Congratulations then!" I felt my face get hot. "You have something special in mind?"

I rubbed the ring box in my pocket one last time before digging my key fob out of the other one. My voice was quiet as she pulled the door to the room shut behind us. "I do actually."

Sarah waved toward the front door of the office. She had mentioned the previous month that she was closing early after this appointment, since her and her wife were starting their vacation. "Good, good." I started to walk out the main door, but didn't get more than a step. "Oh, and Ash?"

I turned to look back at Sarah. My psychologist's eyes were crinkled at the corners and she looked like she was holding back a grin. "Yeah?"

She winked. "I hope she says yes."

My face flushed again but I grinned back at her. "Me too."

About the Author

Born and raised in Michigan, Kelly is a latecomer to the writing scene. She works in the automotive industry coding in Visual basic and Excel. Her avid reading and writing provide a nice balance to the daily order of data, allowing her to juggle passion and responsibility. Her writing style is as varied as her reading taste and it shows as she tackles each new genre with glee. But beneath it all, no matter the subject or setting, Kelly carries a core belief that good should triumph. She's not afraid of pain or adversity, but loves a happy ending. She's been pouring words into novels since 2015 and probably won't run out of things to say any time soon.

Other K. Aten titles to look for:

The Fletcher

Kyri is a fletcher, following in the footsteps of her father, and his father before him. However, fate is a fickle mistress, and six years after the death of her mother, she's faced with the fact that her father is dying as well. Forced to leave her sheltered little homestead in the woods, Kyri discovers that there is more to life than just hunting and making master quality arrows. During her journey to find a new home and happiness, she struggles with the path that seems to take her away from the quiet life of a fletcher. She learns that sometimes the hardest part of growing up is reconciling who we were, with who we will become.

ISBN: 978-1-61929-356-4
eISBN: 978-1-61929-357-1

The Archer

Kyri was raised a fletcher but after finding a new home and family with the Telequire Amazons, she discovers a desire to take on more responsibility within the tribe. She has skills they desperately need and she is called to action to protect those around her. But Kyri's path is ever-changing even as she finds herself altered by love, loyalty, and grief. Far away from home, the new Amazon is forced to decide what to sacrifice and who to become in order to get back to all that she has left behind. And she wonders what is worse, losing everyone she's ever loved or having those people lose her?

ISBN: 978-1-61929-370-0
eISBN: 978-1-61929-371-7

The Sagittarius

Kyri has known her share of loss in the two decades that she has been alive. She never expected to find herself a slave in roman lands, nor did she think she had the heart to become a gladiatrix. But with her soul shattered she must fight to see her way back home again. Will she win her freedom and return to all that she has known, or will she become another kind of slave to the killer that has taken over her mind? The only thing that is certain through it all is her love and devotion to Queen Orianna.

ISBN: 978-1-61929-386-1
eISBN: 978-1-61929-387-8

Rules of the Road

Jamie is an engineer who keeps humor close to her heart and people at arm's length. Kelsey is a dental assistant who deals with everything from the hilarious to the disgusting on a daily basis. What happens when a driving app brings them together as friends? The nerd car and the rainbow car both know a thing or two about hazard avoidance. When a flat tire brings them together in person, Jamie immediately realizes that Kelsey isn't just another woman on her radar. Both of them have struggled to break free from stereotypes while they navigate the road of life. As their friendship deepens they realize that some-times you have to break the rules to get where you need to go.

ISBN: 978-1-61929-366-3
eISBN: 978-1-61929-367-0

Waking the Dreamer

By the end of the 21st century, the world had become a harsh place. After decades of natural and man-made catastrophes, nations fell, populations shifted, and seventy percent of the continents became uninhabitable without protective suits. Technological advancement strode forward faster than ever and it was the only thing that kept human society steady through it all. No one could have predicted the discovery of the Dream Walkers. They were people born with the ability to leave their bodies at will, unseen by the waking world. Having the potential to become ultimate spies meant the remaining government regimes wanted to study and control them. The North American government, under the leadership of General Rennet, demanded that all Dream Walkers join the military program. For any that refused to comply, they were hunted down and either brainwashed or killed.

The very first Dream Walker discovered was a five year old girl named Julia. And when the soldiers came for her at the age of twenty, she was already hidden away. A decade later found Julia living a new life under the government's radar. As a secure tech courier in the capital city of Chicago, she does her job and the rest of her time avoids other people as much as she is able. The moment she agrees to help another fugitive Walker is when everything changes. Now the government wants them both and they'll stop at nothing to get what they want.

ISBN: 978-1-61929-382-3
eISBN: 978-1-61929-383-0

Running From Forever

Sarah Colby has always run from commitment. But after more than a year on the road following her musical dreams, even she yearns for a little stability. Her sister Annie is only too happy to welcome her back home. When she meets Annie's boss, Nobel Keller, she's immediately drawn to the woman's youthful good looks and dangerous charisma. The first night together leaves Sarah aching for more, but the second shows her the true price of passion.

ISBN: 978-1-61929-398-4
eISBN: 978-1-61929-399-1

The Sovereign of Psiere:
Mystery of the Makers Book 1

Psiere is a world of intrigue where old ideology meets new. The Makers built massive pyramids on each continent and filled them with encrypted texts and advanced technology. The two suns, Archeos and Illeos shine down on a mostly undiscovered planet with a psionic race of people living on land, and violent sea people below the water. The Queen seeks to make the world a better place for all Psierians but her daughter, Royal Sovereign Connate Olivienne Dracore, seeks only to solve the Divine Mystery.

The connate makes her living as a historical adventurist and wants the answer to two important questions. Who were the Makers and where did they go? Because she is the heir, Olivienne travels with a security force and resents it every moment. Every one of her captains has either quit or been injured trying to keep up with the risk-taking woman. That's where Commander Castellan Tosh comes in. Capable, confident, and oh-so-dashing, she is forced to switch career corps to take charge of Olivienne's team. Sparks fly from the moment they meet and things only get hotter as they chase down the clues to the greatest mystery of all time

ISBN: 978-1-61929-412-7
eISBN: 978-1-61929-413-4

MORE REGAL CREST PUBLICATIONS

Melissa Good	Thicker Than Water	1-932300-24-4
Melissa Good	Terrors of the High Seas	1-932300-45-7
Melissa Good	Tropical Storm	978-1-932300-60-4
Melissa Good	Tropical Convergence	978-1-935053-18-7
Melissa Good	Winds of Change Book One	978-1-61929-194-2
Melissa Good	Winds of Change Book Two	978-1-61929-232-1
Melissa Good	Southern Stars	978-1-61929-348-9
Jeanine Hoffman	Lights & Sirens	978-1-61929-115-7
Jeanine Hoffman	Strength in Numbers	978-1-61929-109-6
Jeanine Hoffman	Back Swing	978-1-61929-137-9
K. E. Lane	And, Playing the Role of Herself	978-1-932300-72-7
Kate McLachlan	Christmas Crush	978-1-61929-195-9
Kate McLachlan	Hearts, Dead and Alive	978-1-61929-017-4
Kate McLachlan	Murder and the Hurdy Gurdy Girl	978-1-61929-125-6
Kate McLachlan	Rescue At Inspiration Point	978-1-61929-005-1
Kate McLachlan	Return Of An Impetuous Pilot	978-1-61929-152-2
Kate McLachlan	Rip Van Dyke	978-1-935053-29-3
Kate McLachlan	Ten Little Lesbians	978-1-61929-236-9
Kate McLachlan	Alias Mrs. Jones	978-1-61929-282-6
Lynne Norris	One Promise	978-1-932300-92-5
Lynne Norris	Sanctuary	978-1-61929-248-2
Lynne Norris	The Light of Day	978-1-61929-338-0
Nita Round	A Touch of Truth Book One: Raven, Fire and Ice	978-1-61929-372-4
Nita Round	A Touch of Truth Book Two: Raven, Sand and Sun	978-1-61929-404-2
Nita Round	Fresh Start	978-1-61929-340-3
Nita Round	Knight's Sacrifice	978-1-61929-314-4
Nita Round	The Ghost of Emily Tapper	978-1-61929-328-1
Schramm and Dunne	Love Is In the Air	978-1-61929-362-8
Rae Theodore	Leaving Normal: Adventures in Gender	978-1-61929-320-5
Rae Theodore	My Mother Says Drums Are for Boys: True Stories for Gender Rebels	978-1-61929-378-6
Barbara Valletto	Pulse Points	978-1-61929-254-3
Barbara Valletto	Everlong	978-1-61929-266-6
Barbara Valletto	Limbo	978-1-61929-358-8
Barbara Valletto	Diver Blues	978-1-61929-384-7
Lisa Young	Out and Proud	978-1-61929-392-2

Be sure to check out our other imprints,
Blue Beacon Books, Carnelian Books, Mystic Books, Quest Books,
Silver Dragon Books, Troubadour Books, and Young Adult Books.

VISIT US ONLINE AT
www.regalcrest.biz

At the Regal Crest Website You'll Find

~   The latest news about forthcoming titles and new releases

~   Our complete backlist of titles

~   Information about your favorite authors

Regal Crest print titles are available from all progressive booksellers including numerous sources online. Our distributors are Bella Distribution and Ingram.